THE NORWAY ROOM

Mick Scully grew up in Birmingham, the city where he still lives. His story collection *Little Moscow* was highly praised. *The Norway Room* is his debut novel.

THE NORWAY ROOM

MICK SCULLY

Tindal
Street
Press

Parts of this novel originated in the short stories 'Ash', 'The Night of the Great Wind' and 'Bonebinder and the Dogs', published in the collection *Little Moscow*, Tindal Street Press 2007

A complete catalogue record for this book can be obtained from the British Library on request

First published in 2014 by Tindal Street Press,
an imprint of Profile Books Ltd
3A Exmouth House
Pine Street
London EC1R 0JH

www.tindalstreet.co.uk

ISBN 978 1 90699 448 8
eISBN 978 1 84765 979 8

Typeset by Tetragon, London

Printed and bound in Great Britain by
CPI Group (UK) Ltd, Croydon CR0 4YY

10 9 8 7 6 5 4 3 2 1

For Helen, Emily and Vicky

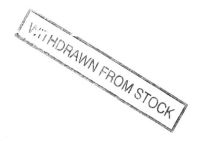

ACKNOWLEDGEMENTS

I would like to express my gratitude to Luke Brown, Ruthie Petrie and Hannah Westland at Profile Books for their help, patience and support. I am grateful to Polly Wright and Rowena Clayton for the use of their house in Clun when I started writing this novel, to Alan Beard for enabling me to work at the Mary Seacole Library in Birmingham, to Dennis Barr for advice on content and to Sheila and Jennifer, and particularly the late Joel Lane, for encouragement.

Birmingham 2007

ASHLEY

1

Fuck it was cold. Everything frozen. Ashley didn't usually light up until he reached Harold North's grave. He didn't know why he always did it there, but he did. Today he couldn't wait. He was shivering. Had to hold one hand with the other to steady the lighter. He inhaled deeply. The hot smoke hit his chest and he held it there for as long as he could before exhaling. It blew back into his face, curled round it into his hood. He looked at his watch. Nearly eleven, the middle of break.

He made for the area of trees and benches beyond the long stretch of graves. There were some trees with wreaths hanging from every low branch; all motionless today in the windless cold. The benches were covered in them too. Christmas cards and messages everywhere, pinned to the trunks and branches of trees, the benches. These were for the dead without graves. Sometimes when he came here a scattering was happening and he had to hold back, but today all was clear, and it was too cold for anyone to be sitting with their memories or their grief on one of the benches – not that there was any room. He had the place to himself.

He headed up the incline to the laurel bush near the top. Here he squatted and let a finger touch the frozen ground. The ashes of his nan who had looked after him had been scattered here. He inhaled again. Perhaps the cigarettes would kill him. He hoped so. That's what it promised on the box.

Shivering he stood and pulled his blazer tighter round himself. He wished he wasn't so skinny. He wished he was clever, and good-looking. He wished he was good at football so he could become a professional and be rich. He was good at snooker, but not good enough for it to come to anything. The same with darts.

He hated school. Hated it.

Sometimes when he came up here he talked to his nan. But not today. It was too cold – and it was pointless anyway. He stamped his feet as he took a last hefty pull on his cigarette, dragging the fire right down to the nub. He flicked it away, held the smoke in his chest until it hurt – someone had told him it was the same burn you felt when you got cancer – then exhaled. He could do a ring: now he was trying to do a question mark. He had tried to work out how you would have to position your lips, what you should do with your tongue, how much suction was needed in the cheeks. He had got somewhere near a few times but not close enough for it to be recognised as a question mark, more like a fat comma. He lit another cigarette. If he could get it right perhaps he could work out how to do lots of other shapes, writing even, go on telly and be famous. He laughed to himself as he imagined taking an enormous pull on a cigarette and *Fuck off* coming out in joined-up writing. That would be a money-spinner.

A procession of black cars was making its way through South Gate. Ashley wondered what that would be like as a job. Last summer he had talked to some of the undertaker blokes as they stood smoking behind the chapel waiting for a funeral to end so they could drive the people home. They were okay. They had joked with him about wagging school, about smoking at thirteen, said what he needed was a bloody good hiding – like they'd had as kids when they'd done those things. But they were all right. He liked the way they were fooling around, swearing and joking one minute, then becoming all serious and kind the instant the chapel doors opened and the mourners filed through. Like his dad changed when the cops turned up and changed in another way when the lads came round.

His phone toned. A message from Karl.

U bin copped. Mad bin lookin 4U. Whit just taken a reg. Got your coat in my bag.

More trouble. So what? Ashley didn't care. They couldn't do anything, not really. Last night Maddocks had kept him behind. Pointless. Just standing there in his office while the headmaster got on with reading and signing a whole stack of forms. For an hour he had just stood there, being deafed-out, like he was invisible. Stupid.

On the way home after his detention Ashley had stopped at a greengrocer's and nicked a banana. He spent ages in the bathroom trying to stuff it into his arse using soap as a lubricant. He remembered a joke about gays using soap; they could use butter as well, but he didn't have any. His plan had been to ram it all the way in, make his arse bleed, then go to the cops. Tell them the headmaster had shagged him. He had formulated the plan while standing, jam-packed with anger, in his office watching him sign forms. It was the perfect plan. If he could get Maddocks sent down for a long stretch Ashley knew the Criminal Injuries Board paid out huge amounts in abuse cases. He'd probably be able to sue the Education too. And if he made out he was so messed up by it he couldn't work he could probably claim invalidity benefit for a few years. A master plan.

But the banana hurt too much. Like fire. Less than a fingertip's length in and he thought he was going to pass out. He gritted his teeth and pushed. The pain consumed his entire torso. He tried again, and then again, but it was useless. Then his dad was banging on the door. 'What you doin' in there, Ash, 'avin' a fuckin' wank? I need a shit.'

The house was empty when Ashley got back. He went across to the Highbury. His dad was in the bar with Kieran. To Kieran and the rest of Crawford's men his dad was the Weasel. From as far back as Ashley could remember his dad had been known as that. Even the coppers called him it when they came round. 'It's like my professional name,' he had explained to Ashley when he was little, when he used to tell him stories, 'a nippy little creature that can get in and out of places quick.'

'What you doin' 'ere?' the Weasel asked. 'You should be in school.'

'Waggin' it.'

'Christ! Already. You've only been back two days.'

'Two days too many.' Ashley sat down on the padded bench beside the men. Baz was behind the bar. He squinted across at Ashley, but Baz was all right.

'Can I have some crisps?'

His dad fished in his pocket, produced a pound coin and banged it down on the table in front of his son. Ashley lifted it and made for the fruit machine where he turned the single coin into three. He went to the bar and bought two bags of crisps.

'I've got enough for two scratch cards now,' he smirked as he rejoined the men. 'What you over here for anyway?'

'Shurrup and eat your dinna,' his dad told him.

4

Baz carried a metal stepladder from behind the bar and started to remove Christmas decorations.

'You never fed the dog,' Ashley accused his dad. 'She's starvin'.'

'Greyhounds are supposed to be thin.'

'The fucking thing can hardly stand.'

'Same again, Weeze?' Kieran lifted the empty pint glasses. His dad nodded. 'Ta.'

'D'you want a drink, Ash?'

'I'll have a Coke.'

While Kieran was at the bar the Weasel turned to his son. 'I'm pleadin' guilty, Ash.'

The boy stopped eating. 'Oh fuck.'

'It's for the best. There's no point going to trial. They've got too much on us. We're goin' for guilty.' Ashley was fighting back the tears. ''Ere,' his dad said, ''Ave a fag.' He pushed his pack across the table.

'How long will you get?'

'Between three and five. Most likely three though.'

'Oh fuck.'

''Ere. Now don't go gettin' upset.' His dad tapped a cigarette from the pack. ''Ere.' Ashley put it in his mouth. His dad struck a match and Ashley inhaled.

'That's better. It'll be all right, son.'

'All right? Of course it won't be fuckin' all right. What's goin' to happen to me? They'll stick me in care.'

'No. No, they won't. I promise. I'm workin' somethin' out.'

Ashley was shaking when Kieran returned with the drinks. 'What's wrong with the kid?' he asked the Weasel. 'Cold?'

'I've just told him. About the guilty plea.'

Kieran sat down and leaned towards Ashley. 'It's for the best, Ash, honest. It'll save him two years.'

Ashley couldn't speak. He had stopped the tears, but he couldn't control the ague that had taken his body, or the snot running from his nose.

Kieran pushed a plastic sachet to the Weasel.

'Go and blow your nose, son.' He dropped the sachet in Ashley's lap beneath the table. "Ere, but only a line mind. Just to make you feel better.'

'You should do something about his spots, Weeze,' Kieran said as the two men watched the boy make his way towards the Gents. 'Take him to the doctor before you go down.'

The Weasel lifted his beer and took a gulp. 'Fat chance. 'E won't even let me squeeze 'em for 'im.'

After school Karl brought Ashley's coat round for him. 'Come in the kitchen,' Ashley told him, 'it's warm in here. I'm making my tea. Want some toast?'

Karl shook his head. 'Whittaker had me,' he told Ashley. 'Asked if I knew where you'd gone. Said he's going to ring your dad.'

Ashley snorted. 'Landline's off and they ain't got his mobile number. He don't care anyway.' St George snuffled round Karl's feet. The boy stroked her head.

Ashley lined fish fingers up on a slice of toast, poured tomato ketchup over them and put another slice on top. He bit into the sandwich. A fish finger slipped out on to the floor. The dog pounced on it. Karl laughed.

'Me dad's pleadin' guilty.'

Karl felt awkward, so he said nothing, just patted the dog's head.

'He'll get three years.'

Karl still didn't know what to say.

'So I'm in the shit. Don't know what to do.' There was no

point beating about the bush. 'D'you think your mom'd let me stay at yours. Till I'm sixteen. A sort of foster. She'd get benefit. Some sort of allowance. At least fifty quid a week. Probably more: I'm Special Needs.'

'Dunno. I'll ask her.'

'I could have Wesley's room. While he's in Iraq.'

'He'll be back in April. The twenty-ninth.'

'I could find somewhere else. For while he's on leave.'

'Dunno. I'll ask her.'

'Thanks.'

'Are we going to nick some stereos tonight?'

'Yeah, all right. When I've finished my tea. D'you want to see *Neighbours* first?'

'Might as well.'

When the programme was finished and the boys were leaving the house Ashley grasped Karl's arm. 'If your mom won't have me, d'you think she'd let you look after the dog?'

'Dunno. I'll ask her.'

Then there was the pigeons. What to do about the pigeons? Taking the tin of feed from under the sink he walked down the narrow strip of garden to the shed. He drew the bolt. The hungry birds swooped around him. Ashley made the squawking sound, *chorkee, chorkee, chorkee*, as he cast the feed in arcs around the shed.

This was stupid; he might just as well let them go. Just leave the door open. Let them join up with the street pigeons. Give them their freedom. There was one week to go till the trial. There would be no one to look after them then. Not that his dad did much of a job of looking after them. He used to, years ago when Ashley's mom was here. He had good pigeons then, looked after them properly, raced them seriously. Ashley remembered when he was a little kid watching his dad taking them one by one and thrusting them away, sending them tumbling upwards, as if thrown by a juggler into the sky. Ashley used to love watching that.

When he returned to the shed none of them had left. They couldn't be bothered. All instinct was gone now. Standing in their midst, he gently lifted the nearest grey bird, a collar of white around its neck, from a perch, stroked with his fingers the length of the head a couple of times, then quickly grasped, tugged, felt the quick jerk of the body, a fluttering of the wings, then stillness. He dropped the bird to the floor. Reached for another. Repeated the action. Reached for another. Until a dozen birds lay dead on the shit-encrusted floor of the shed. Soon he would have to do something about the dog.

Ashley did churches on Sunday mornings, sometimes with Karl. It was easy. If the alarms went off people were slow to return to their cars. You can't just rush out of a church service. He could do half a dozen in a morning, no problem.

Ashley took the CD players round to Easy Ted Nichol's for a fiver a time. Sometimes, now, they got a satnav. Ted paid fifteen quid for those. He flogged them at car boot sales. Ted's maisonette was up on the Mendelssohn Estate, the Mendy, just off the Tallis Road. There was a small stickered Cross of St George, about twice the size of a postcard, neatly placed in the corner of each of the front windows. The Weasel said it made the place look like a first aid centre, but nobody was fooled; everybody knew what it meant. It had cost Ted a few windows now and then, but as soon as they were replaced the flags were back. No windows had been smashed for a while now.

'You're a little bastard,' Ted told him.

'Oh yeah?'

'Yeah. What you did to your dad's birds.' Ted cuffed the side of Ashley's head.

'Piss off.'

'Then you let the fuckin' dog eat 'em.'

'She was hungry.'

'Fuckin' loon you are. Broadmoor's waitin' for you, mate. Got a bed with your name on it.' He put a mug of tea in front of Ashley. 'Want some toast with that?'

'Go on then.'

When Ashley had eaten his toast and collected from Ted he confided his fears. 'Social worker keeps coming round.'

'Trial's Thursday?' Ted checked.

'Yeah.'

'And?'

'I'm in the shit. She keeps goin' on about fosters.'

'They're not gonna let you stay in that house on your own, Ash.' Ted could see the tears in Ashley's eyes. 'Fag?'

Ashley took the offered cigarette from Ted and lit up.

Ted watched him. He felt sorry for the boy. 'It's for the best, kid. You get the right family, they'll look after you.'

'No way.' It was almost a wail.

'Ash, you can't stay in Cecil Road. The house'll be repossessed in a couple of months.'

'No. Crawford's going to look after that.'

'Bollocks. For four years? There's—'

'Three. He'll get three.'

'Ash, you don't know. Anything could happen.'

The boy said nothing. Ted could tell he was thinking; he let him be. Ashley finished his cigarette, drained the remains of his tea. He was calmer now. 'Ted, any chance of me stayin' 'ere for a bit. Just kippin' like. I'll get the radios for my rent,

And satnavs. Other stuff too. I can do the clothes shops easy. Good stuff.'

'Sorry, mate. Marilyn'll be out in a coupla months. We should get the kids back. It'd be too much.'

'Till then. Till she comes home.'

'Sorry, Ash. No can do.'

'The dog then?'

'Same. Sorry. What about that black mate of yours?'

'Karl? His mom won't let him.' Then quietly, as if to himself. 'No can do.'

Fuck it! Fifty quid's worth of lottery tickets and all he had made was twenty quid. It wasn't fair. This had been his last chance. He knew his dad had agreed with the social worker that he should go into care. That's why she was coming round tomorrow before his dad left for court. No. No. No. He wouldn't. He wouldn't be here when she came. He'd be out of the house before his dad got up. He didn't want to have to say goodbye. He didn't want to have to see him in a borrowed suit, his hair all gelled and combed. He wasn't going to be there to hear him say everything would be all right.

He wasn't going to say goodbye and he wasn't going into care. No way. Some poxy family telling him what to do. Making him sit down for meals. Being all nice. *Just think of Jamie as your brother. You can call me Mom if you'd like.* Well he didn't fucking like. He'd been there before. He hated it. No. No. No. He'd lamp Jamie or Josh or whatever the next one was called and he'd be back in the home waiting for the next on the list to come and collect him. No.

Ashley wondered why there was never any smoke coming out of the big crematorium chimney. Perhaps they burnt them at night. No, the undertaker blokes had told him they do it straight after the funeral, that's the law, they said, it must be done straight away.

Sometimes when he came to the cemetery Ashley practised his reading on the gravestones, or the long marble scrolls that held the names of the war dead. Today he went straight to the laurel bush. The cold wind brought tears to his eyes so he couldn't read the face of his watch, but the case would be over by now. With guilty pleas it was just sentencing.

'I won't be back for a bit,' he explained. 'I'm not going in no home, Nan. Nor a foster neither. I'd rather do time. It'll be better that way. Don't worry; I'll be all right. And I won't hurt anyone. I'm going into school tonight. Just Maddocks's office. Torch it. I won't do it till late, when everyone's gone. No one'll get hurt.' He took a cigarette and lit it. 'All I got to do now is keep out the way till it's dark. I've done the dog. There was no choice. She's in the shed, but I'll take her into the school if I can. Leave her in the office.'

He crouched down and let his fingers dance on the cold earth. The shrivelled grass. The hot smoke in his chest was a comfort. As he ditched the nub he rose. 'Oh well. I'm going now. I'll be all right. I'll be back one day. Promise.'

There were other words – he wanted to say them, but what was the point. And it was too cold anyway. But he'd be warm tonight.

2

Ashley stood in the darkness of the headmaster's office. He had put the dog on the desk. A canister of petrol at his feet. He knew this room so well. A patch of darker dark beyond the desk, a filing cabinet. If he moved a pace or two to his left his leg would touch one of the two upright chairs placed before the headmaster's desk. Outside the window another sort of darkness, bluer, not so black.

A surge of tiredness overtook the boy. He wanted to lie down, beneath the desk perhaps, and sleep. It was ten o'clock. He thought about his dad. His first night, so it'd be Winson Green. It's always a local prison to start with. He guessed he would be in bed by now; they went to bed early in prison. He tried to see him in a cell. Two men, or even three, in a cell smaller than this room. He wondered who he'd be in with. What they had done. And in the silence he recalled the sounds he had heard about: slamming and clanking, footsteps – on metal stairs – hundreds of them; keys – jangling and turning – hundreds of them; after dark – shouting and calling, tapping and banging. His dad had told him stories. It was the smell that was the worst. Piss. Sweat and piss. Kieran had told him it was snoring; that's the worst, other blokes in the cell, snoring like trains, like pigs, and no escape.

He guessed he'd probably know for real in a few days. Well it'd be better than care. He wished he were bigger and stronger. He knew that the kids in YD were tough, hard, brutal. His dad always said, weedy blokes like us, littleuns, have to learn to use our gobs, talk our way out.

He'd got a paper, his reading wasn't that good, and he had looked carefully at each headline, searching for key words, *burglary, sentenced*, but he couldn't see anything about his dad. He wondered if they would write about him after the fire. He lifted the petrol canister. He needed to think this out. If he didn't he'd probably go up with everything. Perhaps that – he stopped the thought and concentrated on the matter in hand. If he slopped about half the can over the dog and the desk, then dribbled a thin trail to the door he could light the newspaper in the corridor, throw it into the office and quickly pull the door shut; that should be okay.

Then burning. In his eyes. Or like there was pepper in them. He opened his mouth to gulp air and a sob shook his body, echoed like another presence in the dark room. Something was going. Something from inside him. Slipping away. What was he going to do? If he set fire to the school, who knew how long he would be looking at, a couple of years at least. American kids shot the school up and then blew their own heads off. There were sites for them on the net.

If he didn't do anything? Just laid low. Tried to get by. They might not notice. Or care even. If he set fire to the school they'd have to chase him, even if he didn't give himself up. In the darkness he stroked the brittle pelt of the dog. Wiry. Sort of hard. No point in leaving her here. He heaved her back into the sack. He'd picked the lock so neatly it slammed to and clicked behind him as if he had never been there.

He let himself into the house. Even darker than in the school. Real black, and the tinny throb of music from the students next door. It was freezing. Cautiously Ashley reached for the switch. He jumped at the light and looked around, as if expecting someone to be sitting there waiting for him. It was funny without the dog. And his dad. He went through to the kitchen and lit two gas rings on the cooker. Let his hands hover over them to warm. Saw how close he could get them to the flame before he had to pull away.

There was no bread, but some Weetabix. No milk, so he spread jam on them; he had four, sitting in the dark. He was nervous about the light being on. It would be best if no one knew he was here. If he only came back here to sleep.

He expected someone would come and they did. Mrs Martin arrived, the social worker he had seen with his dad, knocking on the door in her smart striped suit. He peered down on her from the front bedroom window. She looked through the letterbox, then in at the window. But not too close; the window was dirty. She stepped back into the road, peered up at the bedroom window, saw nothing and got into her car. The next day she was back, this time with another woman, dressed like a hippy, with a shaggy coat and a long flowered skirt. The next day she was back, with the hippy and a bloke in a suit. He spoke on his phone, looked the house up and down. Tried to look in at the front-room window but didn't want to get his cuffs dirty. Then a police car arrived. Two officers, a man and a woman. Both young. Laughing. They talked to the social workers, looked at the house, went round the back and looked at the house from there. The social workers knocked on the door again. The police officers came back and banged on the door. Looked through the letterbox. Peered in through the window. Banged on the door again.

Ashley had a plan. If it looked like they were coming in he would go up into the loft. They wouldn't go up there. He watched them all standing round the police car, talking. The hippy kept sneezing. The woman police officer stepped away, didn't want her germs.

Ashley was ready. If the police took anything out of the car that suggested they were going to break in he would make for the loft – but they didn't. They talked for a bit longer, then the police officers got into their car and left. The man in the suit spoke on his phone again, then to the two women. One last look at the house and they got into their cars and drove away.

He sometimes thought about coming clean, phoning Kieran, or Crawford even, telling them he was in the house and asking for help. Just help in staying here. Sometimes he was optimistic – he could get odd jobs, nick a few things, get enough money to pay for his food and the bills when they came in – electric, gas, stuff like that. He'd just take the cash to the post office; you can pay bills like that at the post office. But what about the mortgage? He had no idea how his dad paid the mortgage. And that would probably be a lot. That's why he needed to talk to Crawford; his dad had said he was going to look after the mortgage for him, he was sure he had.

After a few days he started going out more, spending most of the day in the park, wandering round the streets, or in the arcades. Sometimes he went into Cotteridge and wandered around the small workshops and industrial units scattered among the rows of terraced houses there, asking if they wanted any jobs doing. The Asian blokes were best. Ashley felt they wouldn't ask any awkward questions about school, that they wouldn't report him to anyone. Sometimes he got jobs like cleaning cars, or helping to pack away stalls outside shops at the end of the day. A bloke called Mr Ahmad from the box factory told him to come on Friday mornings if it wasn't raining. He could clean the directors' cars, four of them, ten quid.

He took a gamble and went round to Benjy Graham's. An old mate of his dad's. Benjy had a few things going, mostly legit these days, stuff like selling on the markets, and Ashley wondered if he wanted a helper.

'You're too late, kid. If it was before Christmas I might have been able to use you, but things are quiet now. People don't come out so much in the winter. Too cold. Tell you what though. Leave me your number. If I do need a hand any time I'll give you a call.'

Ashley put on his most pathetic and disappointed look as he gave Benjy his number, and it worked. Benjy fished a tenner from his pocket. 'Here you are, kid, this might help.'

'Ta. It will.'

Then Benjy had an idea. 'How's that dog of yours? St George.'

'She died. A virus.'

'I like to walk my dogs myself. Gives me a bit of exercise.' He patted his belly. 'But mornings is busy. How do you fancy exercising 'em for me? A good distance though. Then I won't have to do so much at night. That'll please the missus.'

'Yeah. I can do that. Easy. A really long walk. How much?'

'Well, to start with let's say two quid a go.'

'Four.'

Benjy chuckled. 'Okay. Let's settle at three. An hour's walk, mind.'

'Cool.'

Ashley was at the Grahams' for six-thirty. It was still dark and there was frost on the ground. Car windscreens looked like bathroom windows. He wanted to get the job done and be out of the way before kids started making their way to school. He was still keeping low. Benjy was long gone. There was a damp black oblong in the frost where his van had stood. You have to be an early riser if you work the markets. Ashley could do that. He didn't mind getting up early if there was something to get up for. He thought he might like the markets. Course you needed the chat. More like comedians some of those blokes. But he could do it, he was sure he could. And if he could perfect his smoke tricks, do the question mark – that would go down well with the shoppers.

When Ashley rang the bell the bedroom window above him opened and a woman poked her head out.

'You Ashley?' He could see the top of her blue nightdress bunched in her hand.

'Yeah.'

'Bloody hell, it's freezing. Here's the key to the back gate. The dogs are in the shed, and the leads are hanging up there. You'll see them. A security light comes on from the back door.' She dropped the key and Ashley caught it, no problem. 'And love, don't let 'em shit in the garden will you.'

'Okay.' Ashley wasn't sure how he was going to prevent them from doing this, but still.

'Oh, and Benjy says give 'em a good hour.'

The dogs started barking as soon as he opened the gate. He knew there were three of them. Staffs. And he knew what he had to do. Talk to them through the door till they stopped barking. Open the door and stand still; let them come to him – still talking. Let them take a good sniff. It was easier to coax two or three dogs than one. One guard dog on a site was more difficult than two or three. He had heard lots of blokes say this. Two or three you can coax; just one, they go mad, too defensive; you have to take them out.

The Staffs sniffed around his trainers. He let his hand fall so they could sniff it. Still talking, like to babies. One dog licked his hand, warm and rough but not wet, not slobby like some dogs, like greyhounds for example. Staffs have dry mouths. Ashley turned his hand and started to stroke one of the dogs. Slowly. A pat or two when it was ready. Then, bend the legs at the knees and in one easy movement you're down to their level, still talking. Another pat. Ruffle the coat a bit. *You're a good boy aren't you?* Then you can start moving. *Come on then you lot, come on.* He found the leads. Rattled them a bit. They started to get excited, knew they were going for a walk. They were ugly little fuckers but they seemed all right, Ashley liked them.

He saw Mrs Graham peering down from the back bedroom window, trying to watch him through the early-morning gloom. Checking to see if one of them did a dump probably. But they didn't let him down. They were keen to get started, real getaway merchants, straining at the leash, and they didn't start shitting till they were well down the street.

Ashley had worked it out. He walked them to Norton Playing Field, there was no one there at this time in the morning, and here he let them off the leash for a bit. Then he walked them along the canal up on to the Mendy, and then down along the Pershore Road and through Kinny Park back home. He was pleased with the plan. But he wished he'd had some breakfast. All he'd wanted when he got up was a cup of tea and a couple of fags. The cold was making him hungry. Benjy wasn't going to pay him until the end of the week, but he had enough to go to a caff and have a bacon sarnie.

There were texts from his dad a few times. He wondered how he had managed to get hold of a phone. He knew they weren't supposed to have them. Kieran had told him that blokes used to hide them up their arses. Ashley couldn't imagine his dad doing that. He remembered trying to get a banana up his own. Perhaps he had just borrowed one. But Ashley never opened the messages. He wanted to. In a way. But in another he didn't. Sort of scared. He asked himself what sort of message he'd like to get from his dad, what he'd like him to say. But he couldn't come up with an answer.

Then there was one from KW. KW? Ashley opened it. *I am changing locks on cecil rd tomorrow. be there. kieran.*

More shit. He should have known it was going too easy. But Kieran was okay. He was sure he was.

Kieran threw a tube of something at him when he arrived the next day. Ashley caught it one-handed.

'Catch!' Kieran cheered.

'What's this? Toothpaste?'

'It's for your skin. Get rid of the spots.'

Ashley looked at the tube. He wasn't sure what the word on the front said.

'You put it on in the morning and before you go to bed. And every time you wash your face. Should last you ages. Anyone been round?'

'No. Well, social worker, the day after the trial. Didn't let her in. Hid upstairs. She checked the place over from the outside. Thinks I've gone. Hasn't been back since. How long did he get?'

'Three.'

Ashley nodded.

'Crawford says you can stay here for a bit if you want. So long as your old man does his stuff and keeps his mouth shut. But.' He raised his index finger, pointing upward, then drew a downward arc stopping between Ashley's eyes. 'Stay out of trouble. Don't attract any attention. And. He'll be storing things here. So stick to your bedroom. No snooping. What you don't know can't hurt you – well, that's what they say.'

There was another bloke waiting in a van outside. Kieran called him in.

'Woytec,' he told Ashley. 'Polish. He's working on Crawford's extension. He's going to help me do a little job. Make us a cup of tea, Ash.'

They turned the radio on and got to work changing the locks. They changed the ones on the front and back doors, and then to Ashley's surprise put mortises on the internal doors.

'Here.' Kieran held a pair of keys on a ring. 'For you. Front door. Back door. There's no lock on the kitchen, this room, your bedroom or the bathroom. Everywhere else is out of bounds. Got it? Keep out.'

Ashley looked at the keys. 'It's like that story.'

'You what?'

'For kids. Princess. I think. Couldn't go into any of the rooms in the castle.'

Kieran just looked at him, like he was sorry for him. 'You've got a number for me in your phone from the text?' Ashley nodded. 'You notice anything? Anyone snooping round? Cars you don't know parked outside? Anything? Call me.'

'I've got no credits.'

Kieran sighed, and gave him twenty pounds. 'For calls to me only.' But you could tell from the way he said it, he knew he was wasting his breath. 'This is serious, Ash. Do as you're told and you'll be okay. But.' And the finger was working again. 'Screw things up for Crawford and you'll really be in the shit – buried in it. Understand? This isn't school now.'

Ashley nodded, then grinned. He liked Kieran.

3

She was there every time he went into the arcade. The cancer woman. Sitting feeding coins into a fruit machine. Always the same one – the third from the door in a row of eight. She was bald. Completely. Shiny. The lights from the machine reflected on her head. He knew that baldness – cancer. It reminded him of his nan. Chemo. It had got to be. Her proper name was Jackie, he heard the manageress call her that. The manageress's name was Alma.

A week after his dad got sent down he started going in every day. It was warm and there was a hot drinks machine. One day Alma said to him, 'You're becoming a regular. Shouldn't you be in school?'

'I'm sick.'

The cancer woman laughed. 'Aren't we all, kid?'

'Now, Jack. Stay positive.' Alma turned to Ashley. 'How old are you?'

'Old enough.' He moved towards a machine.

'Cheeky young sod. If anyone checks, you told me you're sixteen. Right? Jackie heard you.' Jackie nodded her head without looking towards them and the huge gold hoops hanging from her ears waved.

'Mind you, they'll probably tell me to get my eyes tested. I only let you in 'cause you come early,' Alma told him.

'Okay.' He fished a quid out of his pocket.

'And ten pound max.'

That took him less than ten minutes. He left a pound on the counter when he cashed in his tokens. 'Ooh style. Ta, love.' Alma dropped the coin into her overall pocket. This was an investment, Ashley told himself; if he did this every time he reached the max, he knew she would increase it. Probably to twenty. And if he upped it to two then, it wouldn't be long before she lifted the max altogether. Let him on the big jackpots. An investment. He looked towards the cancer woman to say goodbye, but her head was down, red and blue light dancing on it.

'Keep warm,' Alma called to him. 'Brass monkeys out there.'

There was a girl at the park bus stop wearing a pink anorak. *Copacabana* was written in blue sequins on the back. Ashley recognised her: Sophie Lyons from school. Obviously wagging it. She was wearing jeans, but Ashley knew a lot of the girls changed straight out of school uniform in Kinny Park. It was probably in the bag she carried.

Ashley crossed the road and moved up behind her. He tapped her left shoulder and stepped to the right as she turned. He tapped the right shoulder and she turned back to face his pointing finger.

'Caught ya.' He wagged his finger. 'You're a naughty girl.'

'Ashley Loop. Ya wanker. You scared the shit out of me.'

She was wearing lipstick, pink. And eye make-up, pale blue. She pouted. Made a pissed-off noise. Twisted her head so that her hair unfurled like a banner and swung around her head. Like hair in shampoo ads.

'Caught ya. Waggin' it.'

'Not,' she said through the returning hair.

'Y'are. You should be in school.'

'Listen to who's talking. I'm on home teaching.'

'Yeah.'

'I am. Three mornings a week. Asian lady, Mrs Syed.'

'Why?'

She tutted. 'I'm pregnant, stupid. Look.' She pulled her anorak up and let her hand trace the curve of her small bump. 'Nearly twenty weeks,' she announced proudly.

Sophie sat on one of the small green seats inside the bus shelter. The ones that looked as if you should be able to move them, tip them back and forth, but you couldn't; rock solid; vandal-proof. Ashley sat next to her.

'Got a spare?' Sophie asked. 'I'm gaspin'. It's the only thing stops me feelin' sick till I've had me dinner.' Ashley took his cigarettes from his jacket pocket. Opened the pack so Sophie could see there were only two left. Pulled them out. Dropped the pack. Gave one cigarette to Sophie and stuck the other in his mouth. Fished his lighter from his trackies.

'You got some money for some more?' she asked.

'Yeah. I just won some at the arcade.'

'How much?'

'A tenner.'

'Where you going now?'

'Home s'pose. It's too cold to hang around here.'

'You can come back to ours if you like, for a bit. Have a coffee.'

'Where d'you live?'

'The Mendy. Walton Tower. The thirteenth. Lucky for some.'

'Is your mom in?'

'She's at work. Greggs. Over there. The cake shop. That's

where I've bin.' She tapped her bag. 'To get me dinner. Sausage rolls. I love 'em. Can't get enough. Got four here. And an éclair. For the cream.'

'All right then.'

They sat together at the back of the bus, which was occupied by only a few old ladies returning from shopping. It made its way along Pershore Road and at the big island disappeared into a tunnel of trees and bushes that led it over the canal bridge and on to the Mendelssohn Estate. Here the bus started its long journey across the estate, weaving its way through chains of maisonettes and between the standing stones of tall tower blocks.

'Whose kid is it?'

Sophie lifted her left hand. A letter was scarred into each of the three middle fingers. Ashley peered in. 'Tyr Hyde,' she announced. Ashley was glad she didn't mind the question. He hadn't known if you were supposed to ask. 'D'you know who I mean? He left last year.'

'Think so.'

Hyde was a big kid, not really trouble at school, but a big kid, strong, looked more like a man than a kid, people were wary of him. Ashley knew he belonged to Mendy West, one of the Mendy gangs, black kids only. But he seemed all right.

'He's made Paige Crutchley pregnant too. She's due at Easter. But he doesn't have anything to do with her any more.'

'Are you goin' out with him?'

'Course.'

'So, you love him?' Ashley said it in a funny voice. It was meant to embarrass Sophie but it didn't.

'Course I do. D'you ever wash your trackies? Look at the state of them.'

The bus dropped them right outside Walton Tower. An Alsatian stood beside the grilled door to the shop at the foot of the tower. Sophie called to the animal. 'Here, Sabre.' She snapped her finger. 'Here, boy.' But the dog wasn't interested. 'It's too cold,' she explained.

'I'll get some fags.'

'You can't here. She won't serve you. She's really strict like that. Nor booze neither.'

Sophie pressed some numbers on the security pad beside the double doors of the tower block. They buzzed and she pushed the doors open. A girl was coming out of the lift with a child in a buggy. 'They've been pissin' in the lift again,' she said. 'Is it very cold out?'

'Freezing.'

The girl was right, the lift stank of piss. Sophie pressed 13. 'Lucky for some,' she said again. 'We might be leaving here. I don't want to. But Mel says—'

'Who's Mel?'

'My mom. She thinks it's a good chance for us to get a house. Me being pregnant and under sixteen. She says I shouldn't be in a place like this, pregnant, 'cause of when this thing breaks down.' The lift came to an unsteady halt and the doors opened. 'They've offered us a place on the ground floor of Elgar, but a woman killed herself in there and Mel's funny about stuff like that.'

Ashley laughed when he saw the mirror that hung above the settee. 'Is that lipstick?' Sophie had written *So 4 Ty* inside a heart, a little flower like a daisy with a long stalk curving beneath it.

'I can't stop myself. Mel went stark when I did this.' She pushed a plant pot across the table revealing another heart scratched deep into its surface.

Ashley traced it with his finger. 'What d'you do this with?'

'Compass. From school. Same one I used for this.' She raised her hand.

'A compass. On your skin. You'll get AIDS.'

'Course I will.' She pouted at his stupidity. 'I put it in disinfectant first.'

In the kitchen there were more hearts on the white tiles above the sink. 'Mel wipes them off, but I just do 'em again.'

'You're a nutter.'

'I can't stop myself. You should see my bedroom.'

Sophie opened the fridge. 'Do you want coffee or hot milk? I've got to drink lots of milk because I'm pregnant. But I hate it cold. Or we've got plenty of Coke.'

'I'll have hot milk.'

Sophie took a carton of skimmed milk from the fridge and filled two mugs and put them in the microwave. She took the sausage rolls from her bag, cut each in half and arranged them in a circle on a plate. She filled the centre with tomato ketchup. She cut the éclair in half and put that on another, smaller plate. When the microwave pinged she replaced the mugs with the plate of sausage rolls.

The milk had boiled over leaving flaky fawn trails down the sides of the mugs.

'I love that smell.' Sophie heaped spoonfuls of sugar into each cup and stirred vigorously. The sausage rolls were ready. 'I'm havin' some whiskey in mine. D'you want some?'

'Ta.'

They sat in the lounge, the plates between them. Sophie carefully lifted a piece of sausage roll, blew at it and dipped it into the ketchup. 'Help yourself, but be careful, they're hot.'

'You're as good as Jamie Oliver you are. This milk is nice.'

There was a tall column of catalogues in the corner of the room. *Littlewoods*. 'Are those your mom's?'

Sometimes, quite unexpectedly, there was a sneer in Sophie's voice. 'Well they're not mine, are they?' Ashley continued to munch his sausage roll. 'She's an agent. Goes round every Sunday collecting.' Sophie's phone toned. She opened the text. 'It's Tyr. He's coming round in a bit.' She saw the look on Ashley's face. 'It's all right. You can stay.'

'It sounds funny. As a name. Tyr. Car tyres.'

'Short for Tyrone. I like it. It sounds better. Hard. Mel takes the piss, but she can talk. Every bloke she's had had a funny name.' Sophie laughed. 'And she's had a few. She's a bit of a slag really. She works some nights at the Fir Tree, and she went out with a bloke from there called Ian Huntley.' Ashley had heard the name. 'The murderer. Of those girls.'

'Oh yeah.'

'He hated it. Well, everyone took the piss. Always said he was going to change it. Officially. He just used to call himself E. Went mad if you called him Ian.' She giggled. 'Threw a cup of tea at me once for that. So you've changed from a murderer to a drug, I said.' Ashley laughed with Sophie. 'And she had a bloke called Linus. It's Irish. He wasn't. From Cannock. It's Gaelic. Mel used to call him Lingus. 'Come on, Aer Lingus. Where you taking me?' When she said that he used to say, 'I'm flying you to paradise with cunnilingus.' Sophie looked across the table at Ashley, a stare really. He rubbed pastry crumbs from around his mouth. 'D'you know what that is?' She waited.

'Course.'

'What?'

'Oral.'

'That's right. Fanny kissing.' And she squealed with laughter. 'You finished?'

Ashley lifted the remaining piece of sausage roll, wiped it through the ketchup and dropped it into his mouth. 'Am now.'

Sophie removed the plate from the table, took it into the kitchen and returned with a cloth to clear the crumbs from the table. She cupped them carefully into her hand. 'D'you want another drink with that éclair?'

'Ta.'

'There's not enough milk for us both to have a cup, so you'll have to have coffee, or tea.'

'Tea. Two sugars.'

'Whiskey in it?'

'Ta.'

When she returned with the drinks Ashley was studying a photograph on the sideboard. 'Is this your mom?'

Sophie came across to stand beside him. 'Mel. Yeah. And that's the murderer. E.'

'She looks young.' Mel's hair was pink and she wore big earrings like the cancer woman's. A stud in her chin and a bolt through her eyebrow.

'It's a good photo. What's your mom like?'

He hesitated. 'She's dead.'

'Cancer?'

'Yeah.'

'Where?'

'Dunno. My nan had it in the lung. But I don't know about my mom. Same probably.'

'There's a woman on the fifteenth with breast. And one of Mel's mates, used to work at Greggs, she's got it. It's everywhere, breast.'

Sophie lifted a catalogue from the pile. 'Look, let me show you what I am going to have.' She flicked through to the maternity clothes section and pointed out the outfits. Then she showed him the buggy and the cradle she wanted.

'I like old names. Like Douglas. I really like that. For a boy.'

'It's a last name. Michael Douglas. Kirk Douglas.'

'And a first name. Like Thomas. Can be first or last. And Lazarus. That's from the Bible. I like that. You could have it for a girl too. And it sounds cool short. Laz.'

'That's Polish.'

'Course it is!'

'It is. There's a bloke me dad knows. He's Polish, and he's called Laz.'

'Where do you live?'

'Cecil Road. Seventy-three.'

'The old houses. By Stirchley.'

'Yeah.'

'Old Birmingham, Mel calls it. Says she likes Old Birmingham better than the estates. D'you get a lot of Asians round there?'

'Not really. A lot of students.'

Tyr had a mate with him when he arrived. 'What you brought him with you for?' Sophie moaned.

'What you got him here for, man?' Tyr jabbed a finger at Ashley sitting on the settee, like he was throwing a dart. 'He ain't from the Mendy, is he? And district.'

'He's a friend.'

'Well Geezbo my friend. Get used to it.'

'Geezbo ain't from this manor neither,' Sophie countered.

Tyr was still pointing at Ashley. His finger held there. A hard look on his face. The words coming out of his mouth sideways. Ashley knew that look. Meant to be tough. Make him feel threatened. It didn't, and Tyr saw this. 'Where he from?' He turned to Sophie so he could release himself from the pose with dignity.

'From school. My class. Ashley Loop. He's lying low so he won't have to go into care. He's cool.'

Tyr pulled Sophie's head towards him and kissed her, then led her to an armchair where she sat on his lap. The kid behind him, Geezbo, wearing long baggy shorts with his thick red bomber jacket and blade boots, sauntered across and bounced down beside Ashley. 'Ashley Loop.' Said his name like he was tasting it. 'Why they wanna to put you in care, Ashley Loop?'

'His dad's inside and his mom's dead. Cancer.'

'Where you livin', man?'

'Cecil Road. His dad's house.'

'Shut up, bitch. Will you let the man talk for 'is self?'

'I'm staying in my house,' said Ashley. 'Till my dad gets out.'

'On yus own?'

'Yeah.'

''Ow you livin', man?'

'Odd jobs.'

Geezbo nodded, thinking. Tyr pulled his jacket open and peered inside. 'Look what I got in 'ere. Smoke.' He picked cigarettes individually from the pack inside his jacket and threw one to each of them. A lighter followed.

Ashley inhaled. 'Menthol! Shit, man. What you smoke menthol for?'

'They were the nearest to the shop door, man.'

4

Someone was at the door. Ashley muted the telly and tried to work out who it might be. It wasn't the police, wasn't the neat rap of a social worker. He waited, and it came again. Not impatient. Sounded like it was being done with the heel of the hand. That'd hurt if you didn't know how to do it right.

Both the front room down here and the upstairs front bedroom were locked now; Crawford's territory. Out of bounds. So Ashley couldn't check from the windows. So. Soundless. Waiting. Like a cat poised for the getaway. The heel of the hand again. Harder this time. Three fast blows. Then the letterbox flicked.

'Ashley Loop. I knows yus in tere, man. Could 'ear the telly. Knowed yus muted it now.' It was a kid's voice, but Ashley wasn't sure whose. 'I'm the chief social worker for Brum and I've come to take you into care. A nice Christian family. Church every Sunday and clean pants.' Laughter. 'No. It's me, Geezbo.'

Ashley opened the door. Geezbo was wearing his shorts again.

'Don't you get cold?'

'Don't matter, man. It my style. You gonna ask me in? I come to visit you, man.'

Ashley led him through to the back room. 'Who told you where I live?'

'Sophie, man. No trouble is tere? What you watchin'?'

'Snooker. On tape. O'Sullivan and Ryan Day. Last year's championship.'

''Ere,' Geezbo lifted a sachet. 'Got some weed for us. Catch.'

Geezbo removed his hood, put it on the table. Just a blue T-shirt underneath. Ashley noticed the way he filled it. His biceps stretching the sleeves. Ashley wished he had arms like those. Then you could properly take care of yourself. Geezbo was only a couple of years older than him, but Ashley knew he would never have a physique like Geezbo's, even in a couple of years, even if he trained. *Wiry*, his dad called it.

Ashley skinned up. Geezbo watched him like an assessor. 'Yus good, man. Credit to you. Innit.'

'Why you talking like that?'

'What?'

'Why d'you talk like that? Rasta black boy stuff. You all do it, specially when you're together. Why don't you talk proper English?' Ashley folded a roach.

'It my style man. Me. I-den-tit-ee.'

'You all do it.'

'It a 'eritage ting.'

'But you don't do it all the time. You turn it on. Or sometimes make it stronger. You was born in Birmingham, the same as me. You're English.' Ashley handed Geezbo the spliff to light up.

'But it not my culture see. You 'ave to be true to your culture.' He examined the spliff, testing its firmness. 'Nice job,' and lit up, inhaled. 'Yeah, very good.' He passed it back to Ashley. They returned the sound to the snooker; watching and smoking.

Geezbo was nosey. Between making comments on the snooker he wanted to know why Ashley's dad was inside, and how Ashley was managing, especially for money. 'You got it cool 'ere, man. Needs some hygiene. Know what I mean, man? Net curtains at the front, filthy as hell. But it cool.'

'Fuck this is strong stuff,' Ashley said. The snooker balls seemed to be flying out of the screen.

'Triple-wired. You know what I mean, man? Sweet.'

After the snooker they watched some football. 'Something for you to know, man,' Geezbo said as Ashley changed tapes. 'There's murder. In my family. My mom's uncle, innit. The last man to 'ang in Birmingham. Years and years ago, innit. But still family.'

Geezbo was too smashed to get home. They were watching *The Matrix* when he fell asleep. Ashley couldn't wake him so left him sleeping on the settee. He was gone by the time Ashley got up the next day.

'Benjy will be right fucked off with you.'

'I'm sorry I'm late, Mrs Graham.'

'You know he likes his dogs walked early. That's the whole point.' Mrs Graham was up and dressed. 'If we was going to leave it till this time I could do it myself.'

You're too fat to walk for more than five minutes, Ashley thought. 'Sorry.' The dogs, hearing voices, had started to bark.

'They need regularity. All dogs do. Specially Staffs.'

'Sorry.'

'Well make sure you're here at the proper time in future. And after you made such a good start last week.'

The dogs were eager to be away. Ashley leashed them and headed for the playing field. It was hard with frost and when they got down by the canal its surface was pocked black ice.

The dogs, off their leashes now, made for it and Ashley had to shout them back. The ice looked solid enough, but you could never be sure, that's what they told little kids wasn't it, and the last thing Ashley wanted was to have to tell Benjy Graham that one of his dogs had ended up under the ice. He'd probably be joining the animal if that happened.

A group of Asian lads from the sixth form college that lay behind the bushes lining the canal were standing on Kinny Bridge smoking and stamping their feet against the damp cold. The dogs went barking towards them. Ashley could tell the lads were scared but didn't want to show it. Someone had told him that Asians were scared of dogs. 'You never see Asians with dogs,' they said, and at the time he had thought this must be true, but since then he had seen Asians with dogs, usually shopkeepers though, usually with Alsatians, like Mrs Nayer, the woman who kept the shop at the foot of Walton Tower. The Asian lads laughed as the dogs approached them, but stopped stamping their feet. Cigarettes went into mouths and hands into pockets. Nervously they let the dogs sniff around their feet.

'You're all right,' Ashley shouted as he walked past. 'They don't bite.' The lads looked unconvinced. Muttering to each other in Asian.

Further on there was a bloke wearing a woolly hat and a donkey jacket with a toolbag slung over his shoulder and who wasn't scared at all. He crouched down, pushed and pulled the dogs. Made noises at them. Tugged their ears. Put his face close. The clouds of his breath mixed with the clouds of theirs. Ashley could see he was used to dogs, and they liked him. The man looked up. 'These yours, mate?'

'Walking them. For me uncle.'

A dog was licking each side of the bloke's face. The third had his muzzle cupped in the man's hand and was playfully tugging away. Ashley noticed a letter tattooed on each finger of the man's right hand. He could see *S* and *W* but couldn't make the other letters out. 'You're a fine fella,' the man was saying to the dog. He looked up at Ashley. 'Live on the Mendy, does he? Your uncle.'

'Close.'

The man laughed. 'Like you.' He rose. 'Nice dogs anyway. Well looked after. You look after them for him, do you?'

'A bit.' The dogs started to follow the man as he moved away in the opposite direction, but returned to Ashley when he called.

'Well trained,' the man said.

'Why yus got all the doors in your house locked, man? Whaz in dem rooms? Your old man got all his gear in there?'

Ashley shrugged. 'They're just locked. Always have been.'

'No, man. They new locks. Shiny little tings.'

'What you been spying for?'

'I'm not spyin', man. Jus look about me, innit. Know what I mean, man? Know where I'm goin. You get me? Tryin' to get to the bathroom when I stayed ova other night. Every door is locked.'

'The bathroom's downstairs. At the end of the kitchen.'

'I knowed that now. Damn near pissed myself finding out.'

For a moment Ashley wondered if he should tell Kieran about this. But Geezbo didn't know anything. Ashley didn't know anything. There was nothing to know. As far as he did know there was nothing in there – yet. He'd certainly never seen Kieran bring anything in. But that changed.

Ashley came back one afternoon after spending some time with Geezbo and Tyr at Sophie's. On the way back Geezbo had told him a secret. He said he was the one who had made Sophie pregnant, not Tyr. It was his baby. He had been shagging her for ages. But he wasn't going to let on. Tyr was part of Mendy West. 'I got connections myself,' Geezbo said. 'So if it came to it. Know what I mean, man? But there no reason for him to know. If that what Sophie want im to fink, it okay with me, man. It sweet.'

Kieran opened the door before Ashley could turn the key in the lock. He could hear voices in the front room. 'Give us half an hour, will you? Ash. Here.' He fished in his pocket for a tenner. 'Get yourself some chips. Give it an hour. We'll be finished then.'

'Okay.' Ash had had some toast at Sophie's so he went to the arcade. The cancer woman wasn't there. It was the first time he had been there when she wasn't. There were quite a lot of people in but her machine was free. He didn't know whether to use it or not. It might bring him luck – or bad luck if she had got cancer.

There were two Chinese blokes in suits on the big jackpot machines. He wondered if they were part of the Dragons, the Chinese mob that did protection in the clubs and casinos in town. He'd heard his dad talking to Kieran about the trouble Crawford had with them sometimes. But he didn't think they would be out here in Stirchley. They usually kept to Chinatown. Probably waiters from Cotteridge, further up the Pershore Road. Cotteridge was full of restaurants. Indian. Chinese. All sorts.

He had started to move towards a machine when he heard Alma's voice. 'Ten quid max for you. Remember.' He changed his mind and went on the cancer woman's machine and lost everything Kieran had given him. He wouldn't do that again.

When he got back to the house, Kieran was gone. It was all dark and cold. Quiet. He felt sad. He put the gas fire on but didn't bother with the light. He wondered what was in the front room. He supposed they had put something in there. He could pick the lock, but he was sure they would have set something up so they would be able to tell if he went in. He got up and went into the hall. Switched the light on. Carefully he examined the edge of the door. He couldn't see anything. He crouched down and examined the lock. A good mortise, but he should be able to do it. But. He reminded himself who he was dealing with. Kieran was all right but mess him about, and remember what he said – *You'll really be in the shit – buried in it.* Best leave it, for now.

It was pissing down when Ashley pressed Sophie's button beside the main door of Walton Tower. Above him he could hear the slap of the rain on the balconies. There were puddles in the lift. 'Mel's here,' Sophie told him as she let him into the flat. 'It's okay though.'

Mel, in a short, silky robe, pink fluffy slippers, dark glasses and a white baseball cap, was lying across the settee smoking, reading an Argos catalogue and watching *Trisha* on television. A glass ashtray rested on her belly. She inclined her head. 'Hello, love, who are you?'

'Ashley.' Sophie answered for him. 'The kid from Stirchley. I told you. His dad's inside. Mom's dead with cancer. Wanna cup of coffee, Ash?'

'Ta.'

'I'll have another Oxo while you're in the kitchen, Bab.' Mel lifted a mug from the floor beside her. She turned to Ashley. 'I'm off work today, love, with a migraine.' Sophie mouthed *hangover* above her mother's head. 'Feel like death warmed up. And not that warm either.' She took a drag from her cigarette and patted it on the edge of the ashtray.

A woman on *Trisha* had started screaming, a lot of her words bleeped out. 'You tell him love. You tell the bastard,' Mel called to the television. This made her cough.

'Come in the kitchen with me, Ash.' Ashley followed Sophie.

'And no more cigarettes this morning,' Mel called. 'You've had two already. I've put her on six a day, Ashley. Don't let her smoke in there will you, love? Or Christ knows what she'll give birth to.' She began to cough again. A deep rattling noise. 'Oh God!' She rapped on her chest with the side of her fist. 'Die, bitch, die.'

In the kitchen Ashley watched Sophie unpeel an Oxo cube and crumble it into Mel's mug, spoon coffee into two others, pour boiling water into all three. While Sophie took the hot Oxo to her mother Ashley put milk and sugar into their coffees. He looked out of the kitchen window at the estate and beyond it. In the distance stood the metal fretwork of three enormous horseshoes, the new hospital they were building. And above the frameworks, cranes, five of them, reaching high into the cold silver sky then dipping down into the nest of the construction site.

When Sophie returned to the kitchen Ashley stuck his hand up his hoodie. Sophie watched him pull out a red Babygro and put it on the kitchen counter. Then another, white this time. A white cardigan. A blue one. Some white booties. 'Present for you.'

'Nicked.'

'Nah.' He grinned.

'Course they ain't.' She was grinning too.

'The market. I tried Mother's Pride. But everything's tagged so—'

'Mother's Pride?'

'What's it called?'

'Mothercare.'

'Yeah. Well I need to do that when it's crowded. People to weave in and out of. So I can do a runner. I reckon I can get you a buggy though.'

Sophie collected up the baby clothes. 'I'll show these to Mel.' Ashley frowned. 'It's okay. She's cool.' Ashley followed Sophie but remained standing in the doorway. 'Look, Mel. What Ash got me.'

Mel slid her head away from the television and pushed her shades above her eyes. In her other hand she held the remote. She muted the sound. 'Oh Christ. Baby clothes. That's really cheered me up. I feel about forty now.' She reached for the bundle. 'Nan. Christ.' She examined the clothes. 'Nice though. Useful.' She looked towards Ashley still in the doorway. 'Where you knock these from?'

'Market.'

'Be careful.' Then, to Sophie, 'Some people think it's unlucky to get stuff too early. Still. Useful though. Thanks, love. I couldn't half do with a new leather purse next time you're down that way.' She handed the clothes back to Sophie. 'The Somali lads, at the end of the curtains row, do some nice ones.' She returned her shades to her nose, her head to the arm of the settee and sound to the television.

There was confusion in Mrs Graham's eyes. She looked around. 'The dogs. Where are they?' The woman's face seemed to grow. A monster. The giant's wife. Ashley could see the small lines around the mouth, pouches at the end of the lips, some tiny hairs beneath the make-up. When she opened it again he was sure he would fall in.

'Nicked.'

'Nicked?'

'Yes. I'm sorry, Mrs Graham.'

Her hand reached for support, but she was further from the door than she thought, and she stumbled against it. 'What do you mean? Nicked? Three Staffs, nicked?'

Ashley stopped trying to fight the tears and let them fall. 'I'm sorry, Mrs Graham. Really.' He started to shake. 'A bloke I see sometimes when I'm walking them down the canal. He's all right. Least I thought he was. Always stops and talks, plays with the dogs. Friendly. This morning when he was playing with them, two other blokes, well one was a kid really, jumped out of the bushes and got hold of me. The kid had a knife. He held me round the neck. The other punched me, twice, in the belly. They leashed the dogs and took them up the towpath a bit and through the bushes. The kid was saying things like—' Ashley started sobbing. 'Things like could I swim. He pulled me to the edge of the canal and said, it's more difficult with a cut throat. I thought he was going to do it, Mrs Graham.' Sobs halted him again. His body shook. 'I really did. I thought he was going to cut me. But he just pushed me in, and ran after the others.'

Ashley stood crying before Mrs Graham. He wanted her to reach out and forgive him. Tell him it would be all right. It wasn't his fault. Take him inside and be nice to him.

'He pushed you in the canal? But you're not wet.'

'I didn't know what to do. I went home and had a wash. I was covered in shit. Changed.'

The backhanded blow from the woman caught Ashley across the mouth. He staggered.

'You stupid little bastard. Two of those dogs are supposed to be breeding this weekend. Two hundred quid each. And we can get more for Sergeant.'

Ashley could hardly see Mrs Graham through his tears. He didn't know what to say now. She grabbed his arm. 'You'd better stay in the shed.' She started to pull him towards it. 'I'll phone Benjy. Jesus Christ, he's going to do his nut. Murder you he will. Probably have another stroke.'

Ashley broke away. Ran. Mrs Graham was shouting at him to come back, shouting threats. He just ran.

The lake in Kinny Park was frozen. Smooth, and grey as gunmetal, the same as the sky. Ducks huddled together at the end where reeds grew. Today they looked like silver spears guarding the birds. But not very well. On the ice were a couple of dead ones, and there was another on the path. Ashley looked down at it, turned it over with his foot. Airguns; kids with airguns. He bet there would be a couple of squirrels around, and he was right, he found two, one taken right through the head, lying under a tree. A squirrel right through the head, that's not easy.

Ashley stamped into the grey frost-covered grass forming patterns: a zig-zag, a question mark. He started on his name, but got bored after the A. As he got closer to the small wall that edged the park he spotted Karl on the pavement beyond, walking at a pace, Blues scarf round his neck, head down, schoolbag bouncing against his leg.

'Karl!' Ashley's yell disappeared into the frozen air unheard by Karl. He yelled again. Nothing. He started to run. Yelling, 'Karl! Karl!' At last the boy halted, turned, saw nothing behind him, made to start again, then heard another yell from the park. He saw Ashley, stood and waited as he ran towards him.

'Where you going?' Ashley asked.

'School.'

'Bit late aren't you?'

'I've been to the doctor. About my verrucas. I thought you was in Ireland.'

'You what?'

'They said at school you'd gone to Ireland. To live with your uncle.'

'Who told you that?'

'Whittaker. Said they'd got a letter. Taken you off the register.'

Ashley was uneasy at this. Glad he was off the register, but unsure about the letter. Perhaps the school was just saying that so they could get rid of him. Forget about him. Or he wondered if his dad might have written it, if Kieran had told his dad he had stopped going to school. Or maybe Kieran himself. 'I've got some money. D'you want a cup of tea? My bollocks are freezing off.'

'All right then.'

Ashley drew a question mark on the steamed-up window they sat beside, then erased it into an irregular smear showing the world beyond the café, but with soft edges, like it was melting, oozing away. Both boys cradled their cups of tea, letting the warmth seep into the palms of their hands. 'There's no point going back to school now. Let's go into town. Pick up some things.'

Karl blew across the surface of his tea. 'No. I want to get my tech project marked.'

Ashley lit a cigarette. 'What you done?'

'The bird box. Level 3. He's grading today.'

5

Ashley didn't recognise the white van parked opposite his house in Cecil Road. There was no reason why he should. Just another van in the string of parked vehicles that always line roads of terraced houses. There were no front gardens in Cecil Road to be concreted and turned into drives, so there were always cars parked, even though half the houses in the street were let to students or gangs of Polish building workers.

Ashley was listening through his headphones to music Sophie had given him. *DJ Ironic*. He didn't see Benjy getting out of the van until it was too late. Benjy was mouthing something at him, shouting it looked like. His mouth open wide, half his head it looked like. Like Jaws coming up for the kill.

Ashley made a dash for the front door and managed to get it open before Benjy reached him. Grabbed for him. Caught the headphones. They slipped to Ashley's neck. 'You little cunt.' Benjy caught his shoulder, shoved him into the house. Ashley ran down the hall to the back room. Tried to slam the door in Benjy's face, but the man was through, banging the door behind him before the boy could stop him. 'You stupid little bastard.'

He seized Ashley one-handed by the collar, dragged him so his face was up close. Benjy's face was red and sweating.

Ashley couldn't breath. He whimpered, 'I'm sorry Benjy. It wasn't my fault. There was three of them. It was too quick to …'

'Not your fault!' Benjy bellowed, flecking Ashley's face with spit. Ashley squirmed in the man's grasp. 'Course it was your fucking fault, ya cunt. Whose fucking fault was it? Mine?' And he nutted the boy, who fell away from him toppling a chair, knocking a cup and a radio from the table.

'I should kill you, ya little fuck.' Benjy pointed at Ashley. 'You were responsible for those dogs. I trusted you with 'em.'

Ashley was crying. 'I've got some money. Nearly thirty quid. I can get some more. I can give it to you now.'

'Thirty quid. I get two hundred before one of those dogs gets a hard-on.' He kicked out. His boot hit Ashley's ribs.

'Please. Benjy.'

Benjy kicked again. Ashley squealed. Benjy kicked again. Ashley curled up to protect himself. His arms wrapped round his head, knees into his chest.

'I'm sorry, Benjy. Really I am.'

Benjy bent over him. 'Shut up, you little cunt.' Ashley sobbed, blood and snot seeping into his mouth. His body shook. Benjy kicked at his knee. 'Listen.' He was panting. 'Tell me exactly—' The door behind Benjy opened. Benjy turned. Ashley turned his head, looked up. Saw legs. Benjy straightened up. There was silence. A man stood in the doorway. Suited. Booted. No tie, just an open-necked shirt. Smart though. He was Chinese. Ashley turned to see properly. The man held a gun. A small silver pistol, no bigger than a fist. Benjy was panting. Wheezing.

'Open your mouth,' said the Chinese. The mouth stayed shut. Benjy was confused. Scared to shit. He couldn't keep up. A gun. A Chinese bloke. In a suit. Here. The kid's place.

The Weasel's place. Where had he come from? What was happening?

Ashley didn't care where he had come from. 'Let him have it,' he shouted. 'Blow the bastard's head off.' Benjy's appalled face turned to Ashley. Turned back to the Chinese bloke. Now he began to shake.

'Open your mouth.'

Nothing.

The Chinese took a step towards Benjy and lifted the gun a little, no more than a tilt really. 'You had no trouble opening it a moment ago. Mouth. Fist. Feet. All in working order.'

'I'm sorry.' Benjy whimpered.

The Chinese guy moved. Grabbed the neck of Benjy's shirt, bunched in one hand. The gun came to Benjy's temple. The man whelped. The Chinese spoke. Right into Benjy's ear. 'I'm going to let you live. It's more than you deserve, but I am. But that mouth.' The gun pushed against it. Ashley saw Benjy's legs shaking like shit. He'd probably piss himself in a minute. 'You open your mouth, breathe a word of anything you've seen here and you're dead. Get it?'

Benjy tried to nod, but the gun prevented him. 'Yes,' he said to the barrel of the gun. Just a flutter of the lips, like he was praying. As they stilled, the gun rested against them. Benjy flinched. The lips tightened.

The Chinese whispered some more. 'You keep your mouth as shut as it is now. Forget all about whatever brought you here and never come back. Never come anywhere near this kid. That way – you will live. But that's the only way. Got it?' He moved the gun far enough away for Benjy to nod. 'Now fuck off.' The Chinese lowered the gun, let Benjy stumble away. They heard the front door bang.

Free of Benjy, Ashley's relief was gone in an instant, as he looked at the man with the gun. Now it was he who was trying to make sense of it all. But he wasn't shaking like Benjy. He noticed he wasn't shaking. Then Kieran appeared in the doorway. 'You little tosser,' he said to Ashley, 'didn't I tell you stay out of trouble? A right fuck-up you've made now.'

SHUKO

6

My name is Shuko, in the English tongue *Bonebinder*. It is an ancient name, given to healers. There is no word in Chinese for irony.

I serve Hsinshu, Emperor of the Ninth Dragon. For him I fulfil many roles. There is nothing he could ask of me I would refuse. And he sets me many tasks. At their tribunals all seven Lords of the Ninth Dragon assemble in the red room above the casino, seated three each side of the long table, Hsinshu at its head. I stand behind and to the left of him; this is my honour and a statement of my servitude.

The energy that drives my nature belongs to the element of Wood, and I, like each tree of the forest, stand alone. When meetings are concluded and the first six Lords of the Dragon have left the room I remain in position. I stand and watch the hours Hsinshu sits in silent thought – his responsibility is great. The principal energy of his nature is Metal; it is the source of his strength. He sits. I stand. The sounds of the casino beneath us belong to another plane, the voices beyond the great door of the red room to another world.

The element of the Ninth is Fire. For this reason we kill

with guns. It was wise of Hsinshu to choose me to serve the Ninth – it is in the order of things for Wood to serve Fire.

Sometimes even Metal must move. When an important decision is close, Hsinshu will rise from his seat at the head of the table and collect three arrows from beneath the dartboard that hangs on the wall at the back of the red room. He will pace back to the line and stand, focused on the board. This is often the way when he is making big decisions, and I love to see it. He did this before the order on the Norway Room was given. It was the only subject on the agenda that evening: *Should the Dragon Move to Take the Norway Room?*

Some around the table were against. One club, they sneered, however successful. An immediate decision became necessary when Ding Chuang informed the Dragon that there were now others intent on taking the club: some legitimate, operating in the British way, others not. Ding Chuang has humour in his character and showed this when he referred to those others as *our friends we love to hate.*

But Reng Zan was not convinced. 'It is only one club. Why get involved in what may become a turf war? We know Mr Stretton, the proprietor, doesn't wish to sell. We know there are those who will try to make him, or take the club anyway. Why involve ourselves? It is only one club. It will make no difference to the Emperor's personal reputation in this city or beyond, or to that of the Dragon. The success of the casinos, the dogfighting, and our import business are all well known and admired, as is the Emperor's facility for fearless and ruthless action.' Reng Zan should have stopped there. 'If the Dragon attempts to take the club and fails, that would be damage indeed, not just to the Dragon's standing in Birmingham, but also to the Emperor's reputation beyond.'

48

The word *fail* should not have been used. It was offensive to the assembly of the Dragon, and particularly to its Emperor. Ding Chuang paused, sensitive to the unease that had been created, before speaking. 'It is not just another club. The Norway Room is the most fashionable and profitable of the clubs in Birmingham. Most importantly it is in the Eastern triangle close to Chinatown and the only establishment here of any importance that we don't control. *But* of equal importance – at least in my opinion and experience,' and at this point there was the smallest of bows towards Hsinshu, a humble gesture and a clever one, 'if we don't take it others will. And soon. If someone, Crawford for example, with his ambitions, were to take the club, enter our territory, it could not be tolerated.' Sensing the feeling of the table was with him Ding Chuang went on to urge the Emperor that the business be completed before the Year of the Boar started in just a few weeks. It is unlucky to leave business unfinished as the year turns.

When all had offered their thoughts to the Emperor the Lords left the room. Hsinshu sat for a long time, considering. Twice he lit and smoked an American cigarette, but these actions were executed with such exquisite slowness they hardly seemed like movement at all. The smoke seeping from each cigarette snaked languidly up above the Emperor, to curve and rest for a second like a crescent moon before fading.

Eventually Hsinshu rose. He stood uneasily for a moment, as if his spirit were returning from a trance – this is not uncommon among those of the Metal element – and collected his darts. When he was ready he turned to face his target and placed his left hand inside his shirt to rest on the Chinese character for power tattooed in black inside a blue circle in his lower jia, just beneath the umbilicus. Taking his energy to his right hand, he breathed deeply, breathed again, then fired the arrows one by one. All three reached the House of Twenty and stood quivering together in the board as close as Siamese brothers. Hsinshu relaxed; he was a true leader.

He returned to perch on the corner of the table, and taking a third cigarette from his silver case he offered me one. American cigarettes are not to my taste, they are too smooth, too sweet, but this was an honour. I lit Hsinshu's cigarette and then my own. Then a further honour: I was to be the first to learn of his decision.

'I think Ding Chuang is right, Shuko.' Hsinshu spoke now in English. 'If Crawford should take the Norway Room it will not be good for us. Ding Chuang is right – it makes economic sense. It was weak and foolish of my predecessor to let the Lopez brothers have the protection rights on the Southside clubs when they were already losing their grip in the city and Crawford was waiting in the wings. Stretton is no longer contracted to anyone; he claims he will pay no one. If Crawford intends to move then we should go before him.'

I nodded. There was nothing useful I could say, so I said nothing.

'I will put you in charge of this business and will talk with you tomorrow about how we will proceed.' The words were a joy to me, as such words always are. It is not boastful to report that he places many responsibilities upon me.

7

It is less than two years since Hsinshu called me to his side. 'The gambling is good business here in Birmingham, Shuko. Lucrative.' As he finished the word, which he always pronounced slowly, breaking it apart to three syllables, a small smile took his mouth; very satisfying to see.

'Shuko, there is a market for another sort of gambling, that could also be very lucrative.' I waited. There was a task coming.

'There are those who prefer a more dangerous way to lose their money. They tire of cards, dice, the wheel.' He looked at me. 'Dogs I think will take their fancy. Fighting dogs. To the death.'

I use two white English women, Diesel and her partner Pauline. Diesel, who is built like a sumo, sources suitable venues. It is of amusement to me that despite the money our venture has brought her she still keeps her snack wagon near the M40. It is called Bite-Inn and is popular with lorry drivers. Her grey hair is cut very short and she wears dungarees. I can rely on her to find venues that are ideal. They are usually old industrial spaces where three or four hundred may gather. There are many such places in Birmingham.

The dogs used to come from a variety of sources. Pauline raised a number of both pits and tosas, but these were unlucky dogs – unlucky for her; destroyed too quickly for her to replenish her stock. Now I use Knighton, a white English from the Mendy. He is reliable, and provides good fighting dogs of several aggressive breeds, mostly Staffs, very strong dogs, admirably stubborn. I don't know where he gets them from, nor do I need to, for he never lets me down.

We are neighbours of sorts, Knighton and I. I live on the sixteenth floor of Nimrod House; Knighton in one of the streets of houses that circle the tower. It is not inconceivable that a firecracker thrown from my back window could be carried by the wind to his home. Or is that just fancy?

I do not spend much time in my flat. I keep very little there. My needs are simple. A bed. My shrine. A chair, a low floor table, and a television. Some books: classics in Mandarin, modern works in Cantonese, the *I Ching* of course, some English books on chess and poker, both interests of mine. I rarely eat there so there is little in the kitchen. Teas. A bottle of vodka, some beers. I buy my Chinese cigarettes in bulk, through the Dragons, cigarettes without filters, and it is the blue-and-gold packs of these that occupy most of the space in the kitchen cupboards.

It is the flat in which we executed Jimmy Slim, and I have lived there since that night. After Jimmy Slim, bound and gagged, had been thrown from the window into the silent blackness of the night, collected from the ground below and disposed of, I set up within the room a small shrine beneath the window from which we threw him, which was only right and respectful, and part of the Code of the Dragons. Having behaved treacherously, working as a spy for one of the black gangs in the city, the Dobermans, he tried to hide in this flat on the Mendy. At that time it was completely empty. Jimmy Slim sat hiding on the floor here for many hours before we found him.

The term *on the Mendy* is interesting. It is used obviously to refer to the Mendelssohn Estate, which is on the west side of Birmingham, but it is also a term used frequently in the city to refer to the practice of sub-letting a flat or a house while its legal tenant is in prison; a practice that apparently started here, and continues, although it is just as prolific on other estates.

My flat was empty for a long time before Jimmy Slim sought refuge there. My feeling is that its last tenant died in jail. A feeling only, for I have not investigated the matter. I pay no rent. No one bothers me. It must have been sorted. At some time someone has been paid – or threatened – to see that it drops off the city council's records. There are a lot of sorted flats on the Mendy, as there are on all the estates. Jimmy Slim's friends from the black gangs must have told him about it. The three other flats on this floor are unoccupied, and have been for a very long time, at least by human beings. The smell and the heat emanating from them suggest other living forms flourish.

The 16 button in the lift does not work, so it never stops here. It is no bother for me to climb the stairs from the fifteenth floor. Sometimes if I have occasion to return here in the daytime I may see some hooded figure entering or leaving one of the other doorways of the sixteenth; youths not much beyond school age. We Chinese are more careful of our youth I think.

Since I supervised the clearing away of Jimmy Slim from the tarmac at the side of Nimrod House I have never seen any connection between my life serving Hsinshu and my sleeping arrangements, for that is pretty much all they are, here on the Mendy. There are a few Chinese in this vicinity; Feiyang, who keeps the takeaway on the estate, and to whom I am related. Feiyang himself is British-born Chinese but his mother is the cousin of my father. There is also Pian Li, who is known to the English around here as Charlie Chann and keeps the gym on the estate known as The Works, and Zusanli who runs the martial arts centre. Wei Lin, the hairdresser.

Occasionally I visit my relatives: at New Year of course, and at Ching Ming each April; six months ago I attended Feiyang's wedding. I do what is right by custom but no more.

8

Envoy. It is a special word. For a special role. Hsinshu was speaking English. 'You will be my envoy. Go as a business-man. Offer Mr Stretton the sum agreed; it is not ungenerous. Explain there is time. A month for a decision. Two further months to vacate. There will be a generous bonus if he agrees to go immediately.'

And so it was – businesslike. That word is correct for Stretton too. Not hostile, not aggressive, but cold, abrupt; short words, quickly spoken, quietly spoken – no nonsense. There is certainly something of the Metal element about Mr Stretton, but that is not, I think, his true element. I believe that his principal energy, like my own, is Wood, but whereas mine is of the strong tree, his is of the seed, full of potential, full of plans, consumed by the instinct to grow.

There was no doubt that the beautiful woman beside Mr Stretton was of the Metal element. She sat at a desk side-on to Mr Stretton, her blonde hair seeming to glow in the gloomy room; scarlet fingernails. I told Mr Stretton that I would to prefer to speak with him alone. 'There is no need, Mr Wood,' he said, using the name with which I had made my appointment. 'Trudy is my assistant. She knows everything about the business. I wouldn't make any decisions without discussing them with her.'

But he discussed nothing with her. 'The club is not for sale, Mr Wood. Nor is it going to be. It's my business and that's the way it will stay. In fact, I may shortly be looking to expand. You might slip me the word if you are aware of anything coming on the market.' There was a roughness of tone in Mr Stretton's voice, as if the words were churned out industrially from some workshop located at the bottom of his throat.

'It is possible that this offer, although already generous, may be improved upon, sir.'

'Not interested. No deal, Mr Wood. You'll have to tell your boss, it's no can do. See the gentleman out, Trudy.'

'It is a very good offer,' I said to Trudy as we made our way downstairs. 'And as I said, financially it is not the last word.'

'No,' she said. 'But what Mr Stretton says is. He's not a man to change his mind.'

Usually I have no difficulty at all in keeping my mind on my work. There is little else I wish to think of. But as I made my way back to the casino I found that the image of Trudy had found a place in my brain; one which I feared would be difficult to dislodge.

I am wary when it comes to women, and try now not to follow inclination. From the time he was a very young boy my brother, whose birth contravened the family laws of our country, was with the Chinese Circus of Chengdu Province. At eighteen he married Tai Yuan, a former Young Pioneer gymnastics champion, three years his senior, who joined the circus as a tumbler. I met her for the first time on the day of her wedding. I was not prepared for my feelings. Lust certainly, a mountain of it, but besides that, and more alarming for me at that time, a lake of tenderness. Within a few weeks we were making love whenever we could. I looked at my brother's face of happiness and felt nothing, but for Tai Yuan it was an agony.

She was sure the son she gave birth to a year later was mine. 'Break the law,' I told her. 'Soon it will be spring and the circus will be on the road again. Have another child. Your husband's child.'

It was towards the end of summer when I visited them in Guillin. From the audience I watched her throw her body into the air, turn it into a circle, leap high through hoops and raise it from the ground straight and true and at an angle to her head. The audience cheered loudly.

The next day when we met in some place I could make love to her, I had condoms. 'There is no need,' she said when she saw them. 'I am sterilised now. I am a tumbler. I don't want to stop my work again. I don't want to break the law.'

On the fourth day of my stay I sat in a practice tent watching Tai Yuan throw herself around the sand circle there, yelling as she did so, fierce as the tigress. And as she paused for rest, slumping forward so that her arms swung beside her legs, and breathing deeply, she raised her head and caught sight of me. It was not hatred in her eyes as she rose to an upright position, but it certainly was not love. And now the word people use, certainly in the West, when they speak of right, of wrong – moral. If I can find meaning in what those eyes conveyed, it was something to do with that word, moral. But alone it is not enough. Moral something. Moral exhaustion? Perhaps. It is close. Or possibly that other word they are so fond of here, disgust.

*

It was not the last time I saw her. I saw all three of them each New Year at my parents' house. I used to watch Tai Yuan looking at her husband playing with his son; the boy up on his shoulders, throwing him into the air. The boy's birthday fell too close to New Year to justify a special visit, so I waited until the August Moon Festival when I could take gifts for the boy. And it was not the last time I made love to Tai Yuan. It happened every time we were together, and I do not regret it. They are memories I love. But with each visit we spoke less, and nothing of consequence, and so I do not know whether she intended to kill the boy or not. The van she was driving went over a cliff edge in Fujian Province. There was only her and the boy in it.

My brother now has another wife, and another son. It was in the year of Tai Yuan's death that I left China and came to find my friends here, so I have never met my brother's second wife, or their son, although each New Year I receive a photograph of all three and their good wishes. It would be unlucky for them not to send it, and I in my turn send gifts and wishes. I have now passed forty and so can add the word blessing to my greeting to my younger brother. There is no need for a photograph, he knows how I look.

CARROW

9

Carrow was back. The city hadn't changed. Why should it? It was only a year. No: all the changes were his own.

Copper – no more.

Highly paid bodyguard – no more.

Jamaican beach bum – no more.

Grieving son – well he'd take a check on that.

Was he unhappy? No. Happy? Well he'd take a check on that too.

But the night was good. The dark wet cold Birmingham night. He'd stepped outside the Norway Room to breathe the city's damp air – to mix it with some nicotine. A month ago he had been breathing the salty Caribbean winds of Bluefields Beach. But he was glad to be back. The muted throb of electronic music seeped out through the old walls of the Norway Room, something to keep him company beneath the blue lamp.

He inhaled. Good. But a spliff would be better. And a woman. He looked at his watch. Three a.m. The time door duties slowed down. No one would mind if he went for a shufty round, see what he could fix up. He'd be back at the door before four – throwing-out time.

A nurse. Perfect. 'Ruthie,' she said. And he knew he was in even before she said 'I've got a weakness for black guys.'

And she obviously had. He noticed the framed photograph of one with his arm around her on the sideboard as soon as she led him into her flat. 'Is he yours?'

'Yes.'

'Where is he?'

Ruthie put the picture in a drawer. 'Away for a bit.'

'Inside.'

'Inside,' she repeated.

The next day when the time came to leave – toast, coffee, cigarettes all finished – he didn't want to go.

'What's his name?'

The question surprised her. 'Howard. Howie.'

'How long?'

'Another three months. If he behaves.'

'I'd like to come back some time.'

'Tonight if you like.'

'I used to be a copper.'

'Yeah.' Thoughtful. 'I can see that.'

It was blatant – these things always are. The Rover snails up Firth Street. Eases to a halt outside the Norway. Empties four Chinks. All in suits. The lanky one pulls the gun. Carrow feels it jab into his forehead before his vision can focus the moving object.

'The boss.'

No point arguing. Day eight, Carrow thinks. Eight days here, and now I've got a gun slapped into my head. He drops his cigarette. He understands the score. He is not in danger so long as he obeys instructions – at least that's what he tells himself. He turns. Slow. And easy. Leads them in. 'It's okay'

– he nods to Mia at the desk – 'they're with me.' Round the dance floor. Up through the Oslo Lounge. He feels like a boxer on his way to the ring for a prizefight, flanked by his entourage. Along the corridor. He stops at Stretton's door. The gun comes out again. Rests on the back of his collar. Kisses his neck. He bangs his fist on the door.

'Yes?' Bad-tempered.

Carrow tries the handle. Unlocked. Opens the door. Stretton looks up from his desk. Counting cash. Trudy side-on to him doing the same. The gun slips from Carrow's collar to rest on his shoulder. Stretton's fingers leave the notes. He leans back in his chair. Takes in the picture in his doorway. Not too surprised it seems. Trudy stops counting. Reaches out to a cigarette smouldering in the ashtray. Hard blue eyes. Scarlet fingernails, with glitter. Slowly she brings the cigarette to her lips. Cool, Carrow thinks.

'Go and have a drink, Carra,' Stretton says. 'Take Trudy with you.' The gun slides from his shoulder. The Chinks shuffle a path for them to leave. He hears the door slam shut. Trudy leans against the corridor wall. 'I'm staying here,' she says. Still smoking.

At the bar he orders a Bacardi. Ice and lime. Thinks Jamaica. Thinks Bluefields Beach. Thinks Fort Clarence. Tries not to think of his mother. He takes a hefty slug. Toga comes across. 'What's goin' down?'

'Search me. Gun in my head and they want the boss.'

'Dragons.'

'I thought this place was clean.'

'It is.' A sneer curves his lips. 'Must be business. I'd heard there was a spot of interest. Takeover.'

Danger. It was in the way he kissed her. That's how you know.

Especially on the second night. The kissing. And touching. Slow. Smiles and sighs. That's dangerous.

'Old people?'

'Yes.'

'And you like it?'

'I've done all sorts. You have to. A&E. Gynaecology. Intensive care. But I'll stick with this. Geriatrics. It's what I like.'

When he'd first seen her, dancing in the Norway Room, she'd been in a silky black dress. Now he thought nurses' uniforms. Imagined her in one, pushing a wheelchair. He didn't want to see what was in the chair.

It was more than lust. Or there was an interceptor. A feeling that he wasn't looking for. Not right now anyway. He'd had enough of feelings. But it was there. She played with his ear. 'I'll see you around,' he said.

It was inevitable that Carrow would come across some Birmingham faces here on the door at the Norway. They had their own pubs, places like the Little Moscow in Tyseley, the Last Morsel in Aston and the Earl in Newtown, but the younger guys liked a night out in the clubs as much as anyone. And there were the opportunities: watching; checking out what was what – something to take back to the boss; networking. Then, his third Saturday in, he sees Kieran and Pricey from Crawford's mob lining up to come in – all nicely dressed and well behaved. They recognised him. A sort of nod from Kieran. Now he wasn't the law it seemed he could at least be acknowledged.

A little later Kieran came up to him. 'Crawford heard you was back. Dutchland didn't work out then?' Carrow said nothing. He saw Pricey lurking in the background. 'I suppose he thought you'd go back on the force. But it looks like you've decided against that?'

'That's right.' He didn't add – for now.

'Well, Crawford would like a word. It's no good asking me what about. I don't know. He could be offering you door work at one of the clubs. But I doubt that, somehow.' Kieran took a card for the Spotted Hippo from inside his jacket. On the back was written a mobile phone number in blue biro. 'Give him a ring. Make an appointment.'

The Spotted Hippo at eleven in the morning – dull and dingy. The scarlet stage curtains, rich and vivid in stage light, were just garish in the gloom of the standard overhead lighting that exposed stains on the carpets, cigarette burns on tables, brown plush seating the colour of dried blood. The glittering poles were pointless without their female pendants. The bars that edged the room were shuttered and locked. A strong smell of air freshener. Two heavy-eyed young women pushed Hoovers around.

The guy who had let Carrow in – all bouncer gear, at this time in the morning – led him through the club to Crawford's office.

Stretton's office at the Norway was a grubby, windowless little room. Crawford's office was spacious and light; you could see the Rotunda from a tall window behind Crawford's desk.

Crawford had a reputation for being immaculately dressed, the price he paid for suits. Today it was a blue suit, white shirt, red silk tie. He rose beaming, arm outstretched. 'Mr Carrow. Good morning. It is Mister now, isn't it? You're not working undercover for Dowd, or anything like that?' He laughed, but it was only just a laugh. Sean Dowd had been Carrow's boss on the force, another man known for being well dressed – and for his ruthless ambition. Quite similar, Dowd and Crawford; just on opposite sides of the line.

'It's Mister. Carra to my friends.' He'd see what he made of that.

Crawford led Carrow to a pair of leather armchairs and a small table that held an open pack of cigarettes, a couple of lighters and a glass ashtray. 'I was sorry to hear about your bad news. Your mom. Especially coming right on top of the Holland business.' Carrow was taken aback. How the hell did he know all this about him? Holland, yes. It had been in the papers here. But his mother?

Crawford lifted the cigarettes, selected one and put it in his mouth. He lifted the packet to Crawford, like a tennis player showing new balls. 'Fag?'

'Thanks.' Crawford lobbed the pack towards Carrow.

When both men had lit their cigarettes Crawford started. 'Why I've got you in here Carra is to offer you a little job. Nothing to worry about. It's all legit. Just because you're no longer in the force doesn't mean you're not the same honest bloke you've always been.' He looked hard at Carrow. 'You know I've either got an interest in, or own, quite a number of the clubs in the city centre?'

Carrow nodded. He could have said, And those you don't own are paying you protection, but he left it, for now. Just see what the man was up to.

'Now a place I've had my eye on for some time is the Norway Room. Your own place of work. Negotiations with Stretton are in the very early stages. He's a wily bird. You don't know him very well yet, but believe me he is. This little incident last week with the Chinese, he said nothing to me about it, I've had to discover it through other sources. But I hear you were involved.'

Crawford leaned forward, put his cigarette in the ashtray, put his elbows on his knees, clasped his hands. A friendly smile on his face. 'In the drawer of my desk over there is an envelope with two grand in fifties in it. It can be in your back pocket in five minutes. What I want is information. Nothing more. The Chinese turn up I want you on the mobile straight away. That's another thousand. Also any comings and goings.' Carrow was about to speak but Crawford cut him off. 'The reason I'm dishing you such a payday is because you're experienced enough to know exactly what I mean by comings and goings. You'll be well paid for anything you put my way. All I want from you is information. It's not going to lead to anything unsavoury, and even if it did there is no way you would be implicated.'

So there it was. Carrow knew now what Crawford was after. It was a job offer – of sorts. And he knew pretty well immediately that he was likely to accept. If he was going to stick around at the Norway and take the risks, he might as well make some money out of it – and Crawford was offering big bucks. He wasn't getting into anything he couldn't get out of. He could sniff a few things out for Crawford, go along so far, then cut out if necessary. Crawford knew that with his connections on the force anything seriously over the line could go to them, so he wasn't likely to try and push him into anything technically unlawful. So why not go with it? It was a boring job most of the time at the Norway and this would make it a bit more interesting; a lot more lucrative anyway.

'It crosses the line and I'm out.' Carrow waited. Crawford nodded. 'But if it's just information – well, I'm happy to oblige.'

'Good man.' Crawford stubbed his cigarette and rose. 'How was home by the way?'

'Home?'

'Jamaica.'

'Home is here, Birmingham, where I was born and raised, just like you. But Jamaica was good.' He phoneyed a Jamaican accent. '*Excellent, mon.*'

Crawford dropped the envelope on the table. This felt like a scene from a film. Was Crawford going to ask him if he wanted to count it? He did, which made Carrow smile. 'I'm sure it's fine,' he said.

How many actors had bagged good paydays saying those words?

'I've a feeling some of the gangs might be trying to get a toe in as well as the Chinese. Not for the place, they're not in that league, but on the supply front. What's it like at the moment?'

'Pretty clean. Some punters doing coke in the toilets, but not much and definitely not bought on the premises. Never seen any evidence of weed or ganga. And certainly not crack.'

Crawford nodded. 'Okay. But you know the crews. Dobermans. Newtown Aces. Any of them turn up for a night out, let me know.'

Crawford rose. 'Come over here.' He beckoned Carrow who followed him over to his desk. 'I would also like a call' – he pressed a couple of keys on his laptop – 'if this girl turns up one night.' And there staring out at him was Ruthie.

10

Call it instinct. The car turned the corner at Pinks. That's when Carrow knew. No time for language – a grunt alerted Toga. Nearside rear passenger window descending – fast slow motion. A gun barrel. A fucking shotgun. Two shots. Roaring through the streets. Roaring up into the sky. Everything shuddered. His ears burnt as the car squealed away. But – he was still standing. And so was Toga. Standing together in silence. The doors flew open and the guys piled out. Neville and Sylvester. The two Lukes. Matty Fallon.

He went away – for a minute. A high. I am not dead. He wanted to weep. Toga grabbed him. Rested his head on his shoulder. 'Man.' He let his head touch Toga's. They had survived together.

'Man,' Toga repeated. A whisper. Hoarse. 'That was close.'

The other guys whipped about them, running this way and that. Toga crouched down. Touched the pavement where a bullet had struck. Felt the shape of the scar.

It's an empty club except for Carrow and Toga sitting at the bar with cigarettes and beer. A novelty – smoking inside. Against house rules, doormen smoking in the club. No music. Another novelty. No bass pounding away. Stretton told them to stay behind after he'd finished his little pep talk to the team.

He's got everything under control, he says. This won't happen again. 'I'm taking the initiative from now on.' Neville looked as if he was going to say something, but didn't. Trudy came round with little envelopes. Her lips high-gloss pink. Her eyes swimming-pool blue. She looked only at the envelopes. 'Carra and Toga, you two hold on,' Stretton said. 'I'll sort you out myself. Pour yourselves a drink. I'll be back.' Everyone knows these two are in for a bigger divvy. And why not? Fair enough. They danced with the bullets, so why not?

Stretton turned up with two wads. Dropped them on the counter. Naked fifties held in a blue rubber band. He pulled himself a whiskey from the optic. 'It's a grand each, lads. And like I said to the others, double time for the next few nights.' He knocked back the whiskey. Stretched to the optic for a refill. 'Just till I can get some hardware in.'

'Hardware?' Carrow was shocked.

'Just a couple of straps lurking in the background.' The second whiskey went where the first had gone, just as quick. Stretton sighed. 'I'll rent. From someone who'll put the word around. Let the Chinese know what they're taking on.'

Toga lifted his bundle of notes from the counter. Slapped it hard into the palm of his left hand. 'This here's appreciated, Mr Stretton.' His voice was slow and deep. 'But this,' he waved the notes, and the blue snake tattooed the length of his left arm slithered, 'double time, treble, whatever. One of us takes a bullet in the eye – it don't mean a thing. I know what you said. And I know it's true. If they'd been out for a kill they'd have made one. This, tonight, sounds like it's just putting on the pressure. Step by step.' His finger ran across the top of the bundle of notes, fanning them. Making just the smallest breeze. 'Yes. I'm sure that's true. But, what's also true, Mr Stretton, for me at least, is that that don't make me feel a whole lot better. When the bullets come flying in my direction.'

They'd taken a few bottles and a little weed back to Toga's place on the Mendy. Seventeenth floor of Elgar. Neither wanted to go home alone. Or sleep. Or be inside. So, sitting wrapped in overcoats on the balcony, with the booze and the weed to keep them warm, they watched the night. The scattered lights of the estate, chains and rings, and other shapes. The changing shade of darkness as behind the tower blocks the night progressed to dawn. Black became blue became a paler blue. Purple appeared, became red, orange, yellow. It wasn't dissimilar to a dawn sky Carrow had seen in Jamaica, or to one Toga had seen in Guyana. Here on the Mendy? In winter? A secret. Just these two guys in their tower block knew about it.

'You thinking of turning it in then?' asked Carrow.

'Tonight was close. But there's too much money starting to flow to quit. And things can change fast. Opportunities for the sort of dough we pocketed tonight don't come around every night. Stretton won't want to lose us. Tonight's hardly the sort of induction that's going to encourage new staff to stay.'

'But what you said about the dangers.'

'Sure. You have to weigh risk against money. But the Chinese aren't stupid. People start getting killed and the whole city becomes a crime scene. Everything tightens up. On all fronts. This is just manoeuvres.'

'You talk like it's a war situation.'

Toga took his big arms up behind his head. Looped his fingers to a cradle. Spread his legs. Like he was taking his ease, looking at the sunrise. Like he was far away from the Mendy watching the sun come up in Georgetown. He smirked. 'No, this ain't no war. Not yet anyway.'

11

With some real money in his back pocket for the first time in ages, Carrow intended his first job to be to look for a decent flat, get out of the Hockley dump he was in. But since the night of the Chinese attack he had gradually moved in with Toga on the seventeenth floor of Elgar.

Perhaps it was going home alone in the early hours, but inevitably as they made to leave at the end of their shifts at the Norway Toga would ask him back for a drink or a smoke, or both, and he would end up crashing there for the night, sometimes two or three nights in succession, leaving stuff there – *I'll collect this next time* – until eventually it was obvious that he should give notice on his own place and bring his stuff over. Not that there was much of that. He had learned to travel light.

Travel? He thought he had come home. Leaving Jamaica after a final visit to his mother's grave, a final drink in Jake's Place looking out at the sea and the sun, looking forward to going home – coming home – here to Brum. But now he wasn't so sure. Did it feel like home? As much as anywhere could, he guessed.

So, why the restlessness? After the gun attack Stretton had brought in an armed team, which seemed to have done the trick. There had been no trouble from the Chinese since. But there was still a lot of tension, everyone alert, waiting for something to kick off, wondering what would happen if it did. The tension extended to off-duty time too. Made you watchful, wary. He and Toga were keyed up, checking everything, ready.

Carrow joined the gym Toga went to on the Mendy. Industrial Training was located in an old factory shell on a unit down by the Pooch. Some boxing but mainly heavy-duty weights.

Carrow called Crawford to let him know he was still on the case. 'All's quiet. No sign of anything going down since they took their pot shots at us. Stratton's got a firm in – all nicely tooled up. Four of them.'

'Who's he using?'

'Don't know. Thought you might. Not local. And he's not keeping it a secret. Wants the Chinese to know he's not rolling over. They're all foreign, hardly a word of English between them. Bulgarians. Run by a London mob probably.'

'Okay. Well, keep me posted. And Carra, that girl I showed you, Ruthie Slayte, she hasn't turned up recently?'

That girl. That girl. No, she hadn't turned up recently. And he was sure of that because he looked for her every night at the Norway. Scanning girls swaying on the dance floor, girls drinking in the bars, searching the faces in the weekend queues. And no, she hadn't turned up.

It took three trips, sitting patiently outside the Gables Nursing Home, before he saw her. He knew that if he turned up often enough he would catch her leaving after a shift. He had seen other uniformed women walking down the long drive of the home to collect cars parked on the roadside, or to make their way to the bus stop beside the church at the top of the hill. He knew that sooner or later she would be among them. And when she was? He wasn't sure. Perhaps just to see her would be enough. Just to watch her for a minute. And if she saw him? Who knows. He'd have to play it by ear. Maybe she'd just say in her cool way, *Come back with me.* And? He'd be there – he knew he would. In a shot.

Then, there she was. An Audi A7 drew up on the other side of the road and Ruthie was in the front passenger seat. He was sure it was her. No. Yes. This was stupid. He shouldn't be doing this. He could hear his heart, and his hands were clammy on the steering wheel. Yes. It was her. Ruthie. About to start her shift. She leaned across to kiss the driver goodbye, then got out. She patted the skirt of her uniform, pushed the strap of her bag up on to her shoulder. Some of the nurses he had seen wore trousers as part of their uniform, but not Ruthie. The car turned. Carrow saw the driver. It was Kieran Walsh. Ruthie waved to him. The horn blared as the car raced away.

She saw Carrow almost immediately. Didn't seem surprised. Walked towards his car. Walked slowly towards his car – deliberately slow. He watched. Then he got out. Rested his arm on the roof. 'Hiya.'

She smiled. That was nice. 'I thought you had gone off the radar.'

'Same here. Crossed the Norway off your list these days?'

'It's getting a bad reputation. A girl might not be safe there any more.'

'There's some good men on the door. You don't have to worry.' He stopped himself from saying, *Not like the piece of shit that just dropped you off.* Instead: 'Who was that?' Carrow's head indicated the direction the car had taken.

'A friend.'

'Boyfriend?'

Ruthie nodded.

'What about your man inside, Howie?'

'Can't wait forever. Time to move on.'

'I thought he'd only got a few weeks left.'

'He'll be all right.' She made to move away, then stopped. 'So? How come you're here? Visiting your granny?'

There was no point in messing about. 'Hoping we might pick up again. Where we left off. Decided I was a bit hasty dropping things.' He waited. 'But I can see now that there's no chance of that.'

There was a pause, but only a slight one. 'No. No, there's not. Sorry.' Her tone was difficult to read. It might have been regretful, then again it might not.

He sat in the car and watched her walk away; make her way up the long drive. Did she look back? Of course she didn't.

SHUKO

12

I took the lift to the seventeenth floor of Nimrod House and descended the stairs. As I did so I heard urgent whispering. On to the landing two young black men were about to enter the flat next to mine. Taken by surprise, one, of sturdy build and wearing long baggy shorts, attempted an aggressive stance, waiting for a challenge.

'No one lives there,' I said. 'Just some plants.'

He was startled by this. 'Who you, man?'

'Their neighbour. I live next door. I haven't seen you here before. Other gardeners, but not you.'

'I bin 'ere,' the boy said, 'lotsa times, man.' The key connected and released the lock, the boy held the door.

'I must have missed you.' I walked past him to my door and opened it. 'I'll probably see you again sometime.'

'Yeah' he said. 'Yeah man, you probably will.'

Inside I took the vodka from the fridge and poured myself a glass, lit a cigarette, lit the ancestors' candle at the shrine beside my bed, and settled down to consider my report. Following the refusal of our offer for the Norway Room Hsinshu called me to the red room. I saw three darts in the House of Twenty and knew he was ready to give me further instructions. 'We have tried to do business with Mr Stretton in the conventional way, but despite your best efforts, Shuko, it has not worked.' He lifted his cigarettes from the long table, but held the pack. 'It was expected of course. The surprise would have been if Mr Stretton had accepted it. No, it was always unlikely that these proceedings would be resolved through negotiation. Also far too expensive. We were merely going through the motions.' *Going through the motions*. It is one of my favourite English expressions. There is, to my way of thinking, something very Chinese about it, very respectful.

'It is time, I think, to use the strength of the Dragon, it's energetic element – Fire. Statements of intent, I think. It is time for statements of intent. Let's try two of them, close together. What is the phrase the President of the United States, Mr Bush, likes to use – *shock and awe* – that, I think, is the reaction we should seek to achieve. But no blood spilled at this stage. Just shock and awe.'

Mr Stretton is a stubborn man. It is the nature of his energy, the element of Wood. Drop a flat stone on a planted seed and it will still seek to grow. The seed will push out around the slab, seeking out light, opportunity. It may become twisted, deformed, less than its natural form. But the urge to grow drives it – and there are two possible outcomes. A deformed and weakened plant that survives a short time and dies, or a thriving plant made stronger and healthier by its struggle.

I wanted to convey to Hsinshu my thoughts on the situation in writing. I felt this was appropriate for such a major Dragon project. In the army my role had been to monitor Australian and Canadian newspapers. From very early in my schooldays I had shown an exceptional ability for languages and I was selected at nine for intensive instruction in English. In the army I wrote reports on articles that dealt with social or political issues. It was work I enjoyed although, looking back, unlike my comrades of that time I never believed in the value of the contribution I was making to the Party. It was in the act of translation that I found satisfaction.

On my way back to Nimrod House I had purchased a notepad. This is what I wrote:

FOR THE PERSONAL ATTENTION OF HSINSHU – HONOURED EMPEROR OF THE NINTH DRAGON

As you are aware Sir, there have been two statements of intent successfully carried out on the Norway Room. The first, eight days ago, when a doorman taken at gunpoint led me to Mr Stretton's office. Here I issued your ultimatum. This was reinforced six nights later by shots at the front of the building. On neither occasion was anyone hurt.

For Mr Stretton, I regret to say, the point has not yet been reached where he can see the inevitable. I hear from sources within the Norway Room that he is looking to recruit – on a temporary basis – a firearms team, four or five men, through one of the eastern European syndicates.

May I respectfully share some thoughts: I feel that despite his determination, Mr Stretton is no fool and given sufficient pressure he will agree to our terms, but for the moment he apparently intends to meet fire with fire, guns with guns.

Something that has been on my mind since my first visit to the club is the rapport that exists between Mr Stretton and his assistant Trudy. He insisted she remain during our meeting. 'Trudy is my assistant. She knows everything about the business. I wouldn't make any decisions without discussing them with her.' On my second visit, when guns were out, his first action was to get her out of the room – out of harm's way?

I have been told that there are stories among the staff of the club, that there was at one time, and may still be, a romantic link between the two of them. This is something I am investigating further.

Mr Stretton is a hard man, and one whose feelings and emotions are not easy to read, but he has a reputation for knowing all of his staff, being liked by them and treating them well, so someone with whom he works as closely as he does with Trudy, literally side by side, is likely to be able to exert some influence on him, especially if there is, as I suspect, a romantic association.

There are two ways you might consider using Trudy. One is for me to make contact with her, and attempt to get her to use her influence for our benefit. This could be done by offering her a sum of money, a senior position in the club under our ownership, both, or leading her to fear for Mr Stretton's safety.

Having given the matter a lot of thought over the past few days, however, I have come to the conclusion that the more effective route would be to take her for a time. An abduction always gives a sense of urgency to a situation, and as we know can lead to quick results. If the Emperor should feel this is a route he wishes to explore further I can prepare a detailed plan for your consideration.

I am your obedient servant,
Shuko

That night it took a long time to fall asleep and when sleep did come I was assailed by dreams. When one dreams of both the past and the future, then momentous events are imminent, or at least that is the wisdom of the generations.

For three nights before the Great Earthquake of 1610 the Emperor dreamed of his late mother the Pearl Empress. In the first dream she was a child, in the second a bride to the future emperor, in the third, aged, she lay on her deathbed. These dreams are known as *The Three Dreams of the Pearl Empress*. For the following three nights the Emperor dreamed of a carpet, as fine and magnificent as any in China. Woven into the beautiful carpet in fine silk threads was a design of his palace and lovely garden. On the night of the first dream he himself walked the carpet, looking down at the palace, at the acacia and laburnum trees of the garden, the ancient ginkgo trees, the hydrangea bushes. In the second dream he walked again, this time accompanied by his wife, the Empress. On the third, he watched, as from a distance, his wife and two eldest sons, the princes Zhu Changluo and Zhu Youjian, walk the carpet without him. These dreams are known as *The Three Dreams of the Emperor's Carpet*.

The Emperor dreamed of such things no more. On the seventh night after his final dream, an earthquake took the Imperial City. A thousand buildings fell, seven thousand of his Majesty's subjects. The Imperial Family was spared.

On the morning after the earthquake, Wan Li watched as his wife, the Empress, and their two eldest sons walked slowly through the Royal garden, picking their way through the rubble of the fallen palace. This story is known as *The Realisation of the Prophesy of the Emperor's Dream* and since that time seven has been known as the number that separates triumph from catastrophe.

In my dreaming that night I first saw Jimmy Slim sailing through the night air. In reality it was a very windy night but in my dream all the trees were still. I dreamed of his smashed face, first looking up at me as it did when Yangku and I went to collect him from the tarmac beside Nimrod House, then looking down on me, as if it were I who had fallen. Then I saw his broken face again, this time raised among a crowd of faces looking up to a tightrope, healing and becoming whole as he watched Tai Yuan fall from the rope. The next time Jimmy Slim entered my dreams he was standing on a hillside watching a white van tumbling from a cliff. When the twisted van came to a halt it was not, as I expected, Tai Yuan who emerged from the vehicle but Trudy, unscathed and unperturbed, her lustrous blonde hair gleaming, dressed in a red silk Chinese shift, a red flower blooming in her hair.

I woke and lay breathless for a while. Sleep would not return so I rose and went to the fridge for another slug from the bottle of vodka. When eventually I was able to fall asleep Trudy came again into my dreams. She was in my arms, my head in her hair. I struggled to see her face but she kept it turned from me, so I kissed her hair.

13

It was a normal business meeting with the managers of all the clubs and bars run by the Dragons in attendance. It is a common misconception that insurance is where our main interests lie. We leave that for the likes of Crawford for whom it is still a sizeable part of his portfolio. In Birmingham we now control all the casinos, and most of the nightclubs. Crawford, of course, still has all the Southside clubs he took over when the Lopez brothers retired. He has developed all of the lap-dancing clubs in the city and seen off any competition that attempted to enter that market.

The agenda for the afternoon was routine apart from the final item – *Health Act: preparation for the smoking ban*. I was surprised that this was being taken so seriously.

Yet as I listened from my customary position behind Hsinshu's left shoulder it became obvious that this new law was being taken seriously – even in establishments where people were happy to contravene others. A member of the casino office reported that many breweries were already making plans to provide areas outside pubs where people may go to smoke their cigarettes, and using this idea as a model the Emperor decided that the management of each venue should draw up an individual plan for their establishment.

When the meeting was over and all were gone, Hsinshu beckoned me to take a seat beside him at the table. He offered me an American cigarette, put one to his own lips. I lit them both.

'You have rung Mr Stretton again today?'

'I have and his answer has not changed. He shouts and swears then puts the phone down.'

'Has his little army arrived yet? What did you say, Romanians?'

'Bulgarians.'

'Bulgarian lunatics.'

'They are here, armed and working. My source tells me he has one positioned on the roof.'

'So, from no security to speak of, he has acquired a militia. He is presuming that this will stop us fighting an outright war. And he is right. A war was never a possibility anyway. This isn't America – we don't have the police force on our payroll.'

'Or Italy.'

'Indeed.'

I know when something important is coming. The Mandarin emperors had seven-finger gestures to indicate to their ministers the level of import of what they were about to say. There are no such gestures from Hsinshu, but there is certainly something about his demeanour that changes, very subtly.

'I have been thinking about the woman – Trudy.'

The vowel stretched to a fracture, as if the Emperor had run out of breath.

'In your report.' I waited. 'I think we should go with your suggestion there.'

'Take her.'

'Yes. His Bulgarian arsenal will not be so useful to him then, and we shall find out if she means anything to him.'

Hsinshu leaned back in his chair. 'It is interesting, isn't it, Shuko, what one might call the cultural differences? To take the staff of a Chinese proprietor, especially connected to the Dragon, would be so offensive to honour and reputation, he would comply with anything to gain their release – comply and plot of course – but not the Europeans. *Kill them*, they will say. *See if I care*. No wonder so many of them are kidnapped abroad. But you don't think that will be the case here? We don't want to be left with her on our hands.'

'I would say that is unlikely. I have investigated, as you would expect, and there is some doubt among those who work for Mr Stretton about the current status of their relationship. He is a very private man. But lovers they certainly have been. I am sure of that now. She works at his side every day, and there is much in their history that binds them. Passions. I have discovered that she left a husband and a child to be with him. Although he is much older. I believe she is likely to be much the most powerful weapon we can use.'

14

Often it is through the power of my physical presence alone that I am able to serve Hsinshu. I am not a tall man, but my physical strength is obvious. *Built like a brick shithouse* is the way some in Birmingham describe me. I am able to use my strength well in combat, but it is the quiet power of my physical presence that has always been most useful to me – and of which I am most proud. It is the expression of my true element, Wood, and I know how to generate that energy to its best effect. In a crowded room I stand at the back near the door; everyone knows I am there, and why.

With surveillance the opposite of those qualities is required so I readily delegate. But with Trudy I was unable to confine my role to what Hsinshu calls *deskwork*.

I had spent a lot of time thinking about Trudy. The image of her sitting beside Stretton, her blonde hair shining, her coolness as she walked me to the door: these things were with me constantly. As I discovered more about her I became convinced that the taking of her would be the key to our success.

Eight years ago Trudy had left a failed marriage and a child to live with Stretton, who was also married, and with two teenage daughters. This was only a few weeks after meeting him when she was employed as a cashier at the newly opened

Norway Room. Each left their marriage and their children, but hard as Stretton appears, hard as I am sure he is, it was he and not Trudy who returned to the marital home – after only six months. Trudy remained in the apartment they had shared and apparently never saw either her husband or her son again. Her relationship with Stretton continued. They worked together, holidayed together, he stayed with her two or three nights a week at the apartment that was now in her name – this presumably was the deal he did with Mrs Stretton. It must have been the daughters. A man would not leave Trudy to return to a wife he was tired of. So he loved his daughters more even than Trudy.

I did, of course, consider the possibility that one of his daughters would be a more effective target, but it was difficult to see how that situation could be contained. The mother, sister, friends would all quickly become aware of her absence and the police would inevitably be involved. Stretton would have no time to consider negotiating with us. Trudy's life, however, seemed to revolve around Stretton and the club. Once she was taken, he would have the opportunity to consider his response without pressure from others.

Cathedral Apartments is a beautiful building. One of three blocks of very expensive apartments in St Stephen's Square, one of the oldest parts of the city, each block named – *Cathedral, Monastery, Priory* – in keeping with the presence of St Stephen's Church at the heart of the square. Yes, lovely to look upon and I am sure wonderful to live in – a mark of success in life. Very different from my own home on the Mendy, which I had decided was also to become Trudy's – for a day or two at least.

On the first morning of my surveillance, a Tuesday, I was in St Stephen's Square in overalls, carrying a tape measure and notepad. I moved among the bare trees at the centre of the square, marking and measuring distances, taking photographs with my phone, the perfect workman, but keeping my attention on Cathedral Apartments. Yangku had provided me with a schedule of the times Trudy arrived at the club, and on Tuesday it was usually about two o'clock.

As English workmen tend to do, I took several breaks for tea in one of the cafés that occupy the square and observed the apartments from the window there.

'Going to be building work is there, mate?' the man who served me green tea asked.

'Possible cable extension. I'm just checking measurements.'

'Still disruption though, ain't it?'

On my second break he had another question. 'So when's all this going to start? You're not going to wait till the summer and first sunny day we get turn up with drills and diggers?'

I knew how workmen respond to such questions. 'No idea, mate. Not my job. Just check the measurements I was told – and take all morning to do it!'

The man laughed.

I was sitting on a bench in the square, eating my sandwiches, when the electronic grille of Cathedral Apartments rose and Trudy's Z4 drove out into the square. It was one-thirty p.m.

The next day, a little before ten, having given most occupants of the apartments time to leave for work, I was in the underground car park looking for the Z4. Mr Stretton's Jaguar was there too. In a relationship as established as theirs people tend to follow a routine. Tuesday was likely to be a night he regularly stayed with her.

I found a spot behind a concrete pillar and squatted down to wait. Just after eleven the door opened and Stretton and

Trudy emerged dressed for business, each carrying a briefcase. From behind the pillar I watched them. He opened her car door for her, gave her a brief kiss. 'See you there.'

Thursday was a busy morning. Again I had taken up my position in the car park. First a resident arrived with the concierge to complain about a buzzing neon strip light, then a couple coming and going loading bags into their car. When the concierge returned with an electrician to inspect the offending light they started to chat with the couple about the few days away they were taking in Devon.

I decided to leave. And it was fortunate that I did, for as I emerged from the car park, I saw Trudy crossing on foot the square ahead of me.

I have said that surveillance is not something at which I excel but there was no denying the exhilaration I felt as I followed her. She wore a tracksuit and carried an exercise mat rolled under her arm. The gymnasium was just around the corner, situated above a row of offices. People on exercise machines could be seen inside the plate-glass windows above.

It was a busy gym for so early in the day. As I watched, several other women followed Trudy in, each with a mat rolled under her arm.

A muscled and tanned young man in shorts and a vest was happy to answer my questions about membership. 'You will have full use of the gym. We can offer a personal trainer, and a wide range of organised classes. Body pump. Body Combat. Zumba. Pilates. There's a yoga class going on right now.'

'A weekly one?'

'Yep, the eleven-thirty, but it's women only. We do mixed ones. The mixed yogas are', he consulted a printed sheet on the reception desk, 'Wednesday afternoons, Tuesday and Thursday nights. Eight o'clock.'

When Trudy left the gym she turned away from her apartment and into Constitution Hill. Halfway up she disappeared into a nail bar. As I took up a position a little further up the hill I considered how nearly I had missed this opportunity of observing what might well be a regular Thursday routine. If it was, this could be an ideal time to take her. The walk between the gym and the manicurist's looked promising. The streets around there, although close to the city centre, were very quiet at that time of day, but obviously there was a lot of CCTV.

An hour after she had entered the nail bar, ignoring double yellows Stretton's Jaguar pulled up and waited. This was interesting. She could have walked back – it wasn't raining. Domestic details like this encouraged my growing conviction that through Trudy we could gain very persuasive power over Mr Stretton.

15

Yangku is a handsome man, tall and slender, his dark hair neatly cut with a side parting. Many of the Dragons prefer to shave their heads. I do myself. For me it is a visual link with Shaolin monks of my Chinese heritage; others see it as a sign of toughness, of being, in the Western way, *a hard man*.

Yangku is a young man, still only in the middle of his twenties, but he conducts himself with the dignity of one who is older and more experienced. His dress is impressive. He uses the same tailor as Hsinshu, a declaration of his ambition, for such suits are very expensive. But his modest behaviour reduces the suspicion with which the openly ambitious are usually regarded. Most importantly, though, he is a man of courage. I saw not a flicker from him as he and I hoisted Jimmy Slim through the window on the sixteenth floor of Nimrod House; it was to here that he had now returned at my invitation.

Sharing food from my cousin Feiyang's restaurant round the corner, I told Yangku of my plan for Trudy. I explained that I wanted him, above all others, to help me in this endeavour. An easy smile took his lips and he bowed his head politely. 'It will be an honour to assist Shuko in anything he requires.'

'We will take her on her way to the manicurist's.' I pointed to the map laid out beside us. 'She turns from St Stephen's Square, here. A few metres down is a narrow passageway. As she passes I will step out – with a gun. You will have the car level at exactly this time. She will not struggle when she sees the gun. She is not a stupid woman. I will tell her she is safe so long as she co-operates.'

Yangku spoke his question confidently, and it needed to be asked. 'If Stretton co-operates then I am sure she will be safe. But if he does not?'

Would I resort to soft words, to euphemism? Yankgu watched. 'Then we will kill her,' I told him.

16

'My name is Shuko. I am the negotiator for the Chinese syndicate. We met when I visited Mr Stretton at the Norway Room.'

'I remember.' The voice was cool. 'What do you want?'

'Merely a couple of minutes of your time. The opportunity, hopefully, to explain to you things we would like Mr Stretton to know, that might help to resolve the current unsatisfactory situation.'

This was a moment of maximum risk. I waited. There was nothing more I could do. The intercom clicked off and the electronic lock of the entrance buzzed its release.

The concierge moved from his desk. 'Good morning, sir. Number eleven. It is on the third floor. The lift is this way.' He made to turn.

'I'll take the stairs.'

'Very good, sir. Over here.'

I wondered as I climbed the stairs if she was now on the phone to Stretton. I had watched him leave an hour ago. This was a gamble. If I could persuade Trudy to make Stretton see the reality of the situation it would save time, money and possibly bloodshed.

When I turned into the corridor she was there, in the doorway of number eleven, leaning against the door to keep it open. A simple red dress, bare feet, bare legs. She glanced, surprised, at the flowers I carried.

'White flowers. A symbol of peace.'

Her golden hair shimmered as she turned pushing the door with sufficient strength for me to follow her in before it started to close.

'In here.'

It was hard to believe that anything had ever been cooked in this large kitchen that shone with magazine perfection. Pop music was playing in another room. I placed the flowers on the counter. She looked at them, then at me.

'Nice music.' I remarked. 'Who is it?'

She pressed an indentation on the unit beside her and a drawer slid open from which she took cigarettes, a gold lighter, an ashtray. She lit a cigarette, inhaled, and leaned back against the counter. 'Take That.'

'Very nice. Thank you for seeing me, Trudy. I don't wish to be familiar, but I do not know your surname.' There was no response. 'It is not I think Mrs Stretton.'

'Trudy is fine.' The smoke rose in a slender, unwavering column above her.

'Not Mrs Stretton, but I know Mr Stretton is very fond of you – that you are fond of each other. And given your affection for him, I am hoping that you might be able to persuade him to negotiate.'

There was a snort of derision and her lovely hair swayed. 'If he knew you were here he would kill you.' The words were aimed. The eyes hard and direct. The gloss on her pink lips shone like everything else in this room – it was just the smoke that changed things.

'The people I represent, who want to buy the Norway Room—'

'The Dragons. I know who you are.'

'– are powerful people ...'

'The Dragon is a mythical creature. Fiction,' she sneered. 'You don't frighten us. I know that might come as a shock to you, but it's true.' Her Birmingham accent was strong.

'Those I represent', I persisted, 'are powerful people, Trudy, with access to resources beyond finance. Mr Stretton has resorted to an almost military style of defence, in response to our initial overtures—'

'Overtures. What sort of music starts with burst of gunfire?'

'I am no expert on European music but I believe that Beethoven starts a symphony with cannon fire, perhaps not—'

'Very clever.'

'Look, Trudy, the people I represent, yes, the Dragons, they are not going away. Mr Stretton may not recognise this fact of life, but I hope you will. Your lover's little army is unsustainable. You know how these people work. We could go in with a better offer and they would change sides immediately. Mercenaries do. We just have to wait.'

'You'll wait till hell freezes over. He's not going anywhere. Don't you understand? It's our club, and it's staying that way. You're not the first, you know. Crawford's been trying to get his hands on it for years, and there have been others too. But it's still ours.'

'An hour ago I watched Mr Stretton leave here. He didn't see me, but I was watching him. I have come unarmed. All I have is a bouquet of flowers – and reason. But you don't seem impressed by either.'

We looked directly at each other. I smiled. She didn't blink, didn't move. But something was changing. She inhaled again. The scarlet nail varnish that she wore on both her hands and feet matched her dress, and in that still moment as she smoked and thought I had to resist the urge to touch her. Just gently. A finger stroking her arm perhaps.

'When a successful transfer of the ownership of the Norway Room is complete, my employer would like you to become its manager. You have worked with Mr Stretton for a long time, you know how everything operates, you know the staff.' I allowed myself another smile. She was listening, but it was impossible to tell what she was thinking. 'You are tough, Trudy, bright. You would do a good job. And your salary would be high, very high.' I could not resist the temptation of the word – though it is not easy to say. 'Commensurate with your responsibilities.' A reaction. Only a movement of the eyes, but it was there. I moved a step closer. Put my hand on the counter, leaned in a little. She didn't move. 'I can see you enjoy a high standard of living, appreciate quality. That you have a taste for the finer things in life.' She turned a little to look at me – always direct. We had reached a point in the road, a junction – and I took the path most travelled by men like me. 'And you have been prepared to pay a high price, a hard price for it.' A different look. Quick. Intense. I think she knew what was coming. Realised she had been lulled. 'To leave a husband, well that is nothing. But to abandon a child for your lover, for the good life…' Her cigarette came down on my hand with sufficient control for it rest for a second before she pressed and turned stubbing it out. It was too quick to prevent a wince, but I kept the hand in place. And she was immediately away from the counter, upright, assessing my reaction, ready, her face raised defiantly; obviously a woman used to violent men, but not one to succumb to them.

Satisfied there would be no retaliation she returned the dead cigarette end to the ashtray which she carried across the kitchen. The press of another indentation opened a cupboard revealing a waste bin. There was a pocket in the skirt of her red dress, as carefully disguised as the cupboards and drawers in the kitchen. She took from it a small vial and sprayed her mouth.

She walked back to the sink and turned on the tap. 'Here.' And this was when she came closest to a smile. I raised my fist into the stream of cold water and watched her looking at it; there was comfort in the moment.

She took a towel from another concealed area and threw it at me. 'Now look Mr Fat Chinaman. You and your powerful mates can make me all the big promises you like. You can obviously find out anything you want. But I could try every trick in the book, every trick' – she repeated the two words clearly and slowly as if I might be lip-reading – 'and there is no way Stret is going to give in to you lot. He's the same as you, that's what you have to realise. He may not be part of a syndicate as you call it, he's not a gangster like the Crawford mob. He's a businessman, but he's just as hard, just as tough as the rest of you, and he's going to hold on to what's his. He enjoys the battles. Like you all do.'

'And you, do you enjoy the battles?'

'I hate to see anyone getting hurt, Mr Fat Man.' She picked up the flowers. 'These are lovely, and thanks, but no thanks. You must have lots of mates in the cemetery, why don't you drop them in there on your way home.'

I counted the flowers before dropping them in a bin. Three white roses, two white chrysanthemums, three white carnations and two white lilies. It is just such bouquets as these, a mixture of white flowers, that one sees Chinese families carrying to cemeteries on the morning of Ching Ming, the festival of the ancestors. The husband carries the flowers, the wife the cleaning bag with which to attend to the family tombs, the child the picnic they will share when their task is done. Three white roses, two white chrysanthemums, three white carnations and two white lilies – I would see that exactly this bouquet awaited her when she came as my guest to the sixteenth floor of Nimrod House. I would go before that time to Miss Blossom's Oriental Emporium in Digbeth and purchase a Chinese pot, one of the large white ones with a pattern of blue dragons. This I would place, filled with her rejected bouquet, beside the futon upon which she would sleep while she was my guest.

It would have been easy then, as I walked away from St Stephen's Square, to let my imagination play, making pictures of Trudy lying on the futon, the dragon jar of white flowers beside her. I resisted, and concentrated instead on the practicalities of my plan. I would get final approval from Hsinshu and then settle on dates and times with Yangku. The purchase of futon, vase and flowers would be the final act of preparation – the last thing I would do for her.

ASHLEY

17

Kieran said nothing as he drove Ashley to Selly Oak Hospital, where the soldiers from Iraq go. There were lots of men and women in uniform about the place. 'Nurses,' Kieran told him. 'Military nurses. They train here before going to the front line.'

There were none in casualty, although it looked like the front line: full of bleeding, broken, sighing people. An old woman sat with her foot up on a chair. It was wrapped in a towel, blood seeping through. Ashley registered; Kieran said he was his uncle, next of kin.

They took it in turns going outside to a little cubicle like a bus shelter that was the only place you were allowed to smoke. Ashley had lit up right outside the casualty doors and was surprised when Kieran had said, 'Behave, Ash. This is a hospital. Go in there.' The first time there were three women in there with him, all in dressing gowns, all patients, the second, two girls and a kid in a buggy, the third a young bloke in a wheelchair with only one leg, and that was only half, thickly bandaged. A bandaged stump really. Ashley asked him if he was from Iraq. 'No,' he said. Then, after a long pause, 'Motorbike.' He was still there the next time Ashley went back, chaining.

The nose was broken. But no ribs. Nothing hurt. 'It will,' the doctor told him. 'Tomorrow. For a few days.' They cleaned him up. Four stitches under his eye. Checked his teeth. 'Seem okay. See how they go.' Kieran told the doctor it was a fight, with the kid next door. 'Big lad. Much bigger than Dean.' That was the name they had given. No, they weren't going to report it. Just a fight between lads. There was a fight going on in the waiting room as they left.

Kieran went quiet on the way back.

'Where we going?' Ashley asked. They were travelling down the Bristol Road.

'Small diversion. Call to make.'

Ashley thought he ought to say something about what had happened. Reassure Kieran that he wouldn't breathe a word. Reassure himself that Kieran would let him stay in the house. Fear. Where was he taking him? It was getting dark. Kieran had his lights on. A police siren. Kieran checked the mirror. Checked his speed. Slowed a little. The police car sped past.

'I'm sorry. About this afternoon. About Benjy Graham.'

'I thought no one knew you were there. I told you to keep a low profile, stay out of trouble.'

'Sorry.'

After a pause. 'So. Tell me. What happened with Graham? I heard some of it through the wall. But tell me.'

Ashley told Kieran about his job walking Graham's dogs. He tried to make him laugh when he described Mrs Graham always going on about not letting the dogs shit till they were in the street. But Kieran remained quiet. Ashley told him about meeting the bloke by the canal, seeing him several times. He was friendly, good with dogs. Then he told him how he was attacked and the dogs were stolen. By the time he was finished they were on Burnside Hill heading for the Mendy. 'What we doing up here?' The fear again.

'Told you. Got to see someone.'

The tower blocks glittered beneath them. Hundreds of tiny rectangles of light in a huge block, the blocks ranked behind each other in neat rows, like perspective lessons at school; little rectangles of light in neat rows. And headlights from the Tallis Road. A chain of headlights, following on from one another, a trail of headlights moving down into and through the estate. Ashley thought about the story of the kids who dropped the seeds on their way through the forest.

They drove over Kinny Bridge past the towers: Grainger, Walton, Elgar, Vaughan Williams, and into the curving groves of maisonettes. Kieran pulled up in the Pooch. Its proper address is Puccini Plaza, but everyone calls it the Pooch. Most of the shops were shuttered now. A few security lights. Sickly yellow. Blue. A fag and booze shop was open behind its iron grille.

'Come on.'

Ashley followed Kieran out of the car. Perhaps they were heading for the pub in the middle of the row. 'Are we going to the Maddy?' Ashley asked. Its proper name was the Madrigal, but everyone called it the Maddy. Sometimes the Mad. 'Will they let me in?'

Kieran secured the car. 'Come on,' was all he said.

It wasn't the Maddy that Kieran was making for – he strode past that, Ashley following, his hood up against the cold – but to Bamboo Garden, the takeaway next door.

There was a Chinese girl behind the counter. About eighteen. Pregnant. Pretty. She knew Kieran. 'You want Feiyang?'

Kieran nodded. 'He said to go straight up.' Her head indicated a mirrored door at the other end of the shop. It made the place look bigger. Ashley saw his bruised face in it. He looked a mess. Kieran placed a fiver on the counter. 'Give the kid some food. Wait here,' he told Ash. 'I won't be long.' And he disappeared behind the mirrored door.

The pregnant girl pushed a menu towards Ashley. He selected a Shanghai Special – chicken, pork, prawns, egg fried rice – sat down on the bench facing the counter and waited.

He was eating his food with a plastic spoon from a polystyrene tray when Kieran put his head round the door. Beckoned him. 'Bring your grub with you.'

Ashley climbed the narrow staircase behind Kieran, followed him into a room illuminated on the one side by a large plasma screen television showing Sky Sports News with the sound off, and on the other by a long fish tank that ran the length of the wall. Brightly coloured fish – blue, pink, yellow, yellow and white, yellow and black, pink and blue, just black – swam through a jungle of green waterweed. In the corner of the tank the oxygenator valve noisily discharged columns of bubbles. It sounded like somebody being sick.

In the space between the tank and the TV a number of people sat around a Formica-topped table. There were two free chairs. Kieran took one. 'Sit down, Ash. You can carry on eating.' Ashley felt self-conscious but was hungry so he did. Next to Kieran sat the bloke with the gun from this afternoon. His suit was gone and now he wore a white vest and dark tracksuit bottoms. Smart ones. His arms weren't big, but muscled. Tattooed. Tiger stripes coated his right forearm.

'This is Feiyang, Ash. And his mom, Mrs Wei, and his nan.' There were two other men at the table, wearing vests like Feiyang, but Kieran didn't introduce them. A copy of

Racing News lay open on the table between them, and one man held a biro. There were marks on the paper against the lists of runners.

The men all looked at Ashley eating. He would have liked to finish it, it was nice food, but he pushed it away. 'That was very nice.' He looked at Mrs Wei as if she had personally cooked it for him. He didn't want to let Kieran down in front of these people. 'But I'm full. Thanks.'

Mrs Wei smiled. Bowed her head. Feiyang's nan collected up Ashley's rubbish and disappeared with it. She was old and bent and walked slowly. Wore black pyjamas and sandals.

'Look, Ash,' Kieran started. 'You really fucked up today.'

'Sorry.'

'A lot of plans. They've all been screwed. So. We, that's Feiyang here and me, we've got to make new ones. And quick. Just in case that tosser you brought round talks.'

Ashley was afraid now. 'He won't, Key. He was scared shitless. Really.' He looked at Feiyang. 'I was too.' Back to Kieran. 'He won't talk. And I didn't bring him round. He knows where I live. He knows my dad.' Ashley was trying not to cry.

Kieran had his hands clasped together, fingers enclosing each other, like the way some people pray, only resting on the table. He leaned forward towards Ashley. 'If I let Crawford know what has happened today,' he paused. 'If I tell him. Do you know what he would say? Do you?'

He looked around the table. They were all watching him. Even the fish seemed to be looking at him from across the room, the bloke on Sky Sports News. 'He'd tell you to throw me out?' Ashley offered quietly. This was a bit like being back at school, being bollocked by the headteacher; but the most dangerous school in the world.

'No, Ash. He wouldn't tell me to throw you out. Or at least not exactly. What he'd say is, kill the kid. Shoot him. Drop him on the railway. Tie him up and dump him in the canal. That's what he would say, Ash. Not a shadow of a fucking doubt.'

Ashley didn't know what to say. His heart pounded, and it felt as if he might bring up his Shanghai Special. Mrs Wei smiled at him kindly.

'So,' Kieran continued. 'Listen good. You're staying here tonight.' Ashley wanted to stop him right there. Shout, no, no way. But he knew it was pointless. 'While Feiyang and me sort things out. Got me? You stay here till I come and pick you up. Probably tomorrow. Take you back.'

Ashley was being punched in the chest. From the inside. And it was hurting. When he spoke he sounded like a baby. 'You will come for me?'

Kieran roared with laughter. Feiyang laughed too. Mrs Wei's smiled broadened. The two men picking winners ignored them.

'Course I will, Ash,' Kieran said kindly. 'I'm not going to leave you here, am I?' He spoke reassuringly. 'It's just till we get everything sorted out. Okay?'

'Okay.'

'Cheer up. At least you'll get well fed here. Anything you like, as long as it's chinky.' Then to Feiyang, 'All right mate, let's get out of here.'

Feiyang said something to his mom in Chinese. She looked across at Ashley.

At the door Kieran turned and threw a pack of cigarettes on to the table before Ashley.

'Bensons. Cool.'

'Mrs Wei will look after you. Behave. See you.'

For a while he just looked at the soundless television. Smoked a cigarette. Looked at the fish for a bit. A big blue one was being chased by a tiny black-and-white-striped one.

The old lady came in with a tray of food. Three bowls of rice. A big dish of Chinese food. Looked like pieces of beef. And vegetables. She placed a bowl of rice before each of the two men. Gave them chopsticks. Spooned the beef and vegetables on top of their rice. She tipped the remaining beef and vegetables into the last bowl of rice and took it to sit cross-legged on the floor beside the television. She reached for the handset and started the video. It was horse-racing. With a Chinese commentary. She watched as she ate, her old black eyes glinting brightly. The two men followed it from the table, shovelling food into their mouths. Ashley wondered at how they could do that with chopsticks. An argument started between the two men. In Chinese. One called to the old woman. She put down her chopsticks and rewound the tape. As it replayed she found something funny and laughed, so she had to push food back into her mouth. The men waved their chopsticks and pointed them towards the television as they made their points.

Ashley looked at the cigarette pack. Bensons, but not English Bensons. Knock-offs. Must be. In a white band across the lid of the pack was *Las autoridas sanitarias advierten.* Ashley sounded the letters. He knew that a lot of knock-off fags were coming in from Latvia. Perhaps this was Latvian. The cancer warning was inside a thick black box like the edge of a funeral card. Foreign as well. Ashley traced the words with his finger, tried to sound them. *Fu-mar per-jud-ic-a.* He gave up after the first line. He knew what it meant anyway – *you're going to die of cancer!* Or, as he'd heard Kieran say – *We've got your money; now you're going to die.* He turned the pack over. Another black box. Another warning.

Fu-mar prov-oc-a. Fumar must mean *smoking* in Latvian. He wondered if the men beside him might know Latvian; but then he hadn't heard them speak a word of English.

He took a cigarette from the pack and lit it. Might as well get on with it. Then he wondered if he should be smoking while people were eating; but nobody seemed to mind. Nobody seemed to notice him at all. He was like the invisible man – the invisible boy. And this, together with the strange languages, Chinese, Latvian, made him feel uneasy. The smell of food, that had been so appetising before, was now horrible, and made him feel sick. His face was hurting again. Hot and stinging. He could feel the stitches. Feel the skin of his face tightening. He was in a room on the Mendy. In the Pooch. The Maddy was only next door. The Maddy on the Mendy, that's what people called it. He'd heard his dad say that a hundred times. Walton Tower and Sophie were just down the road, but he felt very far from everything. Like he'd fallen down a hole into another country.

When the food was finished the old lady turned off the video, turned down the sound and let Sky Sports News play silently. There was something on about Chelsea. Ashley saw the players training. Their kit the same blue as the fish being chased by Stripy; like an Albion defender on the trail of a great big Chelsea forward. The old lady collected the bowls from the table and shuffled out of the room.

A man in a black suit came in carrying a wooden box. He set it on the table and opened it. Removed stacks of small tiles. Ashley watched the men play a game with them. He thought they might invite him to join them – teach him how to play – but they didn't.

Mrs Wei came in and gave him a choc ice. When he had eaten it, she beckoned for him to follow her. She led him along the landing to a room containing five mattresses. The old lady was lying on one. Mrs Wei pointed to a mattress on the other side of the room. 'For you,' she said carefully, moving her finger from the mattress to Ashley.

The fear. He didn't want to stay here. Who else was going to sleep in this room? The men at the table probably. No. No way. And he definitely wasn't going to bunk down yet. It was too early. He lifted his wrist so Mrs Wei could see his watch and pointed to eleven. 'I don't go to bed till late.' She seemed to understand and nodded. She followed him back to the table.

His face was hurting bad. His nose felt hot and huge, like it was growing. He thought about the kid in the story, the wooden one. Or the kids lost in the forest who the witch traps. He tried to assess the men beside him. The one in the suit didn't look too bad. But then you never knew what he was carrying; you don't have to be hard if you've got a gun. The two in vests did look hard. Lean and muscled. Like they could have been in Kung Fu movies. Mean-faced. Both had tattoos on their arms. Chinese writing, and tribal stuff. One had roses on his lower arm, blue and pink, climbing up towards his elbow. He had a mashed-up nose; almost completely flat. And Ashley didn't think he'd had that from birth. He touched his own nose. It hurt. He hoped it wouldn't end up looking like that.

Ashley rose from the table.

'What you want? Where you going?' It was the one in the suit.

'For a piss.'

The man nodded and returned to the game. On the landing Ashley peered down the stairs to the shop below. Three sets of legs. People sitting waiting for their orders. There was no sign of Mrs Wei so he bolted down the stairs. She was behind the counter with the pregnant girl. Some customers were standing at the counter, he tried to make himself small as he dodged behind them, but she saw him. Called something. Maybe his name. Maybe something else. But he was away, out of the door, and into the Pooch. The cold air hit his face like another blow, perhaps the worst so far. He raced down the road towards Walton Tower.

18

'What happened to you?'

'Fell over.'

'Fuck off. You've been belted.' Tyr had followed Sophie to the door and was talking to Ashley over her shoulder. 'Who hit you?'

'Leave it, Ty.' Sophie made way for Ashley.

'Is your mom in?'

'No, she's doing a party. With her mate. An Ann Summers.'

Ashley followed Sophie into the lounge. Tyr followed Ashley, sat down on the settee beside Sophie, put his arm round her.

'You been to the hospital?'

Ashley stood before them like an exhibit. 'Yeah.'

'And?'

'Broken nose.'

Tyr laughed. 'You don't 'alf look pretty.'

'Leave him alone.'

Ashley felt awkward just standing there between them. He wished Tyr wasn't there. This would be easier then. 'I'm in trouble. I can't go home tonight. Probably never. My dad never paid the mortgage. They've taken the house back.'

'And they whacked you in the face while they did it?'

Ashley ignored Tyr's mockery and appealed directly to Sophie. 'Do you think your mom would let me stay here, just for a bit? I could pay for my food. And I could get stuff for her. You know. Like I got her the purse. I'd only be here to sleep.'

'There's no fucking chance of that, Ash. Sorry. She just wouldn't.' Sophie thought. 'You got nowhere to go tonight?'

'No.'

'Well you can stay tonight. She won't be back till late. And she'll be gone by eight in the morning. So I can hide you here tonight. But just for tonight.'

'Ta, Soph.'

It was the dream that woke Ashley. He was being pulled towards a furnace. A furnace with glass doors like an oven. Closer and closer. Hotter and hotter. He couldn't get away. His face was almost touching the glass. The heat was suffocating. He summoned all his strength to jerk away – woke. Breathless. His face was burning up. His nose throbbing. He tasted blood.

He was curled up under the clothes hanging in Sophie's wardrobe, an eiderdown around him. The mirrored door of the fitted wardrobe had been left open a little – *Don't want you to suffocate, Ash.* He could just make out the shape of Sophie's bed in the darkness of the room. He listened for her breathing, but heard nothing. What if she was dead? He'd get the blame.

She could say he had tried to rape her.

She wouldn't do that.

She might.

What the fuck was he going to do when daylight came?

Perhaps they would be searching for him. To kill him.

They wouldn't.

They might.

What he'd say is, kill the kid. Shoot him.

The cold air made his nose start to hurt again. But just an ache this time. Perhaps it was getting better. There was snow in the air. Light flakes dancing like dandruff. *Is it frost or is it snow, that's what the jackdaw wants to know.* The words of a reading book from his first year in school came back to him. He saw again the picture of the big black bird looking from the branch of a tree at the white land below. The words were printed beneath. He remembered the way the teacher used to sing them out, and then all the kids would do the same. How they sat in a circle on the floor every afternoon for story time; he used to love that.

The streetlights were still on. Ashley made for Kinny Park. Slowly. There was plenty of time. Kids had thrown bricks into the lake creating pools of black water. A pair of ducks swam slowly in one. Like the hands of a clock. The falling snow seemed to disappear about a foot above the ice, just dissolve into thin air – magic. Ashley watched the ducks. Smoked a cigarette. Tried to make a question mark. Tried to make some plans, decide what to do. He looked at the cold water, black, and thick as paint. Half an inch of ice. He could always jump in. Shit. No. He laughed. How could people do that? Or jump off high-rises. No way.

He recalled the story of Jimmy Simper who his dad had gone to school with. He had been a good boxer. Turned professional and everything. Then something went wrong with his eyes and he couldn't box no more. He got married and his missis cleared off after he had to do some time. He killed himself. Off the top of Vaughan Williams where his mom lived. But the weird thing was before he jumped he took his glasses off, and his jacket. Left them in a neat little pile by the roof guard before he went over it.

Ashley touched his nose. It was hot. He touched his cheek, cold. He noticed blood on his trainer, gobbed on it, and wiped it against the back of his calf, checked, some still there, gobbed again, wiped again. Gone.

He was late. Ashley feared he'd been cheated, taken for a pratt. He wasn't coming; he'd been done. But then: ten minutes late but there he was coming out of the playing field, over Kinny Bridge and along the towpath. Ashley moved towards him.

'Shit,' he said when he saw Ashley's face. 'Who you upset?'

He carried on walking. Ashley fell into step beside him. 'Who d'you think?'

'The dogs?'

'Course.' Ashley scoffed. 'What d'you expect?'

'Bin to the hospital?'

'Yeah.'

'Broken?'

'Yeah.'

'Oh well, it doesn't hurt for long.'

'You got my wages?'

'Sure have. Up here.'

When they reached the wharf steps that led on to the Mendy, Knighton stopped and pulled a wad of notes from the back pocket of his jeans. Ashley sighed his relief. He knew the man might try to cheat him when he hadn't paid him at the handover. Ashley had walked the dogs back to Knighton's place with him, then once they were penned, 'Can't pay you today. I'll see you Thursday. At the canal. Usual time.'

'Right. Three dogs at twenty quid a dog.'

'Fifty. You said fifty a dog.'

'I don't think so.' Knighton was laughing.

'You did. You did. Fifty each you said. I've been kicked to fuck over them dogs.' He pulled the jerkin of his hoodie up, revealing his blackened ribs.

'All right, kid. All right. Don't get excited. Just testing. You know. Business. We'll call it eighty for the three and we're in business.'

'I can tell him where they are.'

'Your uncle?'

'Yeah.'

'Look, kid. You can tell who the fuck you like.' Ashley saw the snarl that came with the words, the laughter gone now. He recognised that he had no choice. Anyway, eighty was all right. He held out his hand. 'Do you still want me to help you exercise them? Train 'em up?'

Ashley finished his breakfast. A full English with double fried bread; he'd been starving. He tried to think straight. He couldn't stay at Sophie's. He'd texted Karl twice but received no reply. He thought about a train – to London. There were hostels there. Hundreds of kids ended up there. No one bothered. No one checked. But he didn't want to do that. Not really. He thought about his bedroom. He wanted to sleep there, not in a hostel. He wanted to stay here where he knew people, where he knew his way around.

He could just go back to Cecil Road, act as if nothing had happened. No. That was stupid. His stomach turned as he recalled Kieran's words – *What he'd say is, kill the kid. Shoot him. Drop him on the railway. Tie him up and dump him in the canal. That's what he would say, Ash. Not a shadow of a doubt.* But it was more the look on his face. That was as bad as the words. Just saying it like it is. Dead eyes. Turned off: you have to do what you have to do.

He was in the shit.

Kieran wouldn't really do that.

He might.

Crawford wouldn't order that.

He might.

So?

The only answer he could see was to call Kieran and say he was sorry. Say he wanted to go back home. Promise he wouldn't cause any more problems. Briefly – very briefly – the thought passed through his mind that he might try to use their own tricks – threaten to go to the police if they didn't let him live in his own house. But no, that was stupid. That way he could end up dead.

The woman he'd heard the lorry drivers and workmen at the other tables call Maureen came across to him. 'You finished, Bab?' She was Irish and he liked her calling him *Bab*. It was what Mel called Sophie sometimes.

'Yes, ta.'

She lifted his plate. 'You've cleaned this.'

'I was hungry. Can I have another Nescafe?'

'I'll bring it over.'

When the coffee arrived Ashley phoned Kieran. 'I'm sorry, Kev. Really, I am.' He waited. Nothing. 'I just couldn't stay there. It spooked me. I haven't said anything to anyone, honest. I wouldn't.'

'Where did you go last night?' He couldn't work out Kieran's tone of voice.

'I stayed at that girl's. Sophie. She hid me in her wardrobe.' He heard Kieran laugh. It was going to be all right.

But now, walking back. The fear. He could walk through

the front door, and that could be it. He remembered the gun in the Chinese bloke's hand. And they were funny these Chinese. Perhaps he had insulted his mother by running away. His mother and his nan. Ashley had heard about honour killings, seen them in Kung Fu films. They were big on honour, the Chinese. Shit. He stopped on Rea Bridge and lit up. Looked down into the treacly brown river making its sickly way through the litter that had been dumped in it. Tyres. A fridge. Branches that had broken off the trees. There used to be a car door just over there. Ashley wondered where it had gone.

He tried to formulate some sort of plan. He went through all the people he knew, but couldn't come up with anyone who could help him. There was nothing else for it. Just go back, see what happened. And with that he was filled with optimism. Everything would be all right. No problem.

He half expected the locks to have been changed again. But no. And when he gingerly entered the house there was no one waiting with a gun. Everything the same – except cleaner. Tidier anyway. No cups and plates in the sink. No teabags on the side. Bin empty. Upstairs his bed was made, his clothes picked up and folded on the chair. The locked rooms were still locked. Someone had put disinfectant down the toilet. It was weird. Ashley looked around. He still was expecting something bad to happen. But when he switched on the lights, they came on. The telly too. There were some cans of lager in the fridge, a sachet of weed in a drawer.

He sat down. Stood up. Sat down stood up. Looked out the kitchen window. This wasn't right. The place was spooky. Dangerous. He went through the numbers in his phone – no one to ring. He went to bed even though it was still only afternoon.

The next day nothing. He watched telly, smoked some weed, drank a can of lager from the fridge, bought a pizza and a Cornish pasty, a carton of milk and some cocoa, made three cups, bought some biscuits, custard creams, ate them dunked in cocoa. Tiptoed round. Kept thinking something might happen. Then decided – it wouldn't. Everything was all right.

The next day he got a text from Kieran. *Hope your behaving yourself. K.*

Then one from Sophie. *Meet me by the funni shop at 2. So.*

The Funny Shop was Sophie's name for it. On the Pershore Road. An old-fashioned shop that had a variety of items in its window. In one, piles of wool for knitters; pastel colours mostly. Some cheap cups and saucers; plain white mostly, but dusty. Ornaments, like dancing ladies and Tutankhamuns. Aston Villa mugs. Some paintings in gold frames; landscapes mostly. The other window had a notice in it saying *Discounts*, and the goods here changed regularly. Sometimes a pyramid of tinned cat food, or a tower of boxes of biscuits; today there was cleaning stuff, for kitchens and bathrooms, and a box filled with flip-flops for fifty pence a pair.

Her bus had been early and Sophie was standing looking into the window of the Funny Shop when Ashley arrived. Turning the corner and seeing her side-on, she looked pregnant to him now for the first time. He wanted to surprise her but she saw him before he reached her. 'Look at this.' She moved to the wool window. 'That's a cuckoo clock, isn't it?'

'Think so.'

'I've never seen a real one before. You got any money?'

'Yeah. A bit.'

'I've had me dinner, but I'm still hungry. Can't stop. Hungry all the time.'

They went to Mr Sizzle on Burnside Hill. Cheeseburgers and chips and mugs of hot chocolate.

'You got me into a right mental with Mel.'

Ashley wiped his fist across his mouth, examined the grease on it, licked it, and waited for her to explain.

'I had to tell her about the other night.'

He waited for more.

'There was blood on things. In the wardrobe. Tops and stuff. Must have come from your nose. Mel thought it was me. Thought I was trying to get rid of the baby. I had to explain.'

Ashley wiped his fist on his trackies. Waited for more.

'She was all right. Didn't believe me at first. Was a right old cow. But in the end she was cool.'

Ashley opened his cigarettes. Pushed one across the table to Sophie.

'We won't be able to do this soon.'

'We're in the smoking.' He indicated the ashtrays.

'They're banning it.'

'What, smoking? Who are?'

'The government. In the summer.'

'They can't.'

'They are. Cafés. Pubs. Everywhere except your own house and outside.'

'That's daft. They can't do that. No one will stand for it. Blokes in pubs not smoking.' He tried to imagine someone telling Kieran he couldn't smoke. Or Crawford. 'Who says?'

'It'll be the law.'

'No one will put up with that. It's stupid.'

Sophie leaned across the table towards him. Rested her chin on her folded hands. She had that look on her face; she wanted something. 'Ash. Will you do me a favour?'

'What?'

'It's a big one.'

'What?'

'I want you to come with me to the hospital. Will you?'

Ashley was confused. He didn't know what to say.

'Will you? Tyr won't. Will you?'

'Shouldn't your mom be with you or something?'

Sophie squealed with laughter. 'Not when it's born. Div. Now. This week.' The laughter went. 'I just want to have a look at the hospital. I have all my appointments at the Mendy Clinic. I just want to go up the hospital. Queen Elizabeth. So I know what it's like. I won't be scared then. Mel won't come. She says it's unlucky. Wait till the right time.' She mimicked her mother's voice. 'You'll be there soon enough. I wish you couldn't see it from our window. Well the new parts they're building. Cranes and steel and stuff. I look out and it's always there. Growing.'

Ashley recalled the view from Sophie's kitchen window. A massive building site. You could hardly see the old hospital behind it. He thought about his visit to Selly Oak with Kieran. That had been mental. He knew hospitals scared people, especially girls having babies.

'So will you come with me?' Sophie asked.

'All right then,' he replied. 'We can go and have a look sometime.'

Sophie's hand lay flat on the table beside the ashtray. Ashley wanted to reach out and take it, tell her everything would be all right – but he didn't.

19

'All right,' Ashley yelled. Knighton was banging the door down. 'You're early.' It was only just two, and Knighton had said two-thirty. He was holding a proper cat-carrier, pink nylon, a bit like a rucksack, but with a grille at one side. Ashley had expected a sack.

Knighton followed Ashley through to the kitchen. 'D'you want a cup of tea?' Knighton looked around the kitchen. He seemed amused. 'No, you're all right, kid. Where is it?'

'In the shed.' Ashley unbolted the back door and Knighton followed him out into the garden. 'Are you living here on your own?'

'Not really. My uncle looks after me.'

'Oh yeah, your uncle.'

Ashley recognised the tone and grinned. 'He's not here today though. Away.'

'I thought he might be. How long's it been in the shed?'

'Since I texted you. A couple of hours.'

'Fed it?'

'Done nothing to it. Just shut the door.' And now he opened it – just a touch. The cat was there. Ashley hissed, nudged it away with his foot, squeezed into the shed. Knighton followed pulling the door behind him. Cracks in the rotten timber provided sufficient light to see the cat, backed into a corner.

Once the cat was in the carrier Knighton reached into his back pocket. 'Fiver we said, wasn't it?'

'A tenner. You said ...'

'Okay.' The tenner was already in his hand. 'Just testing. Business you know. Let's keep it at one a week if you can for now. That should do.'

'Terry's All Gold. Ooh you little love. I love dark chocolates.'

'You love anything dark.' This was Jackie, standing beside Alma. Both women enjoying a cigarette. A saucer on the counter served as an ashtray. 'The darker the better.' The women laughed.

Ashley had given Alma a card and a box of chocolates for her birthday. She was delighted. 'Come here.' And she gave him a kiss on the cheek. 'How did you know?'

'I heard you saying, last week. About going for a curry. Sorry there's no wrapping paper on the chocolates. I'm no good at wrapping things up.'

'Ooh what a lovely card.' The card showed a bouquet of flowers in a glass vase; above an arch of gold letters said *Happy Birthday to a True Friend*. Ashley got it from the Funny Shop. 'Look at this, Jack. Isn't it lovely?'

When the thank yous were over Ashley went across to a machine. He hoped this was going to work. Maybe he should wait for a few days, so it wasn't so obvious. No. Best try while she was in a good mood. He saw her put his card with three others on a shelf above the counter. His first six pounds went immediately and he thought his plan was dead, but gradually he began to creep towards the ten-pound max.

When he got there his luck was in. Three bells and HOLD flashing. 'Bloody hell!' he said loudly. 'Just my luck.'

Alma looked across. 'What you moaning for? That looks all right to me.'

'I'm at ten.'

Alma laughed. 'Oh go on then. But if you reach twenty-five, stop. Okay?'

He stopped at eighteen pounds and left two on the counter for Alma. 'Buy yourself a cake.'

'Here is something you should know – I is evil.' Geezbo curled the fingers of his right hand inwards and touched the centre of his chest. 'Bad anyway. It true. My mom's gran whood never seed me. She write. When I was born. To my mom. You 'as to treat him 'ard, she sayd. Treat 'im 'ard. He got the gleam of the dollar and the dime all over 'is soul. I know 'e 'as. I dreamed it. 'E like the other one. Our relative that I told you about. The last man to hang in Winson Green Prison, who didn't string hissel up. You get me? An she right. There's something in me. Like a fist I was born wiv. It run all the way through. Grow wit me. Inside. Nuttin I can do. She said my brother, Carlton, would bring credit. And she right there too. He a good upright man. Nation of Islam and all. Principles.' He breathed the word out. Carefully and thoughtfully. Then stopped.

They were in Sophie's flat. Tyr and Sophie were in the bedroom, Geezbo sitting on the floor, his back propped against the settee, his arms around his drawn-up knees. Ashley lay on the settee. Light was fading in the late afternoon. Soon it would be dark. Soon it would be time to go. The weed was done.

''Ere's somethin' else you should know. But it con-fee-den-shal.'

'You're talking that way again. Why don't you talk normal?'

'Confidential. Okay?'

'Okay.'

'You 'eard of the Doberman Crew? Linton, the boss man?'

'Yeah.'

'Well. It can't be said I exactly one of tey. Yet. But I in with tey, innit. More all the time. Linton know me by name. I do jobs for dem. A little business on this estate. Know what I mean, man? Not big. Tey more active in de North. But tey movin all over the city. London too. An Manchester. Well, here, I do a little work for dem. A little runnin' around. Developin' the estate. Lookin' afta tings. Know what I mean, man? A few orders. A few deliveries.' Geezbo stopped. Silence. Well close. They could hear the lift moving up and down the centre of the building. A buzz from the heating.

'I could get you a little work, man,' Geezbo said at last. 'Pay good. Weed sometime. Cash sometime.' Ashley could hear a siren now, from somewhere outside on the estate. And inside Sophie's phone ringing in the bedroom.

'You gotta bike, man?'

'Nah. Not any more.'

'Get one, man. It'd be jus the ting. For deliverin'.'

Another siren. Geezbo got up and looked out of the window. Then he turned on the light. Sophie came out of the bedroom with a can of air freshener that she sprayed around the room. 'What time's your mom coming home?' Ashley asked.

'About half an hour.'

Tyr followed her out. Moved to Geezbo at the window. 'Anyting happenin'?'

'Jus' passin'.'

'You've all got to go now.' Sophie told them. She was on her way to the kitchen. 'I've got to start doing Mel's dinner.'

Sometimes at night he went up to the Parade on Pershore Road. There was always a group of kids there hanging around outside the chip shop. Not Mendy kids usually. At least not Mendy boys. Sometimes a few from the Lea Hill gang turned up. This was about as close to the Mendy as they were able to get, unless a fight was arranged.

Ashley looked out of the window. There was frost already. Silvery white moss glittering in the dark. It was funny, sometimes you didn't feel so cold outside as you did in. He decided. He would finish his lager and go. At least it would be somebody to talk to.

He opened his eyes and Kieran was there, sitting in front of him, all suited and booted, reading text messages. Ashley blinked.

'Hello. Enjoy your nap?'

'Shit. What time is it?' He lifted his arm to look at his watch. 'Nearly eleven. Bloody hell. I was going out.'

'Too late now, mate. Unless it's a nightclub.'

'Funny.'

'Talking of which.' Kieran closed his phone and rose from the chair. 'I'm due at the Hippo in half an hour.' Making for the door he suddenly turned. 'By the way, Ash. Stay in tomorrow morning. I'm taking you somewhere.'

'Where?'

'You'll see.'

Ashley didn't like the sound of this. 'Am I in trouble?'

Kieran laughed. 'No. No you're not. Not with me, anyway.'

'With Crawford. Is he kicking me out? Because of the Chinese. I'm sorry about that. But I couldn't stay there. I was scared. I'm sorry.'

Kieran sat down again, but on the edge of the chair; he wasn't going to stay long. 'Don't worry, kid. You showed initiative. We're impressed if anything.' Ashley thought Kieran was probably being straight with him.

'So where are you taking me?' Then a thought. 'Not to see my dad. I don't want to go there. Not yet. I —'

'It's not to see your dad.' Now, suddenly, as he rose again, he was impatient. 'I'll explain tomorrow. Just be here.' And with that he was gone.

Morning – it was nearly three o'clock before Kieran arrived. 'Okay, let's go.' He was driving a blue BM today. 'Jump in.'

'You going to tell me where we're going?' Ashley was nervous. You could never be sure with these blokes. And it was Crawford wasn't it? He was the boss. If he said something Kieran had to do it, just like his dad had to.

The car stopped. 'What we come here for?'

'You retarded or something?' Kieran pointed out of the window. 'What's that?'

'Barber's.'

'Get out then.'

It was an old-fashioned barber's. Converted from the front room of an old terraced house. Like the one Ashley lived in. You could see from the old tin sign screwed to the brickwork above the door that the shop had been there for years. *Horace Bleed. Barber.* The window was misted over, distorting the figures that moved in the yellow gloom within.

'What we come here for? Are we collecting something?'

'You've come to have your hair cut.'

'Here? No way. He'll be about eighty. Anyway, I'm growing it.'

'Shut up.'

The barber wasn't eighty but he was old. Walked with a limp, and wheezed. There were photographs of haircuts stuck up around the place. From the ark. Black and white. Faded. Curled. Men with Brylcreem haircuts and toothpaste smiles. Perfect perfect teeth. There was a bloke in the chair having his hair cut. Younger than Ashley would have expected in a place like this.

Ashley sat beside Kieran who picked up a copy of the *Sun* and started to read the back page. 'You're going down,' he said to Ashley.

'You what?'

'You support the Blues don't you? All that stuff in your bedroom. You're going down. Another defeat last night. They're on their way. Good as in the lift.'

The men started to talk about the football. Ashley listened but didn't join in; he was trying to work out what was going on. Why was Kieran making him have a haircut? And why here? He remembered a film. Some blokes in America, having haircuts and shaves when suddenly the door bursts open and there's a gang with machine guns. No, he was being stupid.

'So, what's he want?' the barber asked Kieran when Ashley was in the chair.

'Just a nice respectable haircut, H. Make him look a bit tidier. Intelligent, if that's not asking for miracles.'

It wasn't a bad haircut. What Kieran asked for really. It made him look tidy, and wasn't old-fashioned. Not what he would have chosen though. He'd been thinking of having it cropped to Number 1, to make him look harder. This certainly didn't make him look hard. But it was good the way he'd cut the fringe. Over to one side. Floppy.

It was pissing down when they left and they had to make a run for the car. Kieran didn't say much. Just a smirk inside the car as Ashley ran his hands through his hair to remove the rain. 'Very nice, Ash. You'll probably pull now. Pop your cherry.' He turned the ignition and the rock music Kieran always played in cars resumed. He nodded his head in time, the ringless ring finger of his right hand tapping the steering wheel.

Back at the house Kieran told Ashley to run ahead and open the door, he had to get something out of the boot. Ashley was uneasy. He still didn't know why he had been forced to have a haircut. 'What's in there?'

'You'll see. Open the door.'

When he followed Ashley into the hall Kieran was carrying a black bin bag. 'Here,' he said, handing it to Ashley. 'Go and put this on.'

'What is it?'

'School uniform.'

Ashley dropped the bag. Then he bolted into the back room. Kieran lifted the bag and followed.

'You fucker,' Ashley yelled. 'You bastard fucker.' Tears were welling up. He couldn't breathe properly. 'You snot fucker. Bastard. Bastard snot fucker.' The tears were falling now. Kieran moved towards him, and Ashley bolted into the kitchen. 'I'm not going to school. I'm not going anywhere.' Kieran followed him.

'Piss off,' Ashley screamed. 'Piss off you piss fucker. Snottin' piss fucker.' He lifted a cup and hurled it at Kieran. It glanced off his shoulder and smashed on the floor. He lifted another cup and hurled it at Kieran. It glanced off his shoulder and smashed against the wall. He lifted another cup. Kieran jumped him. Grabbed his shoulders, brought his knee up between Ashley's legs. The boy gasped and keeled, but Kieran had his collar. He dragged him into the living room, heading towards the door to the stairs. Ashley thought Kieran was going to ram his head into it. His feet weren't touching the floor. Then the door was open and Kieran threw him into the stairs. The bag followed.

Kieran stood above him in the doorway. 'Get up those fucking stairs and put that fucking uniform on.' He booted Ashley in the arse. 'If you're not down here in five minutes wearing it, the next thing you do wear will be a shroud. Got it. You'll be meat.'

He stopped. Waited. Ashley snuffled. A sob took him. Shook his body. All of it. Like a convulsion. 'Key. Please. I —' Another boot in the arse. Harder than the first. 'Bastard,' the boy wailed, and grabbing the bag he scuttled up the stairs.

'Five minutes,' he heard Kieran shout. 'Or I'm coming up.' Then the door to the stairs slammed.

Ashley dropped the bag on the bed and opened the bedroom window. He had shinned down the drainpipe before, times when his dad was after him. But Kieran had opened the back door before Ashley could get more than one leg out of the window. There was nothing he could do. He withdrew his leg. He closed the window and waited. He looked down again. Kieran wasn't going anywhere. He was leaning against the doorpost, looking up at him. There was nothing for it: he'd have to put the poxy uniform on.

Shoes, trousers, a shirt; there was everything in the bag. He was surprised when he removed the blazer. The badge wasn't from anywhere round here. Oh shit! Where were they sending him? He couldn't get his breathing right. He moved to the window again. Kieran was still in the doorway.

There was even a tie, neatly rolled in the pocket of the trousers. Stripes. Dark blue, light blue. He put it on but left it loose. He waited for the trembling to stop, then went downstairs.

Kieran's anger was gone. 'Sit down, Ash.' Kieran indicated the settee, 'I want to talk to you.' Kieran pulled a chair from beside the table and, placing it right in front of Ashley, its back towards the boy, sat astride it.

I'm trapped, Ashley thought.

Kieran took his cigarettes from inside his jacket, gave one to Ashley, put the other in his mouth, lit them both. Ashley inhaled deeply. Expensive fags. Nice. Kieran exhaled. There was a veil of smoke between them. Kieran let it clear. 'Someone told me the government is going to ban smoking,' Ashley started. 'They're not, are they?'

'Shut up and listen, Ash. This is important. I'm not sending you back to school. The uniform's not for that. We've got a little job for you. We want you to help us with something.' Kieran paused. Ashley said nothing, but waited.

'Something's on next week. In town. And we want you to help us. Nothing much. You just have to hang around. I'll show you where next week. It's a little alley. Pricey will come and give you something. You put it in your schoolbag. You can use your own.' Kieran saw the look on the boy's face. 'You must have a schoolbag? What did you use for your books? Your kit? Shit, Ash, no wonder you're fucking thick. Well I'll get you a schoolbag. As soon as Pricey gives it to you, you stick it in the bag, under your books. I'll get you some of those as well. And I'll tell you what to do next on the day. It'll just be catching a bus and meeting me. Simple. I'll take the bag from you and drop you off here. You skip out of the uniform and I'll take it away and torch it. Job done.'

He waited. Ashley said nothing. 'You'll never have to wear school uniform again. Promise.' Still Ashley said nothing. 'You owe us, Ash. I got you out of school, got the social workers off your back. They think you're in Ireland. With your uncle. You owe Crawford, Ash. He let's you stay here. Don't forget that. That's how these things work. And we'll see you all right afterwards.'

Still Ashley said nothing. He didn't know what to say. He was thinking.

'I'll go through all this with you properly next week. I don't know which day yet. But you don't go anywhere. Got it? You stay here all next week. Got it? You're on call.' He grinned. 'Like a fucking doctor.' Then the grin was gone. 'You stay put till this is done. Understand?'

Ashley nodded. 'Yeah.' Then he asked the question. 'What is it Pricey's going to give me, Key? A package? Will it be heavy?'

'Don't worry about that now. And no, it won't be heavy.'

'Is it money?'

'Leave it, Ash.'

It seemed to Ashley then that the room had gone very quiet, almost as if there was an echo to their voices. 'Is it a gun? Is that what he'll give me? Is that what I'm collecting for you? A gun?'

'I said don't worry about that.' Kieran rammed his cigarette into his mouth. Ashley could hear Kieran inhale, and when he had exhaled he heard him say, quietly, but very clearly, into the smoke, 'Yeah. It's a gun, Ash.'

When Kieran had gone, Ashley went up to his room and took the school uniform off and very carefully hung everything over the back of his chair. He wished he had a photo of his mom now. He would have liked to look at it. But there wasn't one. He wished he had her to talk to. But she was gone. Get over it, he told himself; like he'd told himself lots of times before. Like the Weasel had told him.

Ashley went downstairs. The chair Kieran had used was still in front of the settee. Ashley put it back beside the table. He brushed crumbs off the settee, then curled up in the corner of it. This was where the dog used to lie. He sniffed the fabric, but you couldn't smell her any more. He took his phone from his pocket and went through his messages. Four unopened. All from the Weasel. The last, weeks ago. He deleted them. Put the phone away. And started to cry.

20

Sophie was pissed off with him. 'You promised.'

'I will. But not next week.'

'Why not?'

'I told you. I just can't. The week after for definite. Or maybe the end of next week. It depends.'

'On what?'

'Things.'

'Fuck you then.' He imagined her pouting like she always did when she was pissed off; her hair swinging. 'You needn't bother.' She rang off.

He tried to call her back but got voicemail. Shit. If he said next week, it was bound to be the time Kieran would want him. Sod's law. Like his dad always said. He tried to ring her back again, and again, but only got her voicemail. He texted: *lets go now*. She texted him back: *fuck off. Il get someone else*. He texted: *lets go now*. She texted him back: *fuck off*. He texted: *lets go now*. She texted him back: *meet at funi shp 11*.

There is a sculpture outside the maternity section of the Queen Elizabeth Hospital. Large. Enormous really. Modern. Like a woman and baby were growing out of, curling out of, this great piece of rock.

Sophie stood looking up at it, smiling. Tiny before it. 'D'you like it?'

'Yeah, it's all right. That's better.' Ashley turned to the construction site behind them. If the sculpture was enormous, there wasn't a word for the scale of this site. You could see nothing else. A network of scaffolding and ladders, forming dozens of cells in which men in coloured hard hats worked. Like bees in a hive. He could have stayed there looking and looking for ages. Blokes climbing ladders, sawing wood, lifting, hammering, leaning against scaffolding talking, like on the deck of a ship. And above it all, the cranes. Ashley loved the cranes. Rising and dipping, busy and steady against the cold blue sky.

They went into the reception of Maternity. There was a large waiting area. Lots of chairs. Like school assembly chairs, plastic, but with a padded bit for your bum. 'Useless for pregnant women,' Sophie tutted, like she was an expert.

An Indian woman was being admitted. Her husband was holding her up as a woman behind the desk took her details. A nurse came with a wheelchair and the woman sat in it. The nurse stroked the woman's arm. The woman tried to smile. Sophie watched as the woman was wheeled towards a lift, her husband following. Sophie watched a doctor in a turban and a man with a trolley leaving another lift, another opening to a woman with a tiny baby in her arms. She looked happy. A group of people in the waiting room rushed across to her, cooing over the baby. The woman started to cry. Sophie watched, and Ashley watched her watching.

He took her to the café and bought her a Coke and a Mars Bar. It was full of builders on their break, having cups of tea, eating sandwiches. At one table there was an old bloke in pyjamas and a dressing gown having a cup of tea with a young woman. 'Do you think that's his daughter, or his bit of stuff?' Sophie giggled.

'I dunno, do I? Daughter, I suppose.'

Sophie stroked her belly. 'It's funny. Thinking that I'm going to go up in that lift, and come down with a baby.'

The builders got up to leave and returned their cups to the counter. Ashley could see some of them getting cigarettes out of their overall pockets ready for a smoke outside.

'So are you going to tell me what you're doing next week that's so important?' There was a gleam in her eye. Ashley knew she would nag him until he told her.

'I'm going back to school.'

'No?'

'Yeah. I decided. Get educated.'

Sophie laughed. 'You're taking the piss. Really? You mean it?'

'Yeah.'

On the bus home she leaned in to him. 'Ta for taking me. It's been good. I feel okay now. So ta. And your hair looks cool.'

'Yeah. You said.'

'Well I'm saying again. Is it for school? Is that why you had it done?'

'Yeah.'

'Cool. It makes you better-looking. And now the swelling's gone your nose is better as well. Cheaper than plastic surgery.'

Ashley looked into the mirror. It was him. And it wasn't him. Of course it was him. No, it wasn't. Nothing like him. The uniform wasn't new, but it looked smart. White shirt, properly white. Ironed. A tie, pressed grey trousers, clean shoes. He looked stupid. No – just different. He put the glasses he had found in the jacket pocket back on. Weird. Sort of cool, but mostly weird. It was him, and it wasn't him. He could never be the kid in the glass. He knew his voice didn't sound like his. He opened his mouth. Nothing came out. It was him, and it wasn't.

It was like meeting someone new. Who was he, this kid? Posh? He would be good at school, could read and write. Probably good at maths too. Ashley noticed the room the boy was standing in. Not right, not right at all. And he tried to imagine the sort of home he had. His mother. Then he stopped the thoughts and took the uniform off. Folded it well. Put his tracksuit bottoms and T-shirt back on. His hoodie. Looked again. He was back. It was him. A dirty kid in a dirty room. A scruff. He took his dirty clothes off. Looked at his puny white body in the mirror. Hated it. Hated it. This was him. Hated it. He put a pair of jeans and a jumper on and took his dirty clothes down to the kitchen to wash in the sink. He used washing-up liquid; just as good. Kettles of boiling water. The kitchen filled with steam. Like a sauna. That's what they say. His nan used to say that when it was steamy – *like a sauna in here*. His hands stung as he rubbed away at his clothes. Then he dried them in front of the gas fire. Over a chair. He had to keep turning them. Like cooking steak. Keep turning, don't let it burn. The thought made him laugh. When they were nearly dry, he folded them, rubbing them hard with his hand, pressing them flat to get the creases out. He ought to nick an iron.

Then he put the immersion heater on. Had a bath, as hot as he could stand. A very hot bath could make a pregnant girl come on. That's what they said. When the water got cold he got out. He put the uniform on again. Looked. And looked. *Is it maths next, sir? I'm going to the library*. His mouth opened but nothing came out. You see, it wasn't him. He wanted to laugh, but he couldn't do that either. It was only nine o'clock but he went to bed.

Sunday Karl came round. Knocking on the back door before Ashley had time to do anything. Karl could see him through the kitchen window. There was nothing Ashley could do but let him in. 'Why you wearing that?'

'I'm going to a new school now.' Karl followed Ashley into the kitchen. 'Or I am next week anyway. Don't tell anyone though. It's a special school.'

'Special?'

'Leaning difficulties. D'you want some toast?'

'Nah. Why you wearing it today?'

'I'm going to see my dad. He texted me: *Look smart.* This is all I got.'

'You look different.'

'How d'you mean?'

'I don't know. Different. You don't look like you. Your hair's different. You look different.'

'Good different?'

Karl didn't really understand the question. 'Just different.' Karl walked into the living room. 'Who's living here with you?'

'Nobody. Just me. On me tod.'

Karl looked round again. 'It's cleaner than it used to be.'

'I had a tidy-up.'

There was the sound of helicopters approaching outside, low. The boys went out into the yard. 'Fucking low.' They watched one circle. A pair of binoculars would have shown you the pilot's face. 'They're heading for the Mendy,' Karl said. The noise was changing as the machines got smaller in the sky.

'There's always choppers flying over it,' Ashley replied. 'Like living in a fucking airport up there.' The boys went back inside.

'I'm going to put me trackies on.'

Upstairs Ashley looked at himself in the mirror again before removing the uniform. He'd found a clothes hanger and now kept it on that.

When Ashley came downstairs Karl was sitting hunched up on the settee, his hands in the pocket of his coat.

'You cold?'

'Not really.'

'D'you want to play a game? On the computer.'

'Not really.'

Ashley sat down beside his friend. Waited.

'Have you watched the news?' Karl asked.

'No.'

Karl said nothing.

'Why? What's happened?'

'Our Wesley.' He paused, swallowed. 'It was on the news.'

Ashley realised. 'Oh shit!' He waited for Karl to say more, but nothing came. 'Is he injured?'

'No.'

Ashley didn't know what to say. The two boys sat in silence. Then Karl sniffed, he was sort of crying.

'When?'

'Friday. He was shot on Friday. They came to tell my mom on Friday night.'

'Oh shit.'

'Through the head. And the shoulder. Another bloke as well. Two of them. The other bloke's not dead though. He got it in the chest.' Each word came slowly. Each word took effort. 'They're bringing him to Selly Oak. The alive one.'

Ashley wanted to say something. He wasn't sure exactly what you should say, but he had to say something. Briefly, very briefly, he wondered how the kid in the uniform would handle this. 'Shit, Karl. That's a real bastard.' He'd heard his dad say things like that, but it didn't really sound right. 'I'm sorry. I'm really sorry.' Karl looked down. Ashley left it a moment, then, 'How's your mom doing?' That sounded right.

It took Karl a while to answer; he was trying, Ashley could tell, but it was hard. 'Bad. Very bad,' he managed at last and then the tears took him and he started to cry, a soft snivelly crying, without sobs.

Ashley wished he had some coke. He'd had some yesterday that Kieran had given him, but it was all gone. He got some weed from a kitchen drawer – the next best thing. He rolled the spliff in the kitchen, and took it in to Karl. 'Here, mate. Make you feel better.'

Karl pulled at it like water. Ashley watched the smoke leave his mouth. Streams of it. He pulled again. 'It was on the news.' Smoke left Karl's mouth with the words. 'A photo of him as well. But not of the injured soldier. They never even mentioned his name. Just of Wesley. That's policy. They just give the name and rank of the dead. Not the injured. Maddocks has been on the phone to my mom. The telly wants to talk to him. About what Wesley was like at school. For *Midlands Today*. Tomorrow.'

'I'll watch it.'

Now Karl lifted his head and looked at Ashley. He rubbed the back of his hand across his nose.

'D'you want some bog roll?'

'Ta.'

Karl had recovered a little when Ashley returned from

the bathroom with a handful of tissue. Karl wiped his face. Blew his nose.

Ashley lit another joint. Made some coffee. Sometimes Karl talked, sometimes he didn't. Ashley felt sorry for Karl and for his mom, he liked her, she had always been nice to him, had him over for Christmas dinner last year, but he was also pleased at the way he was reacting, helping his friend; he knew he was doing it right, just like the other kid would.

Karl couldn't stop talking now. 'My mom wouldn't go to church this morning. She's never missed before. Ever. The pastor came round. He was being nice and comforting us. Then my mom just gets up and starts marching round the room. Fucking Iraq, she says. Then again. Fucking Iraq. I never heard her swear in my life before. She'd swipe Wesley or me for swearing less than that. The pastor didn't know what to say.' And now Karl was laughing. Really laughing. Like it was comedy television. Then he stopped. Leaned back. 'That's why I came here. To get out.'

21

At least Kieran said he could leave the house in the evenings. It was doing his head in staying in all day. A fat woman carrying a bottle of wine held the door for him at Walton Tower. He could smell her perfume as he followed her to the lift. 'If you breathe in deep there'll be room for two,' she said. 'God, it stinks like a toilet in here.' She pressed 13. 'What floor you want, love?'

'Same.'

'You going to Mel's? You a friend of Soph's?'

'Yeah.'

'Didn't think she knew any white lads. Ooh, I shouldn't say that should I?' The woman was nice. About thirty, with very big tits, like a shelf, and glossy white hair with dark roots. A lot of make-up. Glasses with fancy frames. She reminded him of someone. Off the telly probably. 'What's your name, love?'

'Ashley.'

'Mine's Sharon.'

Mel was standing at the open door of the flat. As she left the lift and saw her, Sharon gasped dramatically, clasped her free hand to her chest and seemed to just save herself from stumbling. 'God give me breath. Like a gas chamber in there.

You'd be dead before you got to eighteen. All blokes should be fitted with catheters. The law.' She held the wine up to Mel. 'Offering. A touch of Bulgarian magic for afterwards.' Mel took the wine. 'Ta, Shaz.' As Sharon hugged her Mel noticed Ashley.

'I was adopted.' Sharon nodded towards Ashley. 'In the lift. This young man escorted me up. But it's your daughter he's interested in. Doesn't appreciate the older woman.'

'Hello, love. I didn't know you was coming.'

'I texted Sophie.'

'Is she here yet? Jade?' Sharon's voice took on a whisper. Mel lowered hers. 'Been here since six.'

'Oops! Last one to the party again. How is she?'

'How d'you think? Not good.'

Ashley followed the women into the flat. Two others were sitting on the settee, both blonde, one with her hair tied back in a tail. The other had bruises all over her face; her lower lip was cut and swollen. Sharon pushed towards her. 'Oh my poor darling.' She hugged her, nearly falling on top of her. 'If I had a gun,' she said, steadying herself, 'I'd shoot the bastard. I'd shoot all of 'em.'

Sophie was sitting cross-legged on a big cushion on the floor, her headphones in, watching the television. Mel nudged her in the back with her foot. She turned. Saw Ashley. Pulled the headphones down.

'Hiya. Didn't know you was coming.'

'I texted.'

Sophie rose slowly from the cushion. Sharon came to hug her. 'How's my precious?' She tapped Sophie's belly. 'Blooming beautifully I see.'

'Yeah. I'm all right.' Then to Ashley: 'Let's go into the kitchen.'

'Don't let her smoke in there, love, will you?'

'He's got a name you know, Mom. It's Ashley.' Ashley had never heard Sophie call Mel *Mom* before.

'Sorry, love. Ashley. Don't let her smoke in there, Ashley, for Christ's sake.'

'D'you want a milky coffee?' Sophie asked. 'We've got tons of milk. Mel keeps buying it. Every time she goes out. I think she'd get a cow if she could.' Then she laughed. 'She's got three of 'em in there with her now.'

There was a bottle of whiskey on the counter, still more than half full. Sophie saw Ashley looking at it. 'D'you want a drop in?'

'Ta.'

'I'm not having any. Not yet. We're having a séance. That's why they're here,' and she nodded towards the other room. 'Jade's bloke has given her a smack. Mel and Shaz want her to grass him. But she's not sure. 'Cause she loves him. They don't seem to understand that. She doesn't want to get him into trouble. And he'd probably dump her. So she wants to ask her nan what to do. You can't do a séance properly if you've been drinking. The spirits don't like it. Not respectful.'

'D'you believe all that?'

'Course. Well, I think so. Mel does. There's a bloke in Sheldon she goes to. Reads her palm. Every time she gets a new fella she goes. Gay he is. A lot of them are. Gays are good at that stuff. Sensitive.'

Ashley watched her making the coffee. She looked properly pregnant now. Funny. Really thin, but with a bump. Like a cartoon muscle.

Sophie poured whiskey into Ashley's mug. 'I want to see if we can reach Wesley? He might have a message for his

mom. Or Karl.' Ashley said nothing. Sophie brought her face
to Ashley's mug of coffee and sniffed. 'Yesterday the smell
of whiskey made me feel sick. It's okay today. Weird. Have
you seen Karl?'

'He came round yesterday.'

'Me and Tyr took some flowers round this afta. There's a
pile of them outside the house. You can't see the wall. And
there's this big Union Jack. In the middle. Flowers all round
it. Looks lovely. All the curtains are closed. Made me feel
weird; curtains closed in the daytime. Like it was a crack
house or something.'

'Wake up.'

'I'm awake.'

'You don't look it.'

'I didn't think we'd be going this early.'

Kieran grinned at the boy's grumbling. Tired like this, and
curled into his seat, he looked very small; very young. Keeping
his eyes on the road, Kieran reached inside his workman's
jacket and pulled a pack of cigarettes from the pocket of
his shirt, dropping them in Ashley's lap. Bensons. A lighter
followed. 'Here, have some breakfast.'

He noticed the boy's right hand. Swollen fingers. 'What
you done to your hand?'

'Tattoo.'

Keeping his right hand on the wheel Kieran used his left to
bring the boy's hand towards him. Ashley curled the fingers,
making a fist.

'Jesus! What a mess. They've gone blue.'

'That's the ink.' Ashley pulled the hand away. 'Sophie did
it? She's done lots.'

'What she use? A fucking Stanley knife?'

Ashley said nothing.

'What does it say anyway?'

'Mom. M. O. M. One on each finger. And R. I. P. Underneath. Two letters on each finger. The middle one, O I, that stands for a Buddhist word. A prayer.'

'And the last finger, M P, that stands for mad pratt. What you want to go and do that for, Ash? It's stupid. If you wanted a tattoo you should have gone and had a proper one. I'd have taken you.'

'She had a séance. Her and her mom. She told me they got in touch with my mom.'

Kieran looked at the boy. 'Ash. You know that's bollocks. She couldn't —'

'That's what they said. Said they got in touch with her and she wanted me to have it done. To remember her.'

Kieran sighed. 'But, Ash – You know—'

Ashley stopped him. 'That's what they said. So I did it. What else could I do?'

Kieran drove in silence for a while. He knew he should talk with the boy, help him accept what had happened; see that this was all nonsense. But this wasn't the time or the place. 'Just keep it as clean as you can,' he said, 'or we'll be back up the ossie again, applying for a season ticket. Use TCP.'

It was just gone seven and still dark. The night's rain had left a damp black sheen on the roads. Streetlights, headlights, glittered and danced. Kieran was dressed like a builder. A fluorescent work jacket, jeans, boots.

They passed the Spotted Hippo.

'That's where Crawford's got his office isn't it?' Ashley asked.

'One of them.'

At the top of Bromsgrove Street a large construction site was coming to life. Kieran pulled up among a number of cars and vans beside it. A bloke was guiding a van as it reversed out. Kieran reached into the back of the car for a couple of hard hats. 'Here, stick this on.'

'It's too big.'

'Shut it. Just get it on. We're blending in.' Kieran's tone had changed. 'And this too.' He handed him a luminous jacket. 'Right, this is where I'm going to drop you. When the time comes. On the day.' This voice was hard. Brittle. More than just businesslike. There was a force behind the words. Like he was driving them into Ashley's brain. 'Get out and I'll take you through it.'

They walked up Bromsgrove Street turning left into a short street of dilapidated buildings that lay behind the clubs. The darkness was disappearing rapidly, replaced by a grey-blue sky, the colour of some girls' eyeshadow. The street was empty and the pad of their feet echoed a little. 'Right, you come down to the corner, and then so long as no one's around you nip up here.' He indicated a narrow passage between two buildings. Ashley followed Kieran in. It was just wide enough for one person to get through.

'Under here.' They ducked under what was left of a wooden fence into a piece of land that might once have been a garden. Now it was rough and uneven scrub, enclosed by the backs of buildings. Old buildings. Boarded-up windows. Fire escapes. A few bottles and bin bags lying about. Ashley could make out a couple of blue plastic crates stuck in a bush, like they were part of it. 'Once you're here – you wait. Best to squat down I think,' and Kieran went down on his haunches. Ashley did the same. 'If anyone should see you from up there, it'll look like you're taking a crap. And once you're here,'

Kieran was whispering close in to Ashley's ear, 'all you have to do is wait. Keep down. But no one ever comes in here. No point is there? So you just wait. And you stay. It might be ten minutes. It might be twenty. It might be a fucking hour. You wait. Rain. Snow. Fucking earthquake. You don't move until Pricey arrives.'

Ashley listened. It was not just Kieran he could hear; the thump of his heart was making a louder noise.

'When he does, give him your schoolbag. He'll put something – ' Kieran stopped, looked at Ashley. 'He'll put the gun in it, give it you back and be off. You wait. Twenty minutes. Got it? I'll give you a proper watch. Twenty minutes. Then up you get.' Kieran rose. Like demonstrating. Ashley did the same. 'And back we go to the street. But this way.' He made for a bush ahead of them, pushed through it to an even narrower passage, that led into another street of derelict buildings, old offices it looked like. Essex Terrace the sign said. 'Right, Ash, this is the way you go.' They turned into Kent Street. 'Keep going down this road. It's the long route to the bus stop but it's one with no CCTV.' At the bottom they turned into Wrentham Street. 'See what we're doing here?'

'Doubling back.'

'You've got it.' Kieran walked Ashley up to the Bristol Road, past St Catherine's dome, over Pagoda Gardens and through St Jude's Underpass to the bus stops on Hill Street. 'When you get here you phone me. Okay?' Ashley nodded. 'You get off the bus at the ice rink and I'll be in the car park waiting for you. Understand everything?'

'Yeah.'

'You sure? We can do it again if you like.'

'I'm not stupid. I know what to do.'

'You worried?'

'No.'

'Right we'll go and have a cup of tea in the market and then you can walk me through it. Show me you know what you're doing.'

'I'm starving. Can't we have a breakfast? A fry-up?'

As Kieran watched the boy wolf down a breakfast that would have satisfied any one of the navvies working round here, he explained to him the importance of his role. He went into no detail, just pointed out that he absolutely had to do exactly as he was told. If for any reason Pricey didn't turn up, he just stayed there until Kieran called him. He was completely safe. No one ever went in there. Why would they?

22

Ashley looked at the kid in the mirror. He could do anything. Like posh kids can. Anything. And get away with it. He flicked his head – and the fringe flopped. Cool. He did it again. Then turned his head to look at himself side-on. He picked up his schoolbag, felt the weight of books, football boots. Five minutes, Kieran had said when he rang. Be fucking ready, he said. That was ten minutes ago. Easily ten minutes ago.

He dragged himself away from the mirror and went downstairs to wait. Kieran hadn't said anything about money yet, except that he would be looked after – and Ashley hadn't asked. But he wanted a good wad. This must be big, whatever it was. They wouldn't be going to so much trouble if what he was doing wasn't an important part of it. So. He wanted enough to get a good laptop, and some clothes. He hardly let himself think it – like the posh kid would wear.

He heard the front door go. Kieran grinned when he saw Ashley. 'Fucking hell, Ash. You look like you can read and write. The glasses look good. Right brainbox. How you feeling?'

'Okay.'

'Ready for this?'

'Yeah.'

'Here.' He handed Ashley a mobile. 'Put this in your bag. You ring me on this. I'm keyed in.' He sort of smiled. 'And you don't get to keep it afterwards.' And in that attempt at a smile Ashley saw that Kieran was on edge, and he was pleased to realise that he himself wasn't nervous at all, in fact he was excited, and looking forward to the job. It seemed more than just a couple of weeks ago that he had lain on the settee crying with fear at what he had let himself in for. Now he was different. If he did this well everything could change for him.

'Come on then. Time to go.'

Ashley looked at the new watch Kieran had given him. It was two-thirty.

'I'm parked-up down here,' Kieran told him, 'on the corner. The Megane; nothing too flash today.'

It was as they were crossing the road to the car that Geezbo turned the corner. Still in his shorts, he was wearing a zebra-patterned hoodie. He tossed his head so that the hood fell back, revealing his side-on baseball cap. He looked straight at Ashley. Ashley froze. Kieran looked from Ashley to the boy in the long baggy shorts. It took Geezbo a moment to convince himself that the boy before him was actually Ashley. He looked at Kieran. At the car. At Kieran again. 'Fuck man! Whaz goin' on? Wha' you dressed up like thiz for, man?'

Ashley didn't know what to say. 'I'm going to school,' was the best he could manage, and he knew how stupid it sounded before Geezbo came back with, 'Two a clock in dee fuckin' aftanoon? You gonna school? Time-keepin' might not be your ting, man,' he sneered, 'but you ain't goin' to no school at two in dee aftanoon.' All of Geezbo's instincts were at work, and both Ashley and Kieran recognised this. He was almost sniffing the air, as if, like some sort of wild pig, he recognised that he had stumbled across something.

'To register,' Kieran said across the roof of the car. And he was talking in his Irish accent now. Cool and smiling. 'To register at his new school. Private. Going to get him educated if it's the last thing I do. Get in Ash, or we'll be late for Mr O'Connor.' And ignoring Geezbo's attempt at further questions the two got into the Megane and were away. Geezbo stood watching the car disappear into Hobson Road.

Ashley could feel Kieran's tension. He was trying to control himself. Ashley knew. Not let his anger show. It wasn't the time. Ashley thought it best to remain silent. Eventually Kieran could speak. 'So. Who's that monkey?'

'Just a mate.'

'Looks like he should be in a cage. What you knock around with kids like him for? Total trouble.' He pressed the CD player. Rock music filled the car. Loud. When he had calmed down, he lowered the sound so he could talk over it. His eyes on the road ahead. 'Ash, I thought I told you no one was to come to the house. Just you.'

'You can't stop your mates coming round.'

'No one is supposed to know you're there. I told the school you was in Ireland.'

'He's not from school.'

'I could tell that. Looks like he came in from the fucking ark. Crawled off it.' He turned the music up again. It filled the car, completely filled it. Like water. Ashley could hardly breathe. And Kieran was driving too fast. Overtaking. He shouldn't be, Ashley knew this, not when you're on your way to an important job. Then as they approached the city centre, Kieran pulled into Speedwell Road opposite the synagogue and killed the music.

Here Kieran went through everything with Ashley. And again. And as he answered Kieran's questions Ashley realised that despite what had happened with Geezbo, he still wasn't nervous, was still excited, wanted to do a good job, do it properly. And he knew that Kieran recognised this. It was a good feeling. He was part of this. He tried to see himself in the wing mirror, but could only catch a bit of his hair. 'What we going to do about Geezbo?' he asked.

'Is that his name? Sounds like somebody bringing up phlegm. Suits him.' Then Kieran looked hard at the boy beside him, took in the question that had been asked, the way it had been asked, without fear, recognising the problem, no longer the whining, defensive little kid he so often was.

'Dunno yet. See how things go. Might have to sort him out if he plays up.'

Ashley nodded. 'Yeah.'

It was cold, but the sun was shining. But not here in this quiet, shadowy place filled with shrubs and ivy. This is it, Ashley told himself, I am here. And he wondered if fear would come, but it didn't. He felt fine. Calm. He looked around. It was about the size of a cell. He thought about his dad and wondered if he would be proud of him. A couple of clumps of snowdrops were out. It reminded him of the cemetery; there were tons of them up there. There were buds on some of the twigs that overhung the broken fence. Brown ones. Green ones. Some small, black, pointed and tiny. Little black spears. He remembered the story of *Gulliver's Travels*. Tons of tiny arrows being fired into Gulliver's huge body. And no effect. He used to love that film.

He looked above the fence to the back of the old buildings that enclosed this space. Derelict by the look of them. The sun shone on milky brown bricks and black ironwork fire escapes; he counted four of them, just on that side. All with boarded-up doors and windows. Some shuttered with metal, others with pieces of wood. It was like looking out into a ruined world.

He crouched down carefully. He didn't want to get his trousers dirty but he wanted to follow Kieran's instructions exactly. To the letter. All he had to do now was wait. He smoked a cigarette. His thighs started to ache, so he stood up, in close to the fence.

One of his fingers had gone septic and that was aching too; the one with the Buddhist word. The *I* was just a bulge of pus. He sucked at it. Spat.

Waiting. Like in a secret garden. Like in – He heard a noise, just a small sound, from above. A boarded door had opened. A fat man came to the edge of the fire escape. Vest and trackies. He scratched his belly and looked out at the world below him. Ashley pushed into the fence. Became one with the shrubbery. He was still calm. Still very calm. This was the job. You deal with events. You cope. He loved the way he was feeling. It was him and it wasn't him – quietly watching the man on the fire escape smoking a cigarette. Like a spy. Calmly watching the man on the balcony smoking his cigarette. Waiting. Part of the job. Doing the job. He loved the way he was feeling.

The man threw his nub over the metal balustrade. Scratched his arse. Looked around again. But Ashley was invisible. He knew he was. Just part of the stuff in this place. The man's gaze never faltered, just moved on. He turned and went back. Ashley looked at the empty space where he had been.

Then the waiting again. Listening to the small sounds of the city that surrounded him. Until – a closer sound – in the passageway. The shrubbery moved. Ashley thought of jungle films, wildlife, a tiger tracked in the jungle, the creature breaks cover. The word was in his mouth. *Pricey?* But it stayed there. He wasn't stupid. The tiger emerged and it wasn't Pricey. A Chinese bloke. Not Feiyang. But Ashley recognised him. One of the men from the Bamboo Garden. Picking winners. Smashed-in nose and roses on his arm.

Ashley was wary. Had something gone wrong? 'Where's Pricey?'

'Give me the bag.' His Chinese accent was strong. Ashley handed the schoolbag over. The man removed his jacket. Beneath it a shoulder holster with three pouches that he slipped off and held in his mouth as he pulled his jacket back on. He took a mobile phone from the bottom of the three pouches and put it in the inside pocket of his jacket. Then crouched to the schoolbag. He scooped books, football boots, shorts, to one side and laid the holster at the bottom of the bag. Pulled off the leather gloves he was wearing and dropped them in. A balaclava from his pocket. Pushed the books back. And he was on his feet again.

'Twenty minutes. Don't move for twenty minutes.'

It was hardly English, just a jumble of sounds, but Ashley understood, nodded. 'I know.'

Then he was gone. Seconds. It could only have been seconds. Ashley was sweating, a trickle down his back. But he loved how he was feeling. It had been so quick. So good. He looked at his watch. Now all he had – the man was on the fire escape again. Another followed. Younger. Leather jacket and jeans. They were talking, the younger man smoking. Ashley concentrated. Studied them. If they had seen anything he should be able to tell. If they were looking out for anything he should be able to tell. No. If they had seen something they would keep looking back towards him. He'd seen stuff like this in films. They were just talking. When the cigarette was finished they turned and went back to the building. Banged on a door that looked as if it was boarded up. It opened. They went through. No backward glance. They couldn't have seen anything.

Ashley realised he had been holding his breath. He exhaled. Crouching down again as he did. Like gym exercises. He checked the watch. Start the twenty minutes from now.

The bag was there before him. He touched it. *There is a gun in this bag* – the words in his mouth, not out loud. And now his hand was moving across the bag. His legs were aching again. He stood up and rubbed his hamstrings. Checked all the fire escapes. Nudged the bag closer to the hedgerow with his foot. Stooped and opened it. Pushed the books aside. Lifted the holster. Looked at it. Looked. Undid the stud on the middle pouch. A box. He lifted it a little. Ammo. Pushed it back. Closed the stud. Then the gun. He rose quickly, looked around, checked again, slowly, carefully. Down quickly and then the pouch was open. He looked. He felt in the bag for the gloves. Put them on. He had never felt like this in his life. Never. He had a gun in his hand. A real gun. Beautiful. He weighed it; light, really light. Looked at it. So small in his hand. So small, but beautiful. Stainless steel barrel, stainless steel sights. Matt, not shiny. He looked at the letters embedded in the steel. *MK9 KAHR*. He sounded them. Put the sounds together. Made a word. A language. Said it again. Said it again. He would have liked to remove the gloves and let his skin feel the metal, the polymer grip in the palm of his hand. He lifted the barrel to his nose, and sniffed. Deep. Yes. Sniffed again. His chest lurched. Like a ride at Alton Towers. He had never smelt this before, this faint acrid odour, but he knew what it meant. It had been used. By the Chinese bloke. He put it back in the holster. But then took it out again. He wanted to hold it, properly, like a gun. He remembered Feiyang's gun hard against Benjy Graham's lips – very similar to this one, but Ashley knew it wasn't the same.

He wanted to hold this gun like a proper assassin. He stood, held it two-handed. He pointed. Imagined squeezing his finger against the trigger. He made an arc. Went down on one knee. He wanted to squeeze the trigger, but didn't. He pointed it at the balcony where the two men had so recently stood. He waited. He had never felt like this in his life. Like sugar in his mouth. If they came out again. Now. And looked down at him – what would he do? He thought about people he would like to be on that balcony. Benjy Graham. Maddocks. He recovered. He had a job to do. And this reaction pleased him. Professional. He repacked the holster in his bag. Checked the back of the buildings. Nothing. Lit a cigarette. Checked his watch. Waited. He recalled a documentary he had seen on television, last year probably, about Africa. Boy soldiers. In this one country they had kids his age as soldiers, mercenaries really, and they were really feared. More dangerous than the men. Ruthless.

Essex Terrace. Empty.

Kent Street. Empty.

Gooch Street. Big open car park. Cars parked in bays along the road. No people.

The long way. As he has been told. Up Wrentham Street. Past blocks of maisonettes. The blue gates of the breaker's yard. No people. Then, a man in white overalls with a ladder. He props it against a wall. Disappears up an entry. Past the White Lion and the Fountain. Both closed.

Bristol Street. He hears it before he reaches it. Traffic. Tons of it. Buses. Lorries. Cars. Motorbikes. You name it. No pedestrians. He passes St Catherine's dome. Still no people on the street. Until Thorpe Street. Then people. Not many at first. Smokers outside offices. Window cleaner at the kebab shop. Groups of kids. School's finished. A group of Asian lads in hoods and trackie bottoms look at him, smirk. And all the time, the thought in his head – *There is a gun in this bag. I have a gun. I am walking through the streets of Birmingham with a gun.*

Ashley headed for the underpass into Queensway. Dark and dingy and smelling of sicked-up cider, of piss. Up into the Pagoda Gardens. And down into St Jude's Underpass. Just as dark and dingy and stinking as they all are. The Asian kids were coming through the other end. The way they were walking. Filling the underpass, blocking him off. The penny dropped. If he turned and ran they would get him. He'd have to blag his way through. Then the penny dropped. School uniform. Clean face. Floppy hair. A schoolbag. They think this is me. And then they were upon him. Quick as a stabbing. Shoulders banged against the wall. A clout across the gob. The bag gone. Pockets frisked, emptied, the watch pulled from his wrist. And with a whack to the belly that floored him they were away.

SHUKO

23

Winter is the season of the Water element, but fortunately all that remained of the heavy rains of just an hour before was a dampness that hung so thickly in the air one could taste it. Not that it affected numbers. Fights taking place on the dark nights of winter were often better attended than those of the lighter nights of spring and summer: the cold dark perhaps creating an atmosphere preferred by the punters.

I vary the locations of fights over three or four venues throughout the course of the year. This evening we were using a redundant factory that stood within an entire complex of abandoned warehouses, workshops, small factories. The lights of the tower blocks of the Kingshurst estate, a couple of miles away, were blurred and smudged in the wet air; the roar of traffic on the M6 equally subdued.

Irregular black lakes stretched across the cratered ground designated as tonight's car park. The beam of Diesel's spot-light torch briskly swept through each vehicle as she checked with the driver their entry password before her girlfriend, Pauline, guided them with a smaller torch to one of the drier places to park.

I made my way through lines of cars to join her. I like to

have a few words with everyone working during an evening. 'You are doing a good job, Pauline.' I looked towards the line of lights awaiting entry. 'About another thirty to get in. We should be ready to start in half an hour.'

'Before that probably,' Pauline mumbled. Drops of water fell from her plastic rainhat to slide down her glasses.

When Diesel had seen in the last of the cars she pulled her wagon across to close the entrance. Pauline joined us as we manoeuvred our way through puddles and rows of cars to the derelict factory. Remnants of its working past were still evident: several metal hoist-rests high up on each wall; ceiling girders; some chain-holds still in place. Concrete platforms that had once been ramp stands offered the early arrivals prime positions from which to watch the evening's proceedings, like those who held boxes in the old Chinese theatres. But mostly the space was empty brick walls and blackened windows.

Knighton had rigged up a circle of light in the centre of the room, throwing the rest of the space into shadow, a very dramatic effect. At the back, smaller lights illuminated trestle tables holding bottles of beer for sale. There were bottles of spirits too, all served in plastic cups. To the left of these were the betting stands.

This was the second evening that I had put Knighton in charge of fights and there was no reason to regret my decision. He managed to find good dogs and had something of the showman about him, conducting each fight with a running commentary. He was very professional in consulting with his judges about when to finish a fight and declare a winner; there were never any complaints about this.

Betting is always highest on Staffs and tosas, both very determined and fearless fighters. The Chinese in particular, who usually make up three quarters of the house, are excited by these breeds.

I spotted Knighton getting a beer and talking to my relation Feiyang and his brother-in-law. 'Uncle,' Feiyang bowed his head. 'You have a busy night again.' He did not acknowledge Diesel or Pauline.

'We have, I am pleased to say. Despite the poor weather.'

Knighton lit a cigarette and downed a third of his bottle of Tiger. He looked around. 'You've certainly pulled 'em in tonight, all right. Reckon we're ready to go?' he asked me.

'I think so.'

'Right, I'll get things started. Give 'em five minutes then, Dies, will you?'

Cupping her hands to the side of her mouth and moving off into the spectators, Diesel bellowed, 'First fight. Five minutes.' Pauline setting off in the opposite direction repeated the call, breathless and reedy.

'First fight. Five minutes. Place all bets immediately. Last bets now.'

'Last bets,' Pauline called. 'Last bets now.'

'Confucius fights Red Emperor. Last bets. Confucius versus the Red Emperor.'

In the circle of light the first dogs were being paraded. Each dog was walked through the circle alone, then they were introduced to each other, instantly rearing and snarling; a moment much enjoyed by the punters. 'The dogs tonight are better than last time, I think, Uncle,' Feiyang told me. 'I have been having a look at them. As good as you would find anywhere in the country. The Staffs in particular.'

I knew that Feiyang had attended recent fights in Newcastle and used to go to the big ones in Bermondsey that have stopped now. Many of the London Chinese who used to attend those now come here to Birmingham.

It is less the fights themselves that hold my interest than the reactions of the punters. Some follow the progress of the fight breathlessly. Their faces register each bite a dog sustains, they groan or cheer depending on where their money lies. When an animal locks its jaws on the neck of its opponent they raise their fists and shout for a win. And if a dog is then able to lift and shake its opponent there is a roar from those who feel sure their money has been doubled. There are a few I see who squint, or look away at the bloodier moments, but there are also those who will stare unblinking at the whole spectacle. They may as well be watching the oranges and lemons of a fruit machine passing before their eyes. Feiyang is a squinter, a looker-away; his brother-in-law, Chun, on the other hand, the man in the arcade, unmoved, except for a smile of satisfaction when his dog was declared.

It was in the time between the second and third fight that Diesel came to me. 'I don't want to speak out of turn, Shuke, particularly about your relatives, but I'd have a word with Knighton if I was you about your nephew. I know you like to keep up with what's happening round town, and you might already know. But it was just something he said about Feiyang. About a connection with Crawford's people. Like I said you might know—'

'No, that's not something I knew about. Thank you, Diesel.'

I slipped her a twenty-pound note.

With the agreement of the owners the last fight of the evening now went to the death. Knighton made it an exciting spectacle, exhorting the injured dogs to fight on, pushing and prodding with his gauge stick at any sign of retreat. Usually such fights end with both dogs dead, and tonight was no exception; the last dog to expire is the payout. A few regulars voice objections about matches to the death, but Knighton's reply is very simple. 'It's just like bullfighting, mate, in Spain. 'Cept you don't end up with no steaks when it's all over.'

It had been a lucrative night. The punters were all gone and the money had been counted and sent back to the casino. Dead dogs are usually removed by their owners, but tonight one had been left for Knighton to dispose of. He hauled it into a sack and lifted it on to a pallet that Diesel helped him carry to his van. Pauline was moving through the circle of light that had been our arena with a watering can.

Although this is a derelict area, used by no one, it pays to be thorough, so I ensure that all evidence of our event is removed. In daylight Pauline will return to clear away cigarette ends and any bottles that have escaped our attention tonight.

It was wages time. No one counted the notes, they never do; they knew there would be enough. I had said nothing to Knighton of what Diesel had told me; I wanted to see if he would come to me himself. Not a word. I was disappointed.

I was parked just beyond Kinny Bridge when Knighton's van crossed it into the Mendy. I followed for a time then flashed my headlights. Recognising me he slowed and came to a halt, got out. He was wary. 'Something up, Shuke?'

I opened my passenger door for him to join me and he got in. 'I didn't have a chance to mention it earlier, not discreetly, but Diesel had a word with me. She said you knew something about my relative Feiyang that might interest me, some connection with Crawford. But perhaps she has it wrong.'

Inside the car we were in darkness, or at least there was insufficient light for me to observe the man's eyes, any flicker that might indicate unease, suggest deceit. There was sufficient light seeping in from the street for me to notice his left hand twitch, open and close, before resting like the other one flat against his thigh. 'Oh yeah. I knew there was something I meant to tell you. I was going to catch you at the end but it slipped my mind. Sorry.' I said nothing, so he continued. 'I told Diesel I thought you'd want to know. It's just that a few times now I've noticed Feiyang hanging around with that Kieran bloke who works for Crawford, a runner I think. Quite an important one though, judging by some of the cars he gets to drive. Twice I've seen Kieran come into the Bamboo Garden when I've been in there for a takeaway. And he's not there for grub. Or if he is, he eats with the family. He waves to the pregnant girl who's always serving.'

'Feiyang's wife.'

'Is she? He just waves to her and goes straight up the stairs.'

'And have you seen them anywhere else?'

'I've seen them in the Maddy a couple of times. Once they had those other blokes that live there with them, one of them was with him tonight. Another time they were chatting with a black bloke. Dreads.' If he had been uneasy his old confidence was now back. 'Let's have a fag,' he said, opening the car door and stepping out. I joined him.

He offered me one of his Royals but I declined, taking my own from my jacket pocket. I accepted a light though.

'I don't know how you can smoke those things. Rough as Old Harry. God knows what the cancer rates are like in China.'

'You've got to die of something.' The refrain I had heard so often among the English.

'I'd prefer something quicker.'

'I am sure that can be arranged.'

Knighton probably wouldn't describe me as a humorous man but there seemed no doubt in his mind that this was a joke, and so he laughed instantly and loudly. 'Very good.' And then, as if suddenly remembering something. 'Eh, you're not pissed with me are you, Shuke, for forgetting to mention about Kieran?'

'I wish you had mentioned it to me sooner. I like to know such things. It may or may not be important, but connections like that are always worth knowing about. Do you have any idea why they are seeing so much of each other?'

'Well, I don't think they're mates. Not in the proper way. You lot like to keep to yourselves don't you? So, it could be that Kieran's recruiting for Crawford, or that there is some business going on between them. My missus said she seen them parking up in Essex Street one evening. About seven. She does shifts in the Metro Bar.'

24

For the second successive Thursday Yangku and I parked at the end of Rectory Street with a perfect view of Cathedral Apartments.

Again it was 11.20 when Trudy came into view. I had already decided that if she kept to the same schedule this morning as she had for the last two weeks it would confirm our plan and we would take her next week. And there she was – precisely on time again.

Miss Blossom is a tall woman, unusually so for a Chinese. She carried herself with willowy elegance as she drifted across the shop to greet us.

'Casino men.' She bowed her head gracefully, and waved an approaching assistant away. 'I will see to these gentlemen personally.'

Miss Blossom has been a regular canasta player at the casino for many years. Longer than the Dragons have run it, and there are stories that she played a part in arranging the Dragons' acquisition of this and various other places in their early days in Birmingham.

There are many stories about Miss Blossom. It was said that she left China as a child when her family came to Europe in the fifties. Her father was in the diplomatic service but defected before the Cultural Revolution took hold. Miss Blossom claims he was shot down on a street in Antwerp by agents of Mao Zedong. Her first husband was French, her second Irish, and she lived for a time in Dublin where so the story goes she helped eliminate unwanted pregnancies.

'It is so pleasant to see a little sunshine today,' she said, speaking now in Mandarin. 'Hints of spring. I noticed only this morning that the crocuses are coming out in my garden.'

Miss Blossom's Eastern Emporium, housed in an old Digbeth warehouse, is a cornucopia of goods from right across the East. There is heavy ornate furniture from South Korea and stone garden pagodas from Thailand on the fourth floor. The basement is crowded with Buddhas and vases and jewellery. Futons are on the second floor, and we followed Miss Blossom, still wearing high heels in her seventies, up the stairs.

'Is this for yourself?' she asked me, reverting to English.

'A visitor. One who will not be out much during her stay. I want something with a base, that may be used as both a comfortable couch during the day and a bed at night.'

She nodded and raised her hand indicating the futons with a base. 'We have several as you can see. These are all the same, very comfortable. Try one.' I bought a navy-coloured one with cushions, some incense sticks and a blue dragon vase; I had not forgotten my promise to replace my rejected bouquet.

Two of the young black men I had seen going into the flat next door followed us into Nimrod House as Yangku and I carried the box containing the futon towards the lift. 'Look eavy mate,' a boy in shorts said, moving ahead of us and pressing the call button for the lift. 'Whaz in it? Tha's Chinese writin' ain't it?'

'A futon.'

'Waz that? Futon?'

'Sofa bed,' his friend told him. 'A Chinese sofa bed.'

The boy in shorts held the door for us when the lift arrived. 'Fifteen or seventeen.'

'Seventeen. Carrying down is easier than carrying up.'

'You want some 'elp?' the other boy asked.

'Thank you. But we're fine.'

The boys left at the fifteenth and were presumably inside their flat and doing whatever they did there by the time we got the futon down the stairs.

The room in which I have my bed is the room used by most people in this block as their living room. There is also a bedroom, and though I had considered keeping Trudy in the room with me, I decided that the futon should go into the bedroom, that I should respect her privacy.

Yangku, who is very capable with such things, fitted a lock to the door, while I arranged the cushions and the quilt on the futon, brought in the television. When Yangku left, I sat for a time on the futon, considering.

In a few days' time we would take her. She would be here in this room, sitting on this futon, lying on it. There would be white flowers in the vase beside the bed. At Miss Blossom's I had noticed pictures of Chinese landscapes, waterfalls and gorges. I would buy a couple.

The thought of a Chinese room containing only one person amused me. I lay back on Trudy's futon. As a youth my father had been prominent in the Red Guard of the Cultural Revolution, and in the first years of my life such service was still recognised with privilege. Though our flat had only one bedroom it had a separate cooking area, and the rooms were larger than most. Times changed, as they always do. The Red Guard were denounced as counter-revolutionary and Mao Zedong announced his return to the country policy. My father was sentenced to a programme of revolutionary re-education based on physical labour. We were moved to a communal flat: four families, two rooms. The luxury of space. Trudy will be in this room, I will be next door – a room each.

25

The Bamboo Garden opens between eleven and two for the lunchtime trade and then closes until five. It was at three o'clock in the afternoon that I paid my visit. After ringing the bell several times the door was eventually opened by Feiyang's grandmother, my Aunt Lu.

Family ties and traditions are respected properly now by only the oldest in our communities here, and it was a pleasure to see the delight with which Aunt Lu greeted my arrival.

'I fear I may be disturbing the family's rest, Aunt Lu. Is everyone sleeping?'

'It is nothing. Nothing.' She took my arm, pulling me into the shop. 'It is a joy to see you. Everyone will be overjoyed.' The old lady locked the door behind me and beckoned me through the shop. 'It is your cousin Shuko who visits us,' she squawked up the stairs. 'Follow Shuko, follow. It is an honour that you are here.'

The staircase at the Bamboo Garden is narrow and steep and the old lady used hands and feet to mount each step, climbing like an animal or a small child. At the top of the stairs stood my cousin Tan, waiting to help her mother.

'Cousin. You are welcome. Come through. Please.' The old lady now had my hand and led me through into the family's living room. 'Please sit.' She collected the newspapers scattered across the table, folded them and laid them on a shelf under the large television where Sky Sports showed a soundless darts match. On the other side of the room, coloured fish swam languidly in their tank. 'Sit. Sit. We will prepare tea.'

Feiyang arrived barefooted in vest and shorts, bowing before shaking my hand, and taking the seat beside me. 'Uncle. It is good of you to visit us. To take the time.' It was only a few days since Feiyang and I had met at the dogfight but a visit in one's own home is very different. Here the ties of family are affirmed. Soon we were joined by Siyu, Feiyang's pretty young wife, bowing and smiling in a pink silk dressing gown. 'Uncle, it is an honour and a very pleasant surprise.' She took the seat opposite her husband, reaching out across the Formica tabletop to touch his hand. The men who work for Feiyang came through in vests and sweatpants and took their places at the table. My aunt and cousin arrived with a tray for tea and a bowl of steamed buns.

'I come to see you all and to enquire after the health of each one of you,' I said as tea was poured, 'but most particularly to see how your wife fares, Feiyang. The pregnant state suits her for she appears more beautiful each time I see her.'

Siyu smiled shyly, casting her eyes down; Feiyang stroked his wife's hand tenderly. 'The Western doctor tells us the child is due in three weeks, and the acupuncturist agrees, but the clairvoyant says it will come ten days before that.'

'And what do you think?'

'I feel the clairvoyant is right,' Siyu said. 'I think the child will be ready soon.'

With the teas all poured, it was up to me as the guest to drink first. All then raised their cups.

'I will take my tea into the bedroom, Uncle, then you can all smoke,' said Siyu.

'Before you go, I have a small gift that I hope may prove useful in the days before the child is born. Get something you need with it. It is not for the child, that will come later. This is to assist with preparations. It should have been offered sooner.' I took the green gift envelope from my jacket pocket and handed it to Siyu.

'It is very kind of you, Uncle.' She dug a fingernail painted with a gold flower into the side of the envelope and peeled back the top half to reveal a small wad of fifty-pound notes. 'Such a gift!' Tan said.

'Fortune smiles on you and your wife, Feiyang,' said one of his companions, 'to have such a generous benefactor.'

'Which must be lucky for your child,' said the other.

Siyu stroked her belly. 'Will you excuse me, Uncle? I would like to lie down for a short rest before we open the shop?'

'Of course. It has been good to see you. I will await your news with anticipation.'

'Thank you for your gift. As all have said it is very generous.'

Tan said it was time to start her work in the kitchen and the old lady followed.

'I will go now and let you get about your preparations for the evening.' But as I made to rise, Feiyang insisted I stay a little, smoke a few cigarettes – would I like to make up the four at mahjong?

While I stuck to my unfiltered Chinese cigarettes my three companions smoked imported Benson and Hedges and Aunt Lu brought in a tray of beers.

We used a Wind suit and agreed on twenty-pound hands. The first throws of the dice gave me the East Wind, a direction that is lucky for me in mahjong. Feiyang held the North.

I took the first hand with a chow, and repeated my success in the second round. The South Wind took the third hand with a pung.

When we had played the full sixteen hands it was time to leave and I asked Feiyang if he would walk a little way with me. It is possible to make a simple request like that in such a way as to endow it with more than ordinary significance. Feiyang understood, and once we left the Bamboo Garden there was for a time silence between us as we walked. I had asked him to come with me. He recognised I had something to say. He waited. And there was wariness. An atmosphere – which was as I wanted it. We both lit cigarettes. When I was ready I spoke in English: 'I have heard you have a new business partner.'

Each of us moved our head a fraction, glanced at each other, then Feiyang took his eyes to the ground.

'Who you do business with is up to you, Feiyang. But there are family ties between us. Crawford's outfit are not popular with the Ninth. I will be frank. There may be serious business disagreements between Crawford and the Ninth. These could become very difficult. Who knows what I may be called upon to do. Anyone who is part of that outfit...' I stopped. 'Do you understand me, Feiyang?'

The streetlight behind him held Feiyang's face in shadow, but I could see as much of it as I needed. A touch of anxiety. Some defiance. 'Uncle, I don't know what you have heard. But I am not part of Crawford's outfit. Never have been. No, I am certainly not in business with Crawford.'

'But you are in business with Kieran?'

As neat as a hand taken in mahjong. One simple tile from the wall – the eyes narrowed and there was the slightest of intakes of breath, little more than swallowing.

'So Walsh is starting to set up his own deals. That will upset Crawford. That could be dangerous for both of you.'

Feiyang opened his mouth, but did not have words ready.

'Whatever Kieran Walsh and you are arranging is up to you. I wish you success. But if you're planning to take anything away from Crawford, make sure it is of no interest to the Ninth. Understand?'

Now defiance got the better of Feiyang's anxiety. But he needed a smirk to say it. 'Business is business, Uncle. You know that. And as you said, we are family.'

The sound of an ambulance approaching stopped us. Louder and louder. Cars pulled over. A boy on a bicycle stopped and covered his ears. Then the flashing white light zoomed past. This was the moment when ideally I would have put an arm around Feiyang's shoulder, familiar and friendly, and offered some final advice. As he is taller than me a different tactic had to be employed. I threw my cigarette end into the gutter and spoke as we walked. 'How is your Chinese history, Feiyang? You went to history classes as a boy?'

'Of course.'

'Then do you know your history well?'

Feiyang laughed and flicked his cigarette butt high into the air. 'China's is a long history, Shuko, a long long history. No one knows it all. I know of the modern part. Some of that I know very well.'

Shuko – the respect was gone. *I know of the modern part* – was that a reference to my father?

'I think there are more valuable lessons to be learned from China's dynastic history. For what are dynasties, but gangs, family gangs fighting to retain wealth and power? Who founded the Han Dynasty, Feiyang?'

'So now you are a quizmaster, Uncle. Will I get a prize?' His confidence was rising. 'Gaozu was the founder of the Han Dynasty.'

'You are right, Feiyang. But Gaozu was his temple name. His family name was Liu Bang, important I think, as so few of the dynastic fathers were of peasant stock. What is it in a man, Feiyang, that enables him to rise from a plough-pulling peasant to the founder of a great dynasty, Emperor of China? Do you know of the Treaty of Honggou?'

'I've heard of it.'

'The Treaty of Honggou divided China from the East to the West, and was entered into with Bang's ancient enemy Xiang Yu. I am sure you know of him.'

'Yes.'

'Bang governed the West and Yu the East, but both men wanted the whole country and so there were many fierce battles.'

'Shuko, I don't know—'

'No you don't, so listen.' And now I spoke in Cantonese. 'Before one battle Bang learned that his enemy had captured his family: wife, mother, children, all. The following evening an envoy arrived from Yu's camp with a message for Bang: *You have until dawn to surrender. If you do not, as the sun rises I will wring the necks of your wife and mother like hens, cut the heads off your children and a meat stew will be made of them.*

I wonder if you know how he replied. I think it tells us much about the man. From peasant to emperor. The message Bang sent back was this. *Please, take pity on your hungry enemy and when you have prepared your stew send him a bowl to eat.*'

CARROW

26

Up on the roof. That was a song wasn't it? Up on the roof. That was where he had taken to having his cigarette breaks now. Better not to be out on the street alone; you have to move along a bit if you want a ciggy – *No Smoking Anywhere Near The Door* – Stretton's instructions. *Gives The Wrong Impression* – what sort of fucking impression did he think Chinese gangsters with shotguns give? One of the artillery team Stretton had brought in was up there too, and Carrow needed to know what was going on – he hadn't forgotten he was on Crawford's payroll, and he was sure as fuck that Crawford wouldn't have either.

The door to the roof needed a hefty push. It was steel-panelled up on the outside with a whole selection of bolts and mortises on the inside. 'Sergei. It's me, mate. Carra.' The Bulgarian was huddled in his thick combat jacket on the remnant of a defunct chimney that enabled him to peer down into the street at the front of the club. Binoculars on his lap, a flask of hot coffee at his feet and by his side a Kalashnikov that every time Carrow saw it made him feel as though he was going to have an asthma attack.

A voice in Carrow's head kept telling him that for most of

his adult life he had been a cop. He should either be reporting this, or getting as far away from it as possible. And quick. But that's as far as it went. Listening to the voice. Agreeing. *You're right.* But action? Nothing.

The team included two guys working the inside of the club who you wouldn't know from normal doormen except they kept to themselves. Stretton wasn't doing things by halves. This must be costing him a fortune. Carrow had picked up that this was an out-of-town gang with a growing reputation. Run, as he had suspected, by a London firm, but based in Stratford-upon-Avon; the cover was these guys were agricultural workers, out on the farms of Warwickshire pulling spuds from dawn till dusk. The caravan parks surrounding Stratford were full of teams of Eastern European agricultural workers. All working for a pittance. Perhaps these guys did do some spud-pulling now and again, to keep their cover, but they certainly had other skills. Very disciplined. The men inside never got chatting to the girls who gave them the eye; always distant, their mind on the job. And Stretton seemed to have called it right with this one. Everything had been as quiet as you like since they arrived. It looked as if the Chinese had got the message.

Sergei was undeniably a man with a head for heights. Carrow had seen him bend so far forward to observe door activity that he had been convinced he would lose his balance and topple into the street. Other times, belly-flat like a soldier, his head just peering over the edge, he gazed down like a gargoyle, observing all.

'How's it going, mate?' Carrow sat beside him. The cold immediately hit his arse; a shock, but it was so hot down in the club that the chill up here felt good. Though perhaps not for more than ten minutes. Sergei looked pretty cold.

'Good. Quiet.' Sergei only had a few words of English, but these were two Carrow liked to hear from him. He passed him a cigarette and the two smoked in silence, looking out at the lights of the Birmingham night, pinched and pale in the winter cold.

Sergei pointed to the column of lights to their right. 'Row tund.'

'Rotunda,' Carrow corrected him, and Sergei repeated the word accurately. The electronic throb of the music in the club pulsed the roof beneath their feet. 'Shit music,' Sergei said. 'Every night. Shit music.' Every night he said this.

The thought of trying a conversation on music always seemed too much like hard work, so, although Carrow wondered what the man would regard as good music, he said nothing. A car turned the corner below them. The two men rose. Sergei leaned over. The car slowed, but continued. 'Nothing,' Sergei said returning to his seat on the wall.

Carrow had been trying to suppress images of Ruthie all evening, one in particular – but now it broke through and he saw it again: her being dropped off at work, leaning across to kiss Kieran Walsh goodbye. Kieran Walsh. He told himself it didn't matter who it was – she'd got herself a new bloke, even if it was just to tide her over until the man Howie's release.

And would he really want that role anyway – tiding her over? He didn't let himself answer that question. Instead he rose, and made his way back down into the club.

So, when a couple of nights later she turned up at the club with a group of girls, he was cautious. Or at least he tried to be. But – there was just something. He watched her dancing. First with her friends, then with a couple of guys who joined them. But the next time he passed she was gone. Then he saw her chatting to one of the Bulgarians, her arm resting for a moment on his, saying something into his ear. Perhaps she would succeed where others had failed, but a moment later she was dancing with her friends again. When he saw her heading for the bar he caught up with her. 'How's the new boyfriend?'

She waited. Smiled. Teasing. He knew it. She knew he knew it. 'Gorgeous.'

'So, it's love?'

Then, a curious way she had. Her face changed. Something fell away – the humour, the bravado. Leaving something lovely, something vulnerable remaining in the empty face. 'Love? I wouldn't say that. It's just – life. Do you want to buy me a drink?'

'Only if it's an investment.'

The spirit was back in her face.

'I'll have a vodka and lime. A double.'

Each time he saw her she was dancing. Each time he saw her she spotted him immediately. Like she was watching for him.

There was a small smile for him as he passed her, still dancing with her friends, on his way up to the roof for a smoke. He winked. On the roof he just nodded to Sergei before moving across to the other side to light up. He ought to kick this habit. Like he had promised his mother.

He stood leaning on the cold iron rail of the fire escape looking down into the black no-man's-land behind the club. He wanted to think. He needed the cold air and the smoke burning in his chest to do so. Give up? Not for a while anyway. He checked the slide in his memory, watched her kissing Walsh as she got out of the car. Just like a girl does: kisses her boyfriend as he drops her off at work. She didn't know Carrow was there, watching. She didn't know he knew who

Walsh was. It was a genuine act. So, what was he to make of tonight? Maybe she had got tired of him. *It's just life.*

It was the guy inside, Howie, she was really interested in, that had got to be the truth of it. Others, including him, were just to get her through. He remembered that lovely look on her face. Don't be fooled, he wanted to say to himself, women can do that.

Then she was gone! There's a perfume ad that uses that line. Comes on every Christmas. Beautiful woman. Expensive perfume. She runs up a golden staircase and disappears – *then she was gone*, a voice says. The man following left bewildered.

The most embarrassing time Carrow ever had on the force was coming down from a flat in Vaughan Williams on the Mendy to find that his squad car had gone. *Nicked – nicked before he could get it back to the nick.* He was to hear variations of that joke a hundred times. But of course it wasn't a joke, and he'd stood looking, staring, at the empty space where his vehicle had been just twenty minutes before. His mind refusing to accept that it had been stolen. He must have made a mistake. So he walked round the building cautiously, as if the car were engaged in a game of hide-and-seek with him, and if he were careful, he would be able to creep up on it without being noticed. *Got ya!* Helplessly he scanned the area, looking back to where he had looked a few seconds before. Probably, he even looked up.

It felt like that now. Wandering round the club. Round and round. He couldn't see the girls she had been with. Perhaps they had all gone. Why would she leave without telling him? Had she just been teasing him? Up one staircase, down another; nothing golden about these. He checked the street. He asked the Bulgarian he had seen her talking to. He even went up to Stretton's floor. Then up another level to pop his head round the door to the roof.

When all was done and there were just a few staff left around the bar, having a drink as they waited for taxis, he went back up to the roof. Sergei was gone now. He had the space to himself. Thin shavings of snow were trying to fall. He lit up. Inhaled deeply, but that didn't shift whatever it was that was stuck in his chest. So what was the problem? He had been turned down by women before. Something close to a sob took his chest. He held on to the rail of the fire escape. What was happening? This wasn't him.

27

Daytime was tedious. There was only the gym. It seemed like just getting through till the evening. And then it was the job; the Norway. This was Birmingham, his city, he was back. He had friends here, a past. So why was he behaving as if he were an immigrant in a new country? With nothing?

Sometimes he thought about his old mate, Jack Stevens. He was the only real white friend he had ever had. They had done their training together and shared a flat for a time. Jack used to go to Buddhist meditation on Thursdays. Had the piss taken out of him rotten by the rest of the guys. All except Dowd, their gaffer. He respected Jack, made him his number two.

Live in the present, Jack used to say. *Concentrate on that.* Well that's what he was doing wasn't it? Living in the present. Not thinking about the past. Not thinking about the future. Just the now. Today. The gym. The club. But it wasn't right; he knew it. Because it was starting to feel like he didn't have a past, didn't have a future. And he couldn't live like this for very long. It was like the days in Jamaica after his mother's death. Beaches and bars. Sunshine and music. Freedom. But it wasn't. It didn't work. He needed something else. The answer was probably as simple as getting a job. A real one.

This was no life. Sharing a flat on the Mendy with Toga. And not even Toga's flat, it was *a Mendy flat*, he was *keeping it warm*, the phrase round here for occupying someone's place and covering the expenses, while they're inside. When he had asked how long they would be able to stay there, Toga had just smiled and told him it would be a while yet before they had to think about eviction.

These couple of weeks here had been okay. He had liked sharing with someone again. Toga rose late, spent most of his time at the gym or a snooker club he went to, occasionally disappeared somewhere. Carrow didn't ask questions; both men respected the privacy of the other. It was when they got back from the Norway and unwound with a smoke and a drink that they spent time together. And even then, they were careful. The talk was mostly about the night's shift, any door problems, the women that had been in that night, how things were going with the Chinese.

Bit by bit information was leaking out. It *was* the Dragons. They pretty much had the casino scene in the whole of the West Midlands sewn up. Other forms of gambling too. There was a big trade in importing counterfeits. Cigarettes. Perfume. And some drugs. Coke. Heroin. A little bit of pure opium, it was thought when he was on the force, but that was a niche market, very high-class and usually went down south. Now they were moving into the club scene. They had already acquired a couple of places in Wolverhampton without too much trouble and one in Nottingham with quite a lot – a man dead.

Toga was still in bed when Carrow left the flat to head for the gym. He detoured. Made for the Gables instead. He just wanted to see if she was on the same shift this week, if Kieran dropped her off again. If he did, that would explain the other night. He parked his car by the church and walked down the hill. Stopped when he spotted Walsh in an Audi parked up on the other side of the road. Carrow dodged into the shrubbery of the nearest driveway. Walsh was on his own, his fingers tapping the steering wheel.

Carrow watched. Ruthie must be on the morning shift. Walsh had come to pick her up. I might as well piss off, Carrow thought, go to the gym, go back to the Mendy, go and get pissed. She's still with Kieran. The other night – she was just taking the piss.

But he didn't move. There was comfort standing here among the trees and shrubbery, standing in the cold, not even smoking. In the moment. Nothing else. Like working again.

A car pulled up behind Kieran's, a fuck-off maroon BMW, so close Carrow though it was heading for a bump. A whisker away – but a whisker's enough. A woman driving. Grey hair pulled back. Kieran got out of his car. The woman opened her door and Carrow could see Ruthie in the passenger seat. Kieran squatted down beside the open door talking to the two women, Ruthie leaning forward. Then Kieran rose. Ruthie got out of her side of the car and walked round. The woman got out too. Older. Elegant. Perhaps she was Ruthie's mom. She was certainly well off. Not only the BMW but the fur coat she was wearing. Long. Carrow didn't know enough about fur to be able to tell what creatures had copped it to produce her coat, but it looked like film star quality to him.

Kieran watched the three of them chatting. Eventually mommy got back into her car, reversed away from the Audi, did a U-turn and drove down the road and into the entrance of the Gables. Perhaps she wasn't mommy after all. Perhaps she was the owner of the place.

Kieran pulled his cigarettes from his jacket. Gave one to Ruthie, popped one in his own mouth and lit them both. They stood smoking and talking beside the car, leaning against it, leaning against each other. And when the cigarettes were finished, Kieran kissed Ruthie before she pulled away and walked towards the Gables. Kieran watched her. At the drive she turned and waved. Kieran waved back before he got into his car and drove away.

Carrow emerged from the bushes. Took a slow walk down to the Gables. The BMW was in the visitors' parking area. No sign of either its driver or Ruthie.

There weren't many in the gym. A group of blokes sparring in the boxing section, a couple on weights, both very serious about their workouts and recording their performance in their phones. Everyone knew he was an ex-copper. He ran into faces there he had come across in the past. A nod or two, sometimes an ironic grin, but no one said much. He should join a proper gym, where they had women doing aerobics and a café and a swimming pool. This was just a muscle factory. He stopped thinking and got on with it. Don't let the brain take the strain.

He took a drive out to Handsworth to visit Miss Rosa Quirk, his only relative in the city, a cousin of his mother. It was something to do with the afternoon. He and his mother had lived with Miss Rosa until he was eleven when they were given a place of their own. When his mother returned to Jamaica she tried to persuade Miss Rosa to go with her, but she had a son who had been killed at ten, buried here in Witton Cemetery, so there was no way she was going to leave. Eventually she would be placed in the same grave, and when she used to talk about it, it seemed to Carrow that she was looking forward to that day. *Placed*, that's how she used to say it.

Both Rosa and his mother had been proud when he joined the force and did well. Occasionally he stopped by Rosa's place in uniform. Afterwards she immediately rang his mother in Jamaica to tell her how fine he had looked, how well he was doing – *Be proud, sister. Your son a fine man. The Lord has blessed you well.* Rosa had always been big on religion. A stalwart of her church.

The area hadn't changed, and the old instincts were still there. Carrow watching what was happening. Doorways. Street corners. Between parked cars. See if he could spot deals. And what would he do if he did see something? Nothing – he was just a tourist now. But the instinct? The looking? Just habit. He knew where he was then; he had reasons. And it was with this nostalgia that he took a spin down to Brewery Street where the Doberman Crew had their base.

A line of flash cars parked outside 114, Linton's place. There was a meathead kid sitting on the wall, in shorts despite the cold day, swinging his legs, drawing in on a spliff. Only a kid but strong, well built. Attitude you could feel from across the street. A white baseball cap and serious-money trainers. No hoody up – too proud to hide. Carrow smiled. Obviously there to keep an eye on things – a trainee. But a promising one if he was on the gate. If Carrow were still on the force, this kid would be one to watch.

'It is not the place it was any more. Gangs. Gangs and guns and drugs. There has been killin' in this street. I tell you, Craig, people's hearts are hard now. Ruthless hard.' Miss Rosa Quirk was stirring the dutchie, heating up her Saturday soup. Carrow hadn't wanted any food, he wasn't hungry, never was after a workout, but Miss Rosa had insisted. 'Boy, you don't step in my house and not get fed. House rule.' And now it was nice, sitting comfortably in Miss Rosa Quirk's kitchen, the table laid, the smell of the food, being looked after.

Miss Rosa looked across to him. She had eyes like a bird of prey, hooded; softened by her slack mouth. 'Your mommy, she loved my Saturday soup. I do the soup and the bread puddin'. She do the pork jerk, rice and peas. You remember?'

'Yes, I remember.'

'Happy days.'

'Yes.' And Carrow wished now that he had arrived with a gift, some flowers, a box of chocolates, some gesture. Why was he so thoughtless?

'Well, now she rests in Santa Cruz. Back in the parish of Saint Elizabeth. Where she started. Where she'll always remain. And I am glad she is there. In her own place, among her own kind.'

Carrow recalled filling in his mother's grave with the help of friends, distant relatives, the sons of her neighbours, as is the tradition. He dropped the first shovelful of earth in, and he laid the last. Thrust in the spade to show the job was done; the other men followed suit. Then they walked away to join the women of the family. He wished now he had taken a photograph of the grave, to bring to Miss Rosa. Outside the kitchen window English rain was falling.

Miss Rosa ladled soup into a bowl and put it on the table. She cut bread for him. He could smell patties warming in the oven. Being fed like a little boy. Miss Rosa sat opposite him.

'You're not having anything?' he asked.

'Hiatus.' She swept her hand across her stomach. 'I keep to very regular times.'

She watched him eat. He didn't need to tell her it was good, his appetite was back. Then without warning she said: 'So they killed the child.'

Carrow opened his mouth in surprise. Soup spilled over his lip on to his chin. He wiped it away with his hand. Miss Rosa pushed a napkin he hadn't seen towards him. He wiped his fist, dabbed his lips, his chin.

'Eat your soup, boy. One of the last telephone calls I had with your mommy. She tell me how badly affected you were.' His appetite was gone but he kept his eyes down and spooned soup into his mouth. He had always thought of Miss Rosa as wise. Was that what he had come for, her wisdom? Saturday Soup with Miss Rosa on a Tuesday afternoon. He looked up into her face: wrinkles; lines; her skin was taking on the dustiness that comes with age. What had he come here for?

'Guilt, she said. Said you felt guilty. That it was your fault.'

'Not my fault. I was on duty, that's all. I took the boy and his nanny to the kindergarten. It happened on my watch.' He might have expected images of that day in Amsterdam to flash through his mind again. They were always there, waiting for a gap. But instead what he saw was himself lying in the hot sun of San San Beach, the day after his mother died. Lying there. Trying not to think. Not thinking. Trying.

He cast his eyes down to the bowl. Put the spoon in. Waited. 'You have had it hard, Craig. Very hard. And just a year ago everything was going so well.'

She shouldn't have said that. He closed his eyes hard shut. He felt the burn in them like pepper. He kept his head down, spooned soup into his mouth. Miss Rosa rose, opened the oven door; the smell of patties escaped. Taking them from the oven, she tipped them on to a plate and carried them across to the table. There were two of them. 'Be careful, boy. They hot inside.'

She took his soup bowl to the sink and washed it with some other dishes. He cut into the patties, let the steam escape from the green and red and yellow chopped vegetables and started to eat.

A year ago everything was going so well. He first met Martin Okker through his old mate Simmy Turner, an ex-copper who had made a career for himself in personal security. The Dutchman was still playing for Villa at the time. That was five years ago and for a while Carrow was just part of a group of guys who did the nightclubs together. Being with Okker got them noticed. Got them in anywhere. Attracted the girls. Eventually Okker was sold to United and while he was there he married Marjie Veay, the Dutch actress. Turner looked after security for them. By the time Okker retuned to Holland to see his career out with Ajax she had been nominated for her Oscar and they were about as high profile as it comes. All over the celebrity magazines. As Turner said, *Go to the States, the only Dutch woman anyone's heard of is Marjie Veay, and everyone's heard of her. They can't name the Queen of Holland, that's if they know there is one, but everyone's heard of Marjie.*

When Turner put together a small personal security team for the couple he offered Carrow a job. Simple as that. A hell of a lot more than he earned on the force and a lifestyle that excited. He remembered when he told Dowd, and Jack, and Trevor the desk sergeant; he felt like he had won the lottery.

Marjie's kid, six years old, was called Magnus. A picturebook kid. Blond hair, blue eyes. He wore specs when he went to school that made him look clever. Carrow used to see him in the garden sometimes, dressed in an Ajax strip, chasing a football around.

Mostly it was Okker who Carrow was assigned to: he drove him to training, to business meetings – he was the face of a national chain of gyms, had interests in the bulb industry and a stud farm; he was determined to be a successful businessman when his footballing days came to an end.

Okker worked hard but he knew how to enjoy himself too, and Carrow was one of a trio of men he took with him on his nights out in Amsterdam. Sometimes Carrow might be called upon to accompany Marjie, but she had a cousin on the team who was always her first choice of escort. Sometimes, but not often, he would take Magnus and his nanny somewhere: to kindergarten, to a kids' party or, at the weekends when the nanny was off, to his grandparents in Leiden.

Tuesday 17th May. 08.45. At the start of the short drive to the kindergarten they were ambushed as they turned out of Princengracht. A white van in front of the car he was driving, a four-wheel behind. All three were hauled out of the car at gunpoint. Carrow on the ground, face hard against a paving slab. A boot in the balls, a foot in his back, a gun in his ear. He heard Margnus yelling, the nanny screaming. He knew the kid was being bundled into the van. Then a whack to the side of his head and the lights went out.

Carrow looked down. An empty plate. Where did the patties go?

'Walnut cake with your coffee? A drop of rum in it?'

'Yes to the cake. No to the rum, I'm driving.'

The gang didn't waste any time. By mid afternoon the ransom demand for Magnus had been received, sent to Marjie's agent. Okker hadn't blamed Carrow. Had been pretty good about it. Once the police had finished their interviews Okker told Carrow to take some time off, but stressed that he hadn't lost his job. He could come back when he was ready. Carrow listened. Agreed. But he knew that whatever the outcome he couldn't face the boy's mother again.

At first it was all over the papers. Day after day after day. After that first day there was nothing from the kidnappers – or at least that was the official line. But no contact was news. Nothing happening, nothing at all. It was news. Had to be reported, analysed. Photographed. How do you photograph nothing at all? How do you photograph *no new developments*? You do it by getting pictures of everyone who has anything at all to do with the case or the family. If a guy had collected their garbage, there was a story in it. Talk to the nanny. Get her life story – get pictures. She's a pretty girl – get plenty of pictures; stick her in a swimsuit. Interview her boyfriend, then interview her ex-boyfriends. Talk to the bodyguard. Definitely talk to the bodyguard, and get pictures, plenty of pictures. He was becoming the most famous bodyguard since Trevor Rees-Jones.

He holed up in Utrecht for a time – like living in a history book. Cute old buildings. Cute old streets. Beautiful young women. Blondes everywhere. He bought an English paper every day and kept himself to himself. Rang Okker occasionally, rang Simmy Turner regularly. Nothing happening. That's all they said. Even the papers gave up. Nothing happening. There was a story that the nanny had gone back to America. The police had cleared it. A week or two later he heard that his mother had cancer. Serious. No hope. The police returned his passport. He could leave; he wasn't a suspect, but they would appreciate being kept informed of his addresses. Things were happening behind the scenes. The papers said so. Ransom demanded. Paid. Not paid. Different papers said different things.

Walnut cake. A thick slice served on a floral plate, the old-fashioned kind. A little cake fork at the side. Tastefully presented; tasteless in his mouth. A wad of thick material.

Then the sweetness kicked in. The taste came. Then it was cake. 'Another slice?'

'Yes, please.' He took a pull at the coffee. Real coffee. Blue Mountain.

'You know the ol' sayin' boy, *So goes life*.' She had said that when he was a kid, his mother had said it too. In Jamaica they had said it all the time, they had said it at his mother's funeral. But you couldn't say this to Marjie Veay. While he had been in Jamaica they had found the kid, dumped in an old bulb warehouse not far from Delft.

28

Ever since he had visited Miss Rosa Quirk, he had felt like the loneliest bloke in the world. Walking round the Norway each night, he was a zombie – oh, he did the job, he chatted to the punters, he looked at the girls, he'd even fantasise a bit, but never do anything about it.

He bought a couple of sandwiches. Toga was out. He had to stop himself imagining he had Ruthie to share his sandwiches with, a cup of tea. You're turning soft, he told himself, *sharing sandwiches, a cup of tea*. Once he had eaten he put on a tracksuit and threw his door suit into the boot of the car. He'd kill the afternoon at the gym, go on to work from there.

So goes life, boy. Since his visit last week he had heard Miss Rosa repeat the old saying in his head at least a dozen time a day. He wondered if all this wasn't still part of the reaction to his mother's death, all quite normal. Perhaps he should have come back from Jamaica immediately, flown back the day after the funeral. He had thought that by staying there, in her place, everything would work its way out and he could return ready to carry on – a chapter closed. Well, it hadn't worked out like that.

There's nothing like a good workout to get rid of all the crap. As Carrow went through his programme he thought of nothing but the activity in which he was engaged. Was able to lose himself completely in the vigorous exercise – and he loved it.

This is the key, he told himself in the shower. Keep yourself occupied. Come here more. And find something useful to do with your time. He knew he should knock the whole nightclub game on the head. Nightclubs were for a night out, for getting pissed and pulling a woman. He needed to get a proper job. Put some structure in his life.

It was while he was still in Jamaica that he decided he wouldn't return to the force. He told himself he wanted something different when he got back here. But he knew it had something to do with failure. He had left for Holland with such high hopes. He wasn't going to go back with his tail between his legs.

In the changing room two blokes pulling on kit were talking about football.

'You're all dressed up, mate,' one of them said when Carrow had put on his suit and was straightening his tie. 'Going somewhere good?'

'Work.'

'At this time?'

'Door work. Club in town.'

'Which one?' his mate asked, tying his trainers. 'You don't get comps to dish out, do you?'

'Norway Room.'

'What, where the shooting was? Don't think I fancy a night out there. Can't see that attracting the talent.'

How the hell did they know about that? Two blokes in a gym out on the Mendy shouldn't know about that. Best to play dumb. 'You've got the wrong place, mate. Never any trouble there.'

'Norway Room? In town?'

'Yeah'

'That's the place. A shooting. This afternoon. It was on the news as we was coming out.'

Outside the gym he checked his phone. Two messages, both from Toga. Message one: *they've got stretton. shot. ring me.* Carrow read it again: *they've got stretton. shot. ring me.* Fuck. He pulled message two up: *I'm at essex st. meet asap.*

ASHLEY

29

Dusk was turning streets into gloomy passageways. Some streetlights were on, some weren't. Some cars had headlights on, some didn't. Ashley walked. New Street. Corporation Street. Down Bull Street into High Street. Past HMV, down to St Martin's where the market traders were packing away. Bargains to be had. Men held plastic bowls of fruit and vegetables aloft. *Come on girls, finish me off now. Nice bowl of bananas, fifty pence. Now tell me, you can't do better than that.* Ashley usually liked it here. He liked to listen to the blokes with their patter, but not now, so he turned and climbed back up the steps to the shiny bronze bull that Sophie always touched for luck. Ashley needed some fucking luck.

Now he didn't know what to do, so he walked back again through the markets and into Chinatown. The smell of Chinese food. Ashley felt sick. He was heading towards Essex Terrace. Why was he going back there? What was the point? To see. To see what? He didn't know what. He could feel tears pricking his eyes, smearing the streetlights.

He was back in the underpass. It was stupid. As if the kids would still be here. As if here where it happened he could reverse time, return to a point where everything was all right, and proceed from there, only differently. There was cursing in his head. It moved to his lips. He was cursing his dad, the bastard. It was all his fault. The bastard. He thrust his fist into the broken tiles of the underpass wall. Did it again, quickly, before the pain started. And again. Thrust his fist into his mouth. Bit down. Hard. Hard. Now he could think.

He had to have a plan. He bit again. Tasted the blood. He needed to get back to Cecil Road before Kieran. Get the cash he had there and get out. He knew he had to get away. This was serious. He had screwed up. Big time. It wasn't his fault; but they wouldn't see it like that. Kieran. Crawford. Shit – the gun was out there. In the hands of some Asian kids. Shit. They wouldn't forgive him for this. He'd be meat.

He had no money on him, no phone. He would have to jump a bus. He had done it before. Get on at the terminus. As the queue moves into the bus and a crowd paying or showing their passes develops, you just edge round them and step inside, then straight up the stairs; he had got away with it lots of times, everyone did it. Once he got home he could sort out what to do. He was calmer now; it was going to be all right.

He was the only one at the bus stop. Must have just missed one. Then a couple arrived. 'Mate,' Ashley called to the bloke. They both looked over. 'I've lost me bus fare. Can you lend us a quid?'

'Sorry mate.' He turned back to his girlfriend. She laughed and pulled away from him. 'Tom! Don't be so tight. It's only a quid.' The bloke had no choice. He fished a coin from the pocket of his jeans and flicked it to Ashley. The girl spotted his fist as he raised it to catch the coin. 'What you been doing? Your hand's bleeding.'

'A fight.'

'You shouldn't do that. Who with?'

'My dad,' Ashley told her. 'I punched his teeth out.' They both looked confused. Ashley remembered. The uniform. It wasn't him. It made no sense. Tom started to laugh. 'It's a good job I give him the quid,' he said to the girl, 'or he might have punched mine out.' And he pulled her closer to him. Ashley watched them kissing.

Back at Cecil Road. No cars at the front. Ashley went round the back. No lights on. Back to the front. He might not have much time. Kieran could turn up at any minute, or worse, Crawford – any of them. So, the plan. He would go straight through to the kitchen, open the back door; an escape route. He'd get his money, some clothes, his phone. No, just the money and phone. It didn't matter about anything else. And then? Afterwards? He still didn't know. Shit. Still, he'd just have to worry about that then. Get his stuff first.

He let himself in. Closed the door. Locked the mortise. Keep it dark. He felt his way down the hallway and through the living room into the kitchen. The back door was unlocked. And unbolted. Shouldn't be. There was some noise – from the living room. Was there? He listened carefully. Someone was in the darkness. Waiting for him. Definitely. He pulled open the door and fled into the garden. He was nearly at the gate before he heard the running feet behind him. Gaining on him. Ashley swerved, like greyhounds do, doubled back behind the shed. As his pursuer reached the other side of it, he would make a run for the house, back through it and out the front door. Once in the street he would have more of a chance. They wouldn't shoot him in the street, would they?

His pursuer wasn't Kieran, or Pricey, or any of them. But Ashley knew who it was. Geezbo. 'What the fuck are you doing?' Ashley moved from behind the shed bringing Geezbo to a halt. 'What you doing in my house? You broke in.'

Geezbo had him in a headlock before he saw it coming. It took Ashley's breath away. His head was down by Geezbo's balls. If he could have reached them Ashley would have bitten them off.

'Calm down, man. Calm down willya.' Geezbo brought his knee up into Ashley's chest, but not hard, just a bang in the chest, it didn't even wind him. Geezbo kept him held down for a while, squeezing his neck so he would know who was boss. Then he pulled him upright and hauled him back into the house. Pushed him down on the settee. Stood in front of him. 'Now man, I wan' you to level wit' me. Wha' goin' on? What wiv tis school bizziness? The uniform? Tell me, man.'

The relief that it was Geezbo he had to deal with eased Ashley; he could handle this. 'I told you, man. I'm going to a new school. I've got to. My uncle says so.'

'Oh yeah. *Gonna register him. At is new skool. Private. Goin get him educated if it the last ting I do.* Bollocks.'

'Please yourself. But it's not bollocks.'

'So you bin? You bin there? To that school?'

'Yeah. Course I have. And what are you doing breaking into my house? You've got —'

'Whazi called?'

'What?'

'The school, white dummy. Wha' your new posh school called?'

'Highfield,' Ashley said. 'It's called Highfield School. It's on Highfield Road. All right?'

'What the edmasta named? Whaz is name?'

'Price. Mr Price.'

There was a still moment before Geezbo jumped. As if he was taking off, flying nearly. His hands rose, his knees came up. He landed astride Ashley, his arse crashing on to Ashley's thighs, his hands pushing back against Ashley's shoulders, pinning him. Then he smashed his forehead into Ashley's face. 'O'Conna.' Geezbo yelled. 'O'Conna dummy. Iz wha' tha' Irish git say. Mista O'Conna.'

Geezbo rose. Blood was dripping on to Ashley's school trousers. His shirt too. Everything was ruined. Ashley pulled his tie loose, balled it and held it to his nose. His sobs sounded like suppressed sneezes.

Geezbo reached for the chair beside the table. Swung it one-handed to land in front of Ashley. Sat astride it, clasped hands resting on the back. Like an interrogator. Ashley waited. Geezbo said nothing. Then he pulled his kit from his pocket, opened it up and laid it out on his thick knee, broad as a tabletop. His hands moved but his eyes never left Ashley. He could build a spliff with his eyes shut, Ashley thought, unconscious probably.

Ashley dabbed at his nose with the tie. Inspected it. 'Okay,' he whined, 'It's O'Connor. I don't know. Or care. I'm not going again. Don't care what he says.'

'Who?'

'My uncle. Or O'Connor. Any of them. Don't care. Don't give a shit. I'm running away. I only came back to get some stuff. My phone.'

It was working. Geez was listening. Stupid fucker; Ashley had him. He pressed home. 'Don't know where to go though. Thought about Sophie's. If she'll hide me again.' Geezbo was listening. Thinking about it. Ashley had done it. He checked the tie again. Blew his nose with it. Dropped it beside him on the settee.

Ashley watched Geezbo insert the roach, a perfect fit. He was thinking about what he had heard. Making up his mind. He flicked his lighter and took the flame to the spliff. Inhaled. Deep. Deep. His eyes rolled to white. Another hard pull. Long. Ashley knew the way that burn must be feeling and wished it were in his own chest. Now Geezbo was giving Ashley the hard eye. Hard eye. Dead eye. Looking across through the smoke. It was supposed to make him scared. Did it fuck! Ashley thought of the gun. In his hand. That's what he saw in the smoke. He could feel it. If he had it now he would blow Geez's head apart, like Humpty Dumpty. He knew he would.

He had to get out of these clothes. Rolling back into the settee Ashley lifted his legs and pushed them hard into the chair sending Geezbo tumbling backwards, the chair on top of him. For a moment there was the instinct to run – a quick getaway, like he always had in situations like this – but it didn't last. He stood and looked down into the surprised eyes of Geezbo still clutching his spliff, holding it aloft. Unhurriedly Ashley went upstairs.

But as he climbed the stairs the strength he had felt just a minute ago as he toppled Geezbo started to ebb away, fear and confusion taking its place. He caught sight of the boy in the mirror. Gun-boy – well, that was a laugh. He pushed his hair back. He examined his nose. The cut was on his forehead, just above the bridge. Dribbles of blood on his nose and cheeks. He spat on his fingers and rubbed them away. He could hear Geezbo on the stairs. Ashley thought of the window, but he wanted to be free of these clothes before he went anywhere. He touched his nose carefully: sore, kind of numb but not as bad as before when Benjy had had a go at him. Perhaps it had been damaged so much recently he was losing the feeling in it. He inhaled through his nose, held the breath, then let it go. The breath moved freely, no blockage. Geezbo was standing behind him.

'D'you mind?' Ashley addressed Geezbo's reflection. 'I'm changing my clothes. I'm not gay. I'm not doing it with you in here.'

Geezbo accepted this. 'I'll be behind the door.'

Ashley put on jeans, a T-shirt, a woolly jumper and his hoodie. His trainers. He took his money from beneath the mattress, some more from under the cupboard. More from the bottom of the lamp.

'What you doin' in there?'

Ashley pocketed his cash. 'You can come in now.'

Geezbo watched Ashley take some T-shirts and a couple of pairs of tracky bottoms from a chair, some pants and socks from a drawer in a cupboard beside the bed. He rolled the clothes.

'Wha ya doin?'

'Going on my holidays. I told ya. I'm clearing out of here. Before he gets back and finds me.'

'Who? Ya uncle?'

'Yeah. I need a bag for these.'

'Tere some downstairs.'

'Where?'

'In the front room. With all that gear in tere. Cigarettes. Booze. All sorts of stuff.'

'You bin in there? No way. There's no way you should 'ave bin in there. You're gonna get me into all kinds of shit, man.'

Ashley tried to push past Geezbo, but the older boy held him. 'Tell me man. Tell me. Waz goin' on? All that stuff down there. Like a fuckin' warehouse innit.'

'I don't know. It's my uncle's. I've never been in there. I can't go in. That's why he keeps it locked, dummy.'

'Waz locked. Not locked no more, dummy. One shove now, and door will fall right down.' Geez laughed. 'Stay 'ere. I'll get a bag for you.' Ashley's phone rang startling both boys. Ashley looked round for it. Geezbo unzipped a pocket in his shorts and took it out.'

'Don't. Don't answer it. No.' Ashley pushed forward with such panic that Geezbo lifting the phone away from him dropped it. Both boys scrambled, but Geezbo was there first.

'No. Let it go to answer. Please Geez. Or I'm dead. Please.'

Ashley was crying. Geezbo pressed connect and the ringing stopped. He lifted the phone to his ear. Ashley stopped crying and watched. Geezbo said nothing. He was listening. Ashley could hear Kieran's voice, tiny and tinny, heard him say his name, repeat it, but couldn't make out what else he was saying. He watched Geezbo, grinning as he listened to Kieran. The call finished. The two boys looked at each other.

'You nicked my fuckin' phone,' Ashley said.

'That waz you uncle. Kieran, ain't it? Didn't sound so Irish now innit though. Sounds upset. Very upset. Sez he's on iz way. Wants to know what you done wizis strap.'

30

Ashley was crouched in the darkness, listening hard. Kieran was still down there; he was certain of it, although there had been no sound for ages, or at least no sound that was definitely him. He wondered what Geez was doing. He had given Ashley a leg-up into the loft, and then left through the back door. He would watch the house, come back when Kieran left. But that was hours ago; must have been.

There was so much fucking dust up here, it was like fur. And he didn't dare to smoke. It could send the whole fucking house up.

Ashley tried to see things from Kieran's point of view. Even if everything else had gone off okay, a missing gun, a murder weapon – that was bad news, however Ashley looked at it. He realised now that he should have told Kieran straight away. Immediately. But how could he? The Asian kids took the phone. But he should have used his own phone as soon as he was back here. Then he would have told Kieran as soon as he could. They would understand that. Kieran. Crawford. When things go wrong it's how you act that's important. But fucking Geezbo had been here, hadn't he? And now he knew everything. They would see him as a grass and that would be it. But he had no choice, not once Geez knew about the gun.

That had really got Geez. Shit, man, he had said. Like a whistle, a long low whistle of shock. Geez had never thought of Ashley in this way before. A player. Ashley could almost hear Geezbo's brain trying to work it all out. 'Tell me man. What sorta strap? Iz make?'

'A pistol. A small one. An MK9. A Khar.'

Geezbo had eyeballed Ashley, trying to be hard. But things had changed. Too quickly really. 'You twistin' me man? Twistin'? Turnin'? Iz that what you doin'? A storytella innit. A fucking storytella.' But the challenge wasn't real. Ashley could tell that Geezbo knew he was telling the truth. It fitted. What he had been trying to work out all afternoon.

Now there was music. From next door. Not loud but enough to prevent him hearing any movement below him. Ashley sneezed. Suddenly and violently. He grabbed the end of his nose. Swallowed. Tasted blood. From Geezbo's nut.

In the darkness he recalled the magic boots. The story his dad told him when he was still a baby, two or three. A little bloke goes into a pub, where there are all these big hard blokes boozing, and they take the piss out of the little fellow because he's small and they say he's got to stand them a round. He does, but instead of being his mate, they want more. He buys another round, and they still want more. So when they're shouting at him to get the third round in, calling him a tight little fucker, the little bloke moves away from the bar, a good bit away. He's sort of mumbling to himself. They think he's scared and going to do a runner. They call him a nutter. But he takes a gobful of beer, swills it round in his mouth and then lets it dribble on to his boots, really slowly. His dad used to do the action with spit, let it dribble. All the big blokes are looking at him like he's mad, and they're all laughing. But as the beer hits the boots they start to grow, really quick, like fast-forward, and soon they're enormous, with bloody great toecaps. And as soon as they stop growing the little bloke moves round the bar kicking fuck out of all the big blokes who had tormented him. He recalled his dad doing the sounds of breaking bones and blokes shrieking in pain. Sometimes he'd do the actions as well, holding his ribs or grabbing his belly, going *aarh* and shouting, *Mercy. Mercy.* Ashley used to love that story, and he'd try to get his dad to tell it over and over.

Usually he could stop himself thinking about his dad, but it was more difficult now. Stories. He loved it when his dad told him stories, or they watched a film together. Cartoons. Disney.

Ashley wished he had something to swill round his mouth now. Just a cup of water to get rid of the taste of blood and dust. Remembering the story of the magic boots made him think of his mom. When they had all been together. He couldn't remember her telling him stories, it was always his dad. Or his nan. But he remembered them all watching the cartoons together. He didn't want to remember these things, but he couldn't help it.

His mind latched on again to the day she went. He was six. All day they had known it was going to happen. He'd never seen his dad cry before. And his nan came round and spent ages with his mom in the bedroom. Then she came down and said she was taking Ashley back to her flat for the night. She cooked him proper chips in a pan for his tea, with egg and sausage, and brown sauce. The next morning his dad came round and told them that she had gone. His nan acted like she didn't already know, but Ashley had heard her on the phone to his dad last night. He could tell by the sound of her voice that his mom had gone.

Ashley heard a noise at the front of the house. He crawled through the darkness, feeling for a beam with his hand then moving his knee on to it. Dust rising. As he reached for the next beam his head touched something. He raised his hand and felt tiles, traced the pitch of the roof.

Sitting in the darkness, crouched into the roof, he remembered Ethan Cambridge from up on the Mendy. Ashley didn't know him, not properly, but he knew all about him. Everyone did now. He used to deal on the estate. He started off a delivery boy like Geezbo, but ended up dealing. On his bike till he got a car. He did other areas too. He started wearing suits. A real player. But. He must have cheated one of the gangs; he pissed somebody off, because his house was torched. Mom and two sisters dead. He got away, but not for long. They found him on a railway track a few months later.

It was the fear. Bringing all these stories up. He knew it was and he tried to stop it but he couldn't. He remembered the Weasel telling him about a bloke who got torched in his car. Nothing to do with Crawford as far as he remembered, just someone his dad knew about. They tied this bloke up, hand and foot, like a parcel, stuck him in the boot, covered him in petrol, swilled it about inside the car, locked the boot and threw a match. Ashley thought about that. Quicker for that bloke than Mrs Cambridge. But he knew it was coming. Even if he didn't know when they were tying him up, once he saw that petrol, and smelt it, he would know. Inside the boot, hearing the petrol swill about. Maybe Mrs Cambridge never woke up, she might have just been asleep and the smoke killed her; she might not have known anything about it. But that wasn't true. Ashley remembered everyone talking about how the girls were screaming from the bedroom window, but nobody could get close enough.

Ashley had started to shake. He hated it up here in the dark. The fucking fucking dark. What was Kieran doing? He wouldn't do anything like that, would he? He might. Just clear his gear out and torch the place? Course he wouldn't, it was senseless. Crawford wouldn't do something like that. Waste all that money. Then he thought about insurance. If they made it look like an accident, like it was his fault, they'd make a packet.

A noise from below. Ashley held his breath, listened. Someone on the stairs.

'Ash.' Ashley breathed again. 'Ash. Yus can come down now, man. I just sin the Irish git drive away, innit.'

31

Firth Street on the TV screen. Seen from the corner of Esssex Terrace: The Norway Room. Police cars. Tape stretching across the street, hovering in the breeze. Now a copper talking. In a suit. His name came up on the screen. A Detective. He wanted anyone who was in the area to ring a number. It came up on the screen then disappeared. Too quick, Ashley thought. You'd never write that down in time. A reporter was talking now. Suit and tie. The knot crooked. Microphone like a lollipop. Give it a lick, mate, go on. *Murder weapon. The police searching for a murder weapon.* Policemen on their hands and knees in the street. Blokes clad in white – head to foot – came and went behind the reporter. Slowly. Not easy to move in those things. Spacesuits. They looked like they worked in a food factory. Food factory spacemen. They looked like big white plastic bags. A strong wind and they'd just bounce along the road.

Geezbo saw Ashley grinning. 'You big fish now boy. You make the ten o'clock news.'

Ashley's grin disappeared. He couldn't hear what the TV was saying. The music from next door had started again, louder. The item finished. Now a man was talking about smoking. Banning it. Ashley struggled to hear. *The end of pubs.* Then a woman. Posh. *Passive smoking. Workers' right to a smoke-free environment.* Geezbo flicked it off. Ashley looked at the blank screen.

'So. Wha' ya doin' man? You goin' stay 'ere tonight?'

Ashley said nothing. He didn't know what to do.

'I seed 'im take out de boxes. Six. Then a sportsbag. So 'e took what 'e wants. 'E wouldn't 'ave screwed the lock back on if 'e waz comin' back tonight. 'E'll be busy finding a new 'ome for 'iz stuff.'

Unless it's a trick, Ashley thought. The night-time is Kieran's time. He could easily come back. Geezbo pulled a chair across and started to roll a spliff.

'Where do you get all that stuff from?'

Geezbo tapped the side of his nose.

Ashley didn't like this. 'Where d'you live anyway? You know everything about me. You don't tell me nothing about you.'

'That troofless. I tell you my relative the last man to hang in Winson Green Prison Birmingham who didn't string hissel up. I tell you I in wiv the Dobermans. I tell you about my brother Carlton, and what my gran predict for me. I tell you I is evil. So. Not troof you know nothing 'bout me. I tell you. Trust you. Iz you who tell me lies, man. Schools and uncles. I 'ave to work it out for myself.'

Geezbo lit the spliff and inhaled. 'Weird man, this. You know what I mean, man? I would neva expected this. Uz knowin' what we know. We 'ave to trust each other. We am on de same side, man.' He turned to face Ashley. 'You wanna know where I live? Well man, my mudda live in Ward End. Francis Road, Ward End. You know what I'm sayin' 'ere, man? So technically that my address. When I in court, that my address. But where I sleep? Lots of places. Places on de

Mendy. In Handsworth. Wiv Dobermans. Friends in Ward End. Nechells. So now you know even more. You know what I'm sayin', man? Now you tell me somethin'.' Geezbo inhaled again. Deep satisfaction. Let his head fall back on the settee, before he released the smoke. 'I waitin' for another secret, man.'

'My mom —' For a moment Ashley's mouth held open.

'Okay. Your mom?'

'My mom is Kylie Monogue, but don't tell anybody. Give us a blow on that spliff, will ya?'

Ashley reached out, but Geezbo moved the spliff out of range. 'No, not till yus tell me. Finish what you started. Your mom?' He waited. He waited.

Ashley looked at the smoke rising from the spliff. 'She's dead. Dead with cancer. Cremated. Now let me have a blow.'

'That's nothing. I knew that. I know your dad inside. I know your mom dead. That's nothing.'

'That's everything there is. There ain't nothing else to know.'

Geezbo handed the spliff over and watched Ashley pull on it, pull on it. 'Yez, dare iz. Must be. Tell.'

And now it seemed possible to Ashley. To say it. After all this time. Might as well.

'She's dead. But she's not dead.'

Geezbo waited.

'She's dead to me. She cleared off when I was little. Years ago. Just went. With another bloke. My dad's useless. In prison and stuff. So she went. Left us all. Her mom never spoke to her again. Never saw her. That was my nan. She looked after me, but she got cancer. My mom never even came to the funeral. Don't know where she is. So she is dead. Really. For me.' Ashley sucked at the spliff. A huge pull. He threw his head back, holding the smoke tight in his chest. Till it hurt. Then released it. Ashley looked across at Geezbo who he realised didn't know what to say. Then the room revolved.

'Fuck this is strong stuff,' Ashley said.

'Some of it my wages.'

'What?'

'The skunk. That's ow I get it. Some of it my wages.'

The next morning Geezbo was in the kitchen when Ashley came downstairs. 'Why didn't you wake me? I wanted to be out first thing.'

'Only just awake meself, man. Making meself useful innit. Made a drink for yuz uncle too. In de front room, man.'

'Kieran? In the front?' Ashley froze.

'Cleanin' iz gun init. Ready to blow yez ed aways, man. Made im nice cup of tea wiv no sugar. For aftawood innit. When we cleans up de mess.'

'Wanker! You wanker bastard.' Ashley's voice a squeak now. He snivelled. Squeezed his eyes against tears. 'That's not funny.' But Geezbo thought it was and roared.

Ashley had only just woken up, but already he was tired. 'We need to get out of here.'

'We ain't had no wash yet. Yus don't keep much food in yus kitchen do ya? No wonda you like a whippet. Gotta respect your body, man. You 'avin' a drink?'

'I'll 'ave a drink at a caff. I just —'

Firth Street. Essex Street. A voice from the television. Both boys looked towards it. Geezbo sat down. *Shooting. Possible gangland connection.* The same as last night, nothing new.

'I'll have a coffee. Then we'll go.'

'Ooze say anytins 'bout we?'

'You can't stay here.' The top had been left off the coffee and it had gone hard, it looked like lava. Ashley chiselled at it. Poured in hot water. It tasted bitter. Geezbo had used the last of the milk but Ashley was glad he was still here, someone was here, someone who knew.

'What do you think I should do, Geez? I thought about just trying to stay here at night, to sleep. Is that stupid? Should I just – ' But Geezbo's attention had been caught by the television. Ashley looked. The Mendy. Pictures of the Mendy. A police car on the Bax Road. More fluttering tape. Like in Firth Street. A voice explained that the body of a newborn baby girl, possibly born prematurely, had been found behind some dustbins on the Mendelssohn Estate. Then a policewoman talking to camera. She was hard-faced and had a strong Brummie accent. 'What we are most concerned about is the mother. She is probably in need of medical help, both physical and emotional. If she is watching, or anyone who knows her is watching, I would appeal to her to come forward.'

SHUKO

32

It was sometimes the way when the Red Guard went to execute someone that they would make them lie in the family bed, then before the assembled household, neighbours too sometimes, the shots were fired. Then all watched. The Guards, relatives, neighbours. They watched the blood seeping into the bedroll. The stain growing larger. Redder and redder. Larger and larger.

The English phrase *sweet dreams* is common in many languages and cultures. In the China of my youth, *safe dreams* was the salutation. And they were the final words of the jeering Red Guards to those huddled around the sodden mattress. Chin Lou's memoir *Haunted by the Dreams of the Red Mattresses* tells of sleeping with the stains, dried and brown, sleeping with the evidence. I believe the book is still banned.

I slept on the navy-blue futon I had prepared for my guest. And it was sweet dreams indeed that I enjoyed.

At first – and then the mattress turned red. Trudy's blood seeped across it and stained my reputation for faultless competence. A phone call disturbed my early-evening nap, the voice of Hsinshu himself. 'There has been a development, Shuko.' There was no stretching of vowel sounds. Each syllable short and abrupt. 'Rather shocking. Certainly unfortunate. You are not aware of it?'

I am Shuko, who stands strong as an oak at the right hand of the Emperor. But as I heard those hard short syllables, *shock-ing, unfor-tun-ate*, rapid twists of a weapon in a wound, my spirit became more like the willow. 'No, Emperor.' He could hear it in my voice.

'Ah.' A long and disappointed sigh. I had heard that sigh before, but never before provoked by any action of mine. 'Then I must tell you – our plans have met a serious setback. Very serious. It seems you have been outflanked, Shuko. Outgunned. Literally. I have learned that Mr Stretton was shot in his office just an hour or two ago. Through the head. Quite dead of course. His secretary, or mistress, with him.'

His secretary, or mistress – I was still lying on the navy-blue futon. Just seconds before, I had been dreaming of Trudy's golden hair lain across it.

It is a test of the quality of men such as I that we can regain focus so quickly at such times. Or perhaps it was just the triviality of the sentiment that I had allowed to overtake me.

'Crawford?'

'Apparently not. Unless he is playing a particularly devious hand, and I can see no reason why he should. It was he who gave me the news. Delivered in something of a tirade. He is quite sure that Mr Stretton was shot by a Chinese. And therefore of course he believes it to be us. He said his man Kieran Walsh has talked to someone from the club. The assassin was masked, but lifted the mask in a corridor beyond the CCTV. Just a little. Just enough for them to know. The Chinese.' A pause. Then: 'But not us.'

'No, Emperor.'

*

It seemed at first that no one was behind the counter of the Bamboo Garden. Looking in through the window I saw only two customers awaiting their orders: a youth leaning against the counter intent on his phone, and a woman seated, looking up at the television mounted on the wall. Then I saw the top of Siyu's head; she was sitting behind the counter, flicking through a magazine.

'Uncle.' She rose smiling from her seat, dropping the magazine on to her chair. Her hand went for her belly – and rested on it. Yangku followed me into the shop. Siyu smiled at him too. Then, sensing something, 'Uncle?'

'Feiyang.'

'He is not here, Uncle. He has been out since lunchtime.'

'Siyu, you must come with me.' Yangku lifted the counter hatch and held out his hand to her. 'Come quickly now, Siyu. It is important.'

'Uncle, what is wrong?' The customers watched. Siyu's hands covered her belly. Yangku put his hand on her shoulder, gently. 'Mamma,' she shouted, 'Mamma,' and took hold of the back of the chair.

Outside a couple of people stared as we dragged her away. A man coming out of the Madrigal moved towards us then thought better of it. Yangku tipped Siyu into the boot of the Rover and we were away.

Yangku drove. Very quickly. In a side street he stopped. I went to the boot. I could hear the girl weeping. Sobs. 'Siyu? Are you listening? This is very important. Are you listening? If you are sensible nothing will happen to you or the child. We are taking you to my flat to wait for Feiyang. When we get there do not make a fuss. Do you understand? No shouting. No screaming. Nothing. No harm will come to you if you behave sensibly.'

As Yangku continued the journey to Nimrod House at a more cautious speed, I called Feiyang. 'You have behaved very foolishly. Your action is a direct attack on the Dragon's interest.' I had decided not to use the words punishment or revenge. 'You will recall our conversation, Feiyang – about history. The Emperor Bang. I have Siyu.' I ended the call. I had no interest in anything he had to say. Yangku stared straight ahead, concentrating on the road before us.

The girl was quiet as we parked up. Her tear-stained face blinked up at me when I lifted the boot. 'Uncle.' She spoke Chinese. 'Uncle, please. Help me. Look.' She brushed a hand across herself. 'The waters.'

I helped her out of the boot. 'Behave properly. You understand? And all will be well.'

'Take me home, Uncle. Or take me to the hospital.'

I took her arm. 'Say nothing.' I squeezed. 'Do you understand?'

She trudged between Yangku and myself into Nimrod House. The lift was empty. I pressed fifteen. Slowly clutching her belly she padded the steps up to the sixteenth, Yangku ahead of her, me behind. Only once did she stop. And, turning towards me, 'Why? What has happened?'

I was unmoved. 'Keep going.' Inside the flat I led her to the room I was preparing for Trudy. She made for the futon and threw herself upon it. And in that movement the wailing began.

33

At the end of the line Miss Blossom listened to everything without interruption. I was standing at the window looking out at the lights of the Mendy, glittering cheaply in the darkness.

'Miss Blossom?'

'I am here.' When Miss Blossom had answered my call there was sharpness in her tone; why had I phoned her at home? She presumed it was urgent, important. Yes it was. Her voice was softer now. 'I am thinking. Considering.' The silence returned. I tracked the lights of a lorry moving out of the estate towards the Tallis Road. 'You ask a great deal of me.' I let the statement hang. 'But you acknowledge this and say you are ready to pay.'

'Handsomely, ma'am. My driver will collect you from your home whenever you say. He can be with you in half an hour. And of course he will return you to your door.'

'I see. Good.' The lorry was on the Tallis now, merging with other lights, soon it would be indistinguishable. 'My fee for this call-out will be five thousand pounds in cash.'

'Let's call it six.' There was a cry from Trudy's room. 'I think I can hear another contraction. Will it be convenient to collect you in an hour?'

*

Soon I too was among the lights of the Tallis Road driving to the casino. There was no doubt in my mind that the killings at the Norway Room would do grave damage to my status within the Dragon. An unreliable servant is useless. The sigh of disappointment I had heard from the Emperor echoed in my mind and the shame was hard to bear, but for the moment I was overtaken by the desire to punish Feiyang.

There were several police cars parked up in Chinatown and a number of foot patrols, but nothing at the casino itself. I feared my access to Dragon funds might already have been withdrawn, my downfall decided upon. But this was not the case. It was still early in the evening. There was no senior member of the Dragons there. The casino staff and junior Dragons showed their usual respect. The cash was bagged without question; few in the organisation enjoy such trust.

There was no sound from Trudy's room. We had taped Siyu's mouth, tied her arms and legs, secured her to the bed. She heard me enter the room. There was enough light from the window for me to be able to see her, the shape of her. Her head lifted, turned, held for a moment and fell back.

I went to the bed and sat beside her, placed my hand on hers, stroked it very gently; there was noise behind the tape, her body pulled against her cords. 'Hush. Hush now Siyu.' I cradled her head and whispered into her ear, as one comforting a distressed child. 'I am back and can release you. It was, as I said, only for a short time. Soon help will be here. Medical assistance. I am going to—'

Her body contorted. A strangulated squawk, despite the tape. A sound like poultry. When she was quieter I continued.

'I am going to ask you a few questions. They are very important – for everyone. When they are answered we can get on with things. Do you understand?' Her head bobbed against my arm. Without thinking I let my lips touch her head. 'All will be fine.'

She gasped and gaped when the tape came off. 'My arms. My legs. They hurt. I need to move my legs, Uncle.'

'Hush niece. A moment. In a moment. Now tell me about your husband. What time did he leave today?'

'This morning he went out. He came back at about one o'clock, and then left again about an hour later – without having anything to eat.'

'And has he returned since?'

'No.'

'And this morning, the first time he went out. Where did he go?'

'I don't know.'

A squeeze of her shoulder. 'It is important, Siyu.'

'Truly, Uncle, I don't know. Business is all he says. Kieran called for him and he said they were going out on business. That they would not be back. Then at about one o'clock, he returned. Without Kieran. He sat with Chun and Tang Weiguo then he and Tang left the shop. Again he told me business – not sure when he would be back. I ask no questions, Uncle, truly. He says it is business, there is nothing I need to know.' She was becoming upset, starting to weep.

'Does he do a lot of business with Kieran?'

'Recently, yes. Kieran comes a lot, and they talk. Sometimes they go out together.'

'Did he tell you anything about the business?' Another squeeze, harder this time. 'It is very important, Siyu, then I can untie you.'

There was a sigh halted by a sob. 'Only that they have very big plans. For a takeover. That will make a lot of money.

The start of very big things. A big takeover that will change everything for us.' She cried uncontrollably now, aware of what she had done.

I rested my chin on her head. 'You have done well, Siyu. Very well. I will make you some tea and then untie you. Relax.' And I eased her head back on to the bed.

34

Miss Blossom was wearing a black trouser suit, perfectly cut to her height and figure, a red stripe down the outer sides of the trousers, a pink carnation embroidered like a badge on the jacket. She had made her way down on high heels from the seventeenth floor.

Yangku carried her small leather case. Once through the door of the flat she removed her headscarf of pink silk and handed it to me. I folded it, and bowed. She nodded a response, then smiled – such refinements please her. An ivory comb finely carved with Shinto symbols held her black hair in a bun to the back of her head. 'Where is the patient?'

'Through here, Miss Blossom.'

'Ah, the navy futon. And the pictures. Very nice. And you are Siyu. Now have no fear. All will be well.'

Arching her back and bending low she took Siyu's hand, placed her fingers on the girl's wrist.

'Are you –?'

'Let me take your pulse.' Turning to me, 'How long is it since the last contraction?'

'Five minutes, I would say.'

'No, longer. Ten.' Siyu corrected.

'My case please.' Yangku brought the case. 'Here. Put it

here.' From it Miss Blossom first took a leather pouch. She removed her rings and dropped them in. Siyu followed each movement. Miss Blossom noticed. 'Beautiful rings aren't they.' She showed the last one to the girl. 'This emerald is my favourite. Very valuable. All of them. And they did not come easily, I can tell you.' Unzipping a pocket in her jacket she popped the pouch in and rezipped it. She took a white plastic apron from the bag and put it on, a box of rubber gloves, a stethoscope and shears, all of which she placed beside the futon. Two towels she laid beside Siyu. 'I will need some bowls of hot water.'

Standing outside the open bedroom door I listened to Miss Blossom reassuring Siyu. She used the peasant dialect and idioms of Hubei Province. When the contraction came her tone was firmer as she instructed Siyu to push. 'Harder now. Come on. It will be easier for you in the end. This is no time for fears or tears. You must work, push.' Then softly, 'That was good. You did very well. We are nearly there. Soon all will be over.'

The sounds held me. The heavy breaths, panting, wails and sobs of Siyu, the fluctuating tones of Miss Blossom's voice. An image of Trudy came to my mind, lying on the futon, almost smiling.

Miss Blossom came to stand beside me. 'We are nearly there,' she whispered. 'You have the money?'

'Six thousand pounds sterling. In cash. In the other room.'

'I think the light is too harsh for this business now. Let us have candlelight. I have some in my case.'

'I have some too, Miss Blossom.'

'Good, that will be very nice. Shadows and flickering lights. Very nice. It will make the girl feel better.'

*

Miss Blossom knelt on the futon, her hands between the girl's legs. 'Another push, Siyu. You are taking too long. Far too long.' The girl yelled. In the candlelight I watched the shadows of her contortions dance across the walls. I saw the head break free into Miss Blossom's hands, the body slither after it. A yellow parcel, swinging from Miss Blossom's hands, blue-veined and slimy, white and grey, thin red streaks of blood. The woman's hands worked quickly around the head. 'The cord is caught. Tangled around the neck.' To whom she spoke exactly wasn't clear. Siyu? The room? She cut the cord. The room was filled with Siyu's gasps. Yangku and I stood watching the woman at work.

Siyu's breathing became quieter, steadier. Miss Blossom wrapped the child in a towel. Quickly. Took it to Siyu. 'You took too long, my dear. And the cord was round its neck. See.' And she showed her the dead baby. Siyu reached out. 'Better not. It is better you rest.'

Siyu screamed and lunged forward as Miss Blossom moved away from her. 'Let me have her. Let me see.'

Miss Blossom turned. 'Sit back,' she barked. 'Sit back you foolish girl. Sit back and be quiet.'

The shocked girl did as she was told. Miss Blossom sat beside her. 'Look,' she held the child so Siyu could see it. 'No. Don't touch. Just look. The child is dead. Was born dead. It is sad. But there it is. It happens a hundred times every day – around the world.' There was quiet. A tableau. Two women on the bed. Candlelight. Yangku and I standing either side of the open doorway. 'Enough,' said Miss Blossom and rose. 'Stay.' She carried the baby to Yangku. 'Take it away,' she whispered.

Returning to the bed she took Siyu in her arms, and held her. 'Cry now girl. It is over. Let it go.' And she held her as the girl sobbed and wailed. When she quietened, Miss Blossom took her to the bathroom, watched her shower. She made soothing noises, dried her and brought her back to the futon where she covered her with a quilt I had bought for Trudy. Miss Blossom took a sachet from her case. She looked to me: 'A glass of water.' She emptied powder from the sachet into it. 'This is a sedative, Siyu. It will make you sleep. You must get as much sleep as possible. You are very young. There will be many babies. More than you need. Safe dreams.'

Outside the closed bedroom door I handed Miss Blossom her money. She put it into the case. I passed her her scarf. She flicked it to a square and put it on.

'Ring me if you have any concerns. She should sleep for a long time. When she wakes, make sure she is well fed. Soup. Rice. Meat. In a day or two she will be fine.'

I watched from the window of my bedroom as Yangku and Miss Blossom made their way across Nimrod car park, two tiny figures now. Soon the Rover was making its way towards the Tallis Road. I was held again by the lights of the Mendy. Like a thousand New Year lanterns. Next door Siyu was sleeping like a baby.

ASHLEY

35

Geezbo walked with Ashley up the Pershore Road but turned left as Ashley turned right.

'You should be coming too,' said Ashley.

'I got things to do.'

'Sophie's your friend too. You say the kid's yours.'

'It her bizness. She babymutta. She do what she wan'. Run intaya 'nother time, man.'

The sun was out but it was still cold. Ashley jumped a bus then cut through the park. The ice was gone from the lake. Bax Road was taped off. Two police officers stood inside the tape. Ashley skirted the grass bank of the car park of Nimrod and made for the trees at the side of Walton. When the coast was clear he headed for the dustbin stands and the service door.

It was too late to turn and nip back into the lift. The doors were almost closed when Ashley spotted the copper standing at Sophie's door talking to Mel. He had congratulated himself on avoiding the ones outside with all their tapes and stuff – and now one was here, right at Sophie's door – and smoking, both the copper and Mel were smoking. Coppers weren't supposed to smoke on duty were they? His eyes narrowed when he saw Ashley.

Ashley's stomach turned. He must be comforting her. He was comforting Mel. Sophie had lost the baby and he was comforting her mom. Perhaps they had arrested Sophie for getting rid of it.

'What do you want, son? Who let you through?'

Mel peered round the copper. 'Oh, he's all right. It's family. She's in here love, and no, it's not hers if that's what you're thinking. She's all right.'

'Who let you in?' the copper persisted.

Mel answered for him. 'Houdini Part Two, this one. In and out of anywhere. But he's all right. His mom's dead.' She half whispered this sentence, as though it were confidential. 'I'll look after him. Come on, love, she's in there.'

The copper moved to let him pass. 'Paige is in there with her. It's like an antenatal class.' She tapped the copper's chest playfully. 'Either of those two goes into labour, I'm going to need your help.'

An hour ago everything had been terrible, frightening. Now as Mel joked with the copper, as he smelled their smoke, everything seemed safe.

No one in the lounge, or the kitchen. He went to Sophie's bedroom. He knocked. 'Soph.'

The bathroom door opened a touch. 'Hold on, we're having a fag. Be out in a minute.'

Ashley wandered into the kitchen. He was starving. He opened the fridge. Closed it. A cupboard contained an opened box of muesli. He scooped a handful into his mouth, then another.

'Fuckin' thief. What you doin'?' Paige Crutchley filled the doorway. She was enormous. And not pretty any more, her face all spotty, her hair greasy and dead. Ashley hadn't seen her since school, probably over a year now. He knew she was pregnant. It was supposed to be Tyr Hardy's as well. But even her face was fat now. Sophie had told him she'd been texting Paige because their kids were going to be related.

'I'm starving,' Ashley told her. 'Ain't had nothing to eat.'

'Don't mean you're supposed to scab off other people does it? There's shops you know.'

'Where's Sophie?'

'Havin' a piss.'

'Not any more she's not.' Sophie pushed Paige into the kitchen.

'He was stealing your food.'

'Only a handful of cereal. You make it sound like the whole fucking cupboard.'

'Same thing. Principle.'

'Sorry Soph. I'm starving.'

'It's all right. D'you want some toast? There's plenty of bread. Have some Bovril on it if you like.'

Mel called Sophie's name.

'In the kitchen.'

'Blimey, it's crowded in here. Why you all in here?'

'I'm making Ash some toast. He's hungry.'

'While you're at it make a cup of tea for Gareth, will you. Milk, no sugar.'

In the end Sophie made toast for everybody. Mel and Gareth ate theirs in the doorway because he was on inside patrol; Ashley, Paige and Sophie sat in the lounge.'

'I was dead worried when I saw it on the telly,' Ashley told Sophie. 'Thought it might be you.'

'I'd never do that.'

'Thanks a lot,' Paige said. 'So you think I would?' She

turned to Ashley. 'She texted me. First thing. *Have you dumped the baby*? Lovely.'

'I'm sorry. I didn't know what to think.'

'When we doing our therapy?' Paige asked Sophie. 'He's not stayin' is he?'

'No. You'll have to go soon, Ash. We're doing music therapy. It's good for a baby to listen to music. Makes them healthier.'

'And good people,' Paige added.

'So we lie on the floor and listen to music together. If they listen to the same music they'll probably be closer. Shared experience makes you closer.'

Ashley wanted to talk to Sophie on her own. He wanted to say I thought you didn't like Paige. Hated her you said. Now you push me out and I've got nowhere to go. He wanted to say I want to talk to you. Tell you things. I'm in the shit again. Instead he said, 'What music you listening to?'

'Lotsa stuff. "Back It Up" by Beenie Man. Tarrus Riley.'

'And "Gummy Bear",' Sophie added. 'Don't forget "Gummy Bear". We dance to that with our toes.'

Mel came through with the empty cups. 'Here, Gareth's just told me some news. He's only just heard it himself. The baby's yellow. And not jaundice. They thought it was. But it isn't. It's Chinese.'

36

Walton Tower was back to normal except for some police notices giving people a number to ring if they had any information. Ashley walked the long way round to the Pooch then back again. He didn't know what else to do. Twice today he had been to Cecil Road and recognised one of Kieran's cars outside. The third time the street was clear but the locks had been changed. He called in to Easy Ted Nichol's, but Marilyn was back and he didn't even get offered a cup of tea. He had gone to Karl's, just in case he wasn't at school, but he was.

Two or three times today he had wanted to phone Kieran. In Cecil Road he had wanted to go over to the house, try and make things all right. But every time he tried he knew it was the wrong thing to do. Time had run out. That's what they say, isn't it. Your time's run out. In the end he had an idea and rang Geezbo, told him he'd got twenty pounds for him if he could find him somewhere to stay for the night, a couple of nights if possible. Geezbo had thought and said he might have a solution, meet him on Kinny Bridge at ten o'clock. There were three hours to kill and it was getting cold. He would walk across to Stirchley, get some fish and chips and see if he could get in the arcade there.

*

'For one night only,' Geezbo told Ashley as they entered the lift in Nimrod House.

'I know. I know. You already said.'

'Jus' so iz clear. I takin' a risk for ya, man. Wiv Linton. An that serious.' On the seventeenth floor they headed for the stairs. 'Next floor down.'

There Geezbo unlocked a door and beckoned Ashley to follow him through. They were immediately cramped together in a small space between the front door and a ceiling-to-floor black curtain. Geezbo drew it aside to reveal another door that he unlocked. The smell was like a blow to Ashley. 'Fuck me!'

'Good innit. Pure skunk, man. One hundred per cent. Hydroponic, man.' From a bank of electric switches on the wall trails of wires, thick as jungle snakes, led along the hallway and into the rooms. The atmosphere was warm and damp and dark. All the windows were covered with neatly taped black bin bags. Ashley began to sweat. The smell made him light-headed.

'You watch yourself man, on de wiring. Like Alcatraz in here innit.'

'Alcatraz?'

'Where dey keeps de electric chair. Old Sparky dey calls it. One false move round 'ere and ya fry.'

Pulling off his jacket Geezbo led Ashley through to the kitchen. A few original fittings were still there, a sink unit, a fridge, a counter above some cupboards. Above that was another wiring board. From the cupboard Geezbo pulled some cushions and a sleeping bag. 'Sometime kip down 'ere myself, or one of the others do. So I keep these 'ere.' Without warning Geezbo grabbed Ashley's collar pulling him towards him. Ashley felt Geezbo's fist hard against his throat.

'I doin' you a big favour, man. Big. Big. Innit. Remember it. An' you neva seen nothin'. Neva bin 'ere.' He let Ashley go. 'I trustin' you wiv my life, man. To help ya out, innit. Neva even breeve it.'

Ashley wanted to say, *You're taking a risk for my twenty pounds, that's what you're doing. You never mentioned this place before I offered cash*. 'I won't,' he said instead. 'I know. Thanks Geez.'

Ashley looked around. The room that in the other flats would be the lounge bore a forest of cannabis plants, each about four foot high, packed together and supported by a matrix of canes and garden twine. From the ceiling hung lighting boxes and reflector panels roped to pulleys so the height could be adjusted as the plants grew. The floor of the first bedroom Ashley looked into was completely covered with smaller plants, but the big surprise was the other bedroom; here seedling trays covered the floor leaving just a passageway to a hole in the wall to the next-door flat. Geezbo followed Ashley as he looked around, amused by his amazement. 'So is this where the Dobermans grow their stuff.'

'Some of it. We import as well. We got lotsa places like this.'

Ashley opened the bathroom door. The water tank was exposed with plastic piping leading from it, an irrigation pump in the bath. 'There juz enuf room to take a shit,' Geezbo told Ashley. Then, pointing to a blue plastic tub, 'Fertiliser.'

On the cistern was a tray with a magnifying glass and two long narrow pairs of scissors, more like hairdressing shears. 'What these for?'

'Takin' cuttin's offa de mutta plant.'

Ashley was impressed. 'And do you look after all this?' He knew this was something he could do.

'Others do it too man. But this 'ouse, recently – iz mainly my work. Tyr done some 'ere. But im not involved much any more. It not is ting.'

Geezbo left soon after that. Some business he said. But he was coming back. He was going to stay here tonight, to keep an eye on Ashley, he said. He didn't want any trouble with Linton.

At least Ashley had somewhere to stay for tonight. At first he had been pleased and seen this as a solution, easily worth twenty quid. Well away from Cecil Road. He could manage in the day. If he could get Geez to let him stay here at night for a bit everything would be fine. But now he felt closed in. There was a hum all the time from the lights. And the smell, that got to you after a bit. And you couldn't turn the lights off. It was like that prison the Americans had for terrorists. They never turned the lights off there either.

He could hear voices from the flat next door. Ashley wondered who lived there. The lift didn't stop at the sixteenth floor, so it must be people who knew what was going on. Not ordinary tenants. People Linton had put in there probably. He wondered if there was anywhere else where they needed someone to keep an eye on things, like a caretaker. He hadn't wanted to get involved in any of the gangs, but something like that would be all right for a while.

He awoke as he shot Kieran. Kieran had been shouting at him. He had climbed up into the loft at Cecil Road and was yelling at him. Then Ashley saw the schoolbag. It must have been there all the time. There was nothing in it but the gun. Ashley lifted the gun. Kieran was still shouting, swearing. Ashley shot him, but as Kieran fell forward Ashley could see there was someone behind him. Ashley could only see a hand in the shadows holding a gun. So who had shot Kieran? Already the dream was becoming more confusing.

Ashley stood up, stretched. You couldn't walk around properly because of all the wiring. There was nowhere to go. All the space was covered with plants.

He drank some water from the tap and tried to go back to sleep, but sleep wouldn't come. He could hear the voices from next door again. He wondered what time it was. He thought about the watch Kieran had given him. The Asian kids had that now. And the gun. He wondered what they would do with the gun. Sell it? Use it? Get scared and hide it?

Perhaps he should do a runner. This wasn't a good place. But that would just land him in more shit. He decided he would go into the corridor, just for a minute. Put the catch on the two front doors. Just stand there for a minute.

He started to feel better. A few minutes out here and he would be okay. It was just stress. Dreams and stress and stuff. And the smell in there. He was probably stoned. He could think okay out here. He could hear nothing from next door. He went closer. Put his ear to the door. Nothing. He returned to the Dobermans' door. Then wandered down to the window at the other end of the corridor. It must be late. Early hours at least. The only traffic was on the Tallis Road that circled the estate and there wasn't much there. Through the grime of the window he was able to make out the form of Geezbo plodding his way across the grass verge towards Nimrod car park.

Then Ashley heard the lift. Travelling up the centre of the building. He heard it stop at the floor below and someone get out. Footsteps. The lift started again. Footsteps coming up the stairs. Ashley heard the lift stop at the floor above and someone get out. Footsteps. Coming down the stairs. Ashley made for the flat. But not fast enough. As he reached the stairs there was Kieran coming up, gun in hand. He turned. There was the Chinese bloke, the one who had sorted Benjy Graham, coming down, gun in hand. He jumped the remaining stairs and grabbed for Ashley. Too late: Ashley was away, heading for the Dobermans' front door. But Kieran had him, first by the hair, then with his arm round his neck. Ashley ducked. Slipped through. Inside the flat he tried to slam the door. But they were both there now, a push and he was on the floor, both of them inside looking down on him.

CARROW

37

Carrow was driving fast on the Pershore Road when his phone rang.

'What the fuck's your game, Carra?' It was Crawford.

'I'm driving.'

'Well I hope you fucking crash. I pay you a wad to keep me informed and I hear about Stretton from everybody but the bloke who's collecting the cash. What—'

'I didn't know. I've been in the gym all day. I've only just heard. I'm on my way over now.'

He couldn't get the motor anywhere near Essex Street. Police closure notices everywhere. He pulled on to the back of a closed garage forecourt in Gooch Street and legged it from there.

Police barricades closed Essex Street from just below the car park behind Pinks. Carrow spotted Toga inside the cordon, standing on the steps of Pinks with some of the other Norway doormen, Matty Fallon and the two Lukes. He called over. Toga waved, said something to the uniform standing beside them and he came across to the barrier. 'You one of the staff here? The Norway?'

'Yeah. On the door.'

'Name?'

'Carrow. Craig Carrow.'

'Hop over.'

The uniform walked him to Pinks. 'Wait here with your mates. Everyone's being seen in here.'

A crew were setting up a gantry of night lighting. About a dozen press and television reporters were crammed behind a barrier at the top of Wrentham Street, side-on to the Norway.

'They're taking us in one by one,' Toga told him. 'Letting people out through the back. Must think we don't have phones.'

'What the fuck's happened anyway? Stretton's shot, you said? Is he dead?'

'Yes, and Trudy. They got both of them.' This was Luke Jarvis. 'The cops aren't confirming anything, just saying a man and woman shot through the head. The bodies are still in there.'

'But it's them,' Luke Freeman said. 'Stretton and Trudy. If it wasn't, they'd be here with us, wouldn't they?'

'And what's our line once we're in there?' asked Luke Jarvis.

'Neville just texted,' said Toga. He kept his head down as he read from his phone. *'they seem to know about turf war. i answered everything straight. told basics about chink raids. never asked about bulgs. i never said.'*

'So. It's cough, but nothing more than you get asked,' Matty said. 'That's what I'm going to do.'

Carrow looked around, tried to take everything in. 'Where's Uncle Bulgaria now?'

'No one's seen a sign of them,' Toga said.

'On the payroll?' Carrow asked.

'Got to be,' Toga replied. 'Stretton kept at least one inside during the day. Obviously a wedge from the Chinese saw them do a runner.'

'So old Sergei will probably be back in Sofia tomorrow.'

Luke Jarvis frowned. 'Who's she?'

Matty whacked the side of his head. 'It's the capital of Bulgaria, you fucking ape.' They all laughed.

'You lot seem very jovial considering your boss has just been shot.'

Carrow turned to see Sean Dowd, his old boss, standing in front of Pinks's neon panel, as immaculately dressed as ever, and to his side, as always, Jack Stevens.

Between us and the good guys it's a very thin line, Dowd used to say. And now, Carrow, standing here with the other doormen, on the payroll of Crawford, felt he had crossed it.

38

Kieran was parked up in Gooch Street waiting for him. 'Crawford wants a personal word. Told me to run you up to the office. I'll bring you back to your motor. Return service.' The passenger door of the A7 swung open. 'Hop in. I've been here an hour.'

As he drove Kieran drummed his fingers on the steering wheel in time to the music, American punk rock, loud and fast. He swung his head backwards and forwards, joined in with lines he knew, shouting them out.

Carrow had had enough. Any more of this and he'd throw up, or get a migraine at least. He reached out to the volume control and turned.

'Don't you like it?'

'It's crap.'

A finger on Kieran's left hand punched the stereo button, killing the music. 'You got to hear it loud or not at all.'

Now there was just the comfortable hum of the car. There were more police cars in Chinatown. 'Looks like they're closing the place down,' Carrow observed.

'This one's got them worried.'

'Seems like they're reckoning on the Chinese.'

'Did they say that then? When they were questioning you,' Kieran asked.

'No. Course they didn't. But if they're all over Chinatown? You don't have to be a genius to work it out.'

'Or an ex-cop.' A touch of a sneer in Kieran's tone. 'They're right anyway. It was the Dragons.'

'Maybe. Maybe not. Crawford was interested in the place. You could have done it, Kieran.'

Kieran laughed. 'Not me mate. That's well above my pay grade. Anyway, I've got an alibi.'

'Well fancy that. I'm sure whoever pulled the trigger has one too. Woman, was it? You were on the job at the time of the crime?'

Kieran was still laughing. 'Christ. You can tell you were a cop. You've still got the tone. Got it perfect. I'd be bricking it if it was me.' Now the laughter disappeared. 'But you're not a cop any more, are you? You're one of us. On the payroll – just like me. Like the girls on the poles. Anyway, it *was* the Chinese. You must know that by now. Staff in the Norway saw the gunman.'

No one had mentioned this when they were all together outside Pinks. 'Anyone can hire a Chinese gunman, Kieran – or pay someone on Stretton's staff to deliver a script. *I saw him. Lifted his mask to scratch his nose. Definitely yellow.* It doesn't mean anything.'

Kieran said nothing. Carrow wondered what Ruthie saw in someone like him. But that was stupid. Kieran was a good-looking bloke, well dressed, confident, lots of chat no doubt, the Irish charm – and he wouldn't be short of a few wads of cash to splash about. Definitely a plus in Ruthie's book.

*

At the Hippo, Kieran escorted Carrow to Crawford's office.

Crawford was more relaxed than he had sounded on the phone. 'Craig, come in. Take a seat. I bet you could do with a drink. Whiskey?'

'Thanks.' He needed a drink. He could always leave the car where it was for tonight. Get a taxi back.

Crawford poured two glasses and handed one over. Carrow took a hefty gulp and released a satisfied sigh. 'Beautiful stuff.'

'Aberfeldy. A favourite of mine.'

'Right, at the kick-off,' Carrow started, 'I need to make something clear. If there is any way this, *your* organisation, is involved, even to the extent of knowing something about Stretton's killing, let me go. Now. I know you can't go into it, can't *commit* yourself...' And here Carrow paused slightly, just enough to ensure his emphasis on the word was clear. 'But if there is any sort of involvement, just say cheers, we'll clink glasses, finish our drinks and I'll be off. Because I know which side I'm on when it gets as serious as this – and if you mislead me and I discover you are involved in any way, or if you know who is, then all agreements of confidentiality are off.'

Crawford took his time to reply. Carrow couldn't be sure whether his little speech had stirred things up or if this was just the way the man was. 'I appreciate you being so direct, Craig. I always like to know where I stand with people. And it's better for them if they know where they stand with me. Better for all concerned. I'll put it in your terms shall I? We could finish this bottle, go through another and we'd both be unconscious before we needed to clink glasses and say cheers. I know nothing about Stretton's death. Didn't see it coming. Know nothing about it. From what Kieran tells me it looks as if it was a Dragons job. Though I must say it surprises me. I wouldn't have thought anything quite as crude as this was their style, not these days. And it's shut the club down for a while.'

'Perhaps that's what they want.'

'Maybe. Now, what do you know? Show me I haven't wasted my money.' The tone was friendly but Carrow knew the man was moving up a gear.

'Maybe you have. I learned about the killing through a text from one of the blokes on the door. I'd been at the gym all day. Soon as I heard I headed for Essex Street. That's when I got your call. Can't get near the place though so I park up in Gooch Street – as you know, or at least as Kieran knew.'

'Nothing sinister. I told him to circle the area, see if he could find you.'

'A lot of Norway staff had made their way there. We were corralled into a little group outside Pinks, which is where they've set up a first stage incident room.'

'Who's running the show?' Crawford asked.

'Sean Dowd.'

'Your old boss, eh? That could be handy.'

Crawford put his whiskey glass down on the table beside him, lifted his cigarettes, put one in his mouth, threw another to Carrow. Each lit up. As a column of smoke grew between them, Crawford leaned forward, his elbows on his knees. 'When you were back in Jamaica, for your bereavement, did you see much of the place? Travel about?'

The sudden change of subject took Carrow by surprise. 'Not really. A bit. Mostly I just hung around Santa Cruz. The Treasure Beach area a bit. I went up to Hanover to visit some relatives in Luces. Cousins took me fishing over at Belmont. Around Kingston a bit.'

'You never went anywhere near Moore Town? Portland.'

'No.'

'No, I don't suppose you did. A bit of a backwater. A pretty poor place, apparently. That's where my family's from. Mom anyway. Originally. I've never been there.'

Carrow spotted the ash falling from his cigarette just in time to catch it in the palm of his left hand. Crawford rose and carried across the glass ashtray from the table beside him.

'Cheers.'

'Do you fancy a beer? This whiskey's nice but it makes me thirsty. Freshen the palate?'

'Sounds good.'

'Come on, we'll go downstairs for it.'

Although it wasn't yet nine there was quite a crowd in as Crawford led Carrow through the Hippo. It was too early for the pole shows but girls in spangled bikini pants with tassels on their tits were already at the tables, sitting on men's laps.

Crawford led Carrow past the long oval bar at the centre of the club to one of the smaller, more intimate ones, situated around the club, away from the main action. Later girls would bring blokes to these bars for cosy chats and get them to cough up for booze. It was too early in the evening for them to be manned, but when a barman saw where Crawford was heading he came across.

'Couple of Prague Blondes, Darren.' The barman stooped to the cooler cabinet for the bottles of lager.

'Here, Craig, look at this.' There was a dancer tattooed on Darren's thick bicep. Big tits with tassels. 'Watch,' Crawford repeated, delighted. 'Go on, Daz.' And as the barman flexed his muscles, the girl's breasts appeared to swing, the tassels with them. 'Kills me every time. You don't want a glass do you, Craig?' Crawford asked.

'Bottle's fine.'

The two men settled on barstools and Darren returned to his position at the central bar. A noisy group of young men arrived. Three girls rushed to greet them and accompany them to a table. Carrow noticed Kieran standing under a lamp near the entrance reading his phone. And she was back in Carrow's head – Ruthie Slayte; a message from her?

Crawford looked around. He waved over a good-looking redhead in a tight black dress.

'Sadie love, looks like we're in for a busy night.'

'I'd say so.' She caught Carrow's eye. Gave him the once-over – blatantly. Smiled.

'Let's get an extra floor show on,' Crawford told her.

'No problem. They're all in. Who do you want?' She was still looking at Carrow.

'Tania. She'll get them warmed up. Get her on pronto. We don't want 'em moving on.'

'No problem.' And Sadie ran her eyes over Carrow again before she turned to leave.

'She likes you.'

'I got that impression.'

'You can have her tonight if you like.'

'Oh, I don't know.'

'She's a dirty little madam.'

'You're speaking from experience?'

'I've had 'em all mate. All the ones I want anyway. And Sadie – certainly top ten. Let me know if you're interested and I'll let her go early. Time off for bad behaviour.'

Carrow got his cigarettes out. Offered Crawford one, and lit both of them. There was certainly something about Sadie. Perhaps she would be good for him; an antidote to Ruthie. He took a slug of the lager.

'So what were your plans for the Norway?' Carrow asked Crawford as they drank.

'Keep it as it was. A very healthy business. Well run. Good profit. You can't take it away from Stretton—'

'Someone did.'

Crawford smirked. 'That's a bit of a sick joke, ain't it, Craig? He won't be cold yet. But yes, you're right, somebody did take it away from him.'

'But not you?'

'Definitely not me. I wanted to. Intended to. But not in that way. Force if necessary, but not deadly.'

'Yet?'

But Crawford didn't run with it. 'What this does mean, Craig, my old son, is that you're out of work.'

'It means that all right.'

'Come and work for me. You'll be well paid.'

'As what?'

'Start on the door. Do bits and pieces for me. Look, I'll be straight with you. I've been thinking a lot about Jamaica recently. It's where our roots are, ain't it? I'd like to expand over there. Strictly legit. I've done very well in this city since taking over from the Lopez brothers. I've got a lot of resources to invest right now. And I'm thinking I might do it over there. A couple of high-class clubs in Kingston. Supper clubs with a bit of gambling, some good live music. A restaurant or two. Kingston's underdeveloped in that way. There's a lot of money. A business community. But all the investment goes into a few coastal resorts. I'd like to change that. I suppose I see it as a sort of retirement plan. And in the medium term, perhaps in six to twelve months, if you and me hit it off all right, you might be the man to be my agent over there. Investigate what's available. Make connections. Set things up.'

Darren came over. 'Need another drink, Mr Crawford?'

'Ta, Daz. Two more Pragues.' Both men watched the tat-tooed girl on the barman's biceps do her dance as he took the lagers from the cooler and snapped off the tops.

'And in the six months before? What do I do for my top-of-the-range salary?'

'Like I said. Learn the business. Start as door. That's easy to explain with the Norway shut. I'll take on a few of the other blokes as well. Matty Fallon used to work here. And the big Guyanan bloke, Toga is it? And as I said little jobs for me. Learn the business. And – decide on the line.'

'The line?'

'You're ex-blue, Carra. We both know there's shady areas in this business. So you have to decide if you're comfortable with the tightrope, given the opportunities it presents. Like you had to decide with the Holland job.'

Carrow picked something up he didn't like in Crawford's tone of voice, some insinuation. 'What are you talking about?'

'The kid that was taken.'

'That was nothing to do with me.' The lights went up on the central stage, filling it with a crimson glow.

'Weren't you looking the other way when he went?' Carrow was jolted back to reality. Crawford was a nasty bastard, ruthless, and he was letting it show now. If Carrow was going to work for him he needed to see it. 'I'm not suggesting you had anything to do with topping the kid, I never heard that off no one. But the general impression – over here anyway – was that you were on the payroll somewhere. Weren't you on police bail for ages?'

Carrow put down his bottle and made to leave. What he really wanted to do was hit the man. Crawford grabbed his arm. 'Hold on.' Carrow saw Kieran look over. There was Pricey, another of Crawford's men, standing beside him. 'Sit down for a minute.' Crawford pushed him back on to the barstool.

Sadie walked into the spotlight. 'Good Evening Gentlemen! I would like to welcome you all here to Spotted Hippo tonight, home of Birmingham's most beautiful girls. We're already filling up, if you'll pardon the expression, and so we are going to start our entertainment a little earlier than usual. Are you all in the mood? You will be soon, for the fabulously talented and very beautiful Tania is going to get our evening off to an exciting start.' And with a flourish towards the pole nearest to her, Sadie left the stage. Music started, the spotlight narrowed to a circle around the pole, and to a loud cheer from the audience Tania walked into it.

Crawford now leaned very close into Carrow's ear, shouting above the music. 'Look. I'm making you an offer of work. A very good offer.' He nodded towards Kieran and Pricey. 'Those blokes over there would kill for it.'

'No pun intended?'

'I'm just being clear with you. You must know the kind of rumours that circulate when you get into that sort of business. All I am saying is that over the next few days I would like you to continue to earn the money I've already paid. There's a little bonus I will put your way for keeping me in touch with the Stretton case and—'

'How do I do that?'

'Old mates, dummy. Have a night out with your old mate Jack Stevens. He's still Dowd's assistant, isn't he? Just let me know the way things look. Then when I put the word out in the next couple of days that I'm taking on a few doormen you come along for the interview. If you don't turn up – well I'll know, won't I? It'll be like clinking glasses and saying cheers. Fair enough?'

'Fair enough.'

As Sadie walked past, Crawford reached for her wrist, lifted her hand and kissed it. She smiled beyond him at Carrow. 'Darling, you can put someone on here in about ten minutes, but before you go, do me a favour and pop behind the bar for a couple of bottles, for me and my friend Craig here, will you love?'

Both men watched Sadie crouch down and collect the bottles. Placing them on the counter, she looked at Carrow. 'Would you like the top off?'

'Not immediately.'

'Just let me know when you're ready.'

'Get out of here you shameless hussy,' Crawford laughed.

'Yes, sir. Whatever you say.'

They watched Tania going through her routine on the pole. Darren came over and opened the bar. Soon there were several other men around them. 'I'm going to have a word with Kieran, find out why he's on that bloody phone all the time. Darren, look after him.'

When Tania finished to loud cheers, Sadie came back on stage for a bit of banter with the crowd. She mentioned a couple of stag nights that were in, built up the next session of three girls dancing together, and told the men to treat all the girls with respect.

This is all right, Carrow was thinking. He felt relaxed now. This world. Girls. Money. Perhaps he could be part of it. For a while anyway. Despite the effect the booze was having, there was still a voice somewhere telling him to be careful, going on about a line he shouldn't cross. But another couple of swallows of Prague Blonde and he could hardly hear it at all.

Crawford returned. 'He's going to be out the door if he's not careful,' he muttered.

'Who?'

'The fucking Irishman. Kieran. Please boss, can I have a few hours? Got to rush off. These last few weeks he's been all over the place. It's some bloody woman he's taken up with.'

Carrow pushed the thoughts away. He was starting to feel pissed. 'Listen, boss.' Crawford noticed the word. 'I know this may be a bit awkward now that Kieran's done a runner for a bit, but you know what you said about letting Sadie off early?'

39

Carrow heard only the television as he padded down the stairs and opened the kitchen door. Sadie, in a pink towelling robe, her red hair tied up on her head, was at the counter filling lunch boxes. Three children seated at the counter looked towards him. There was a moment when everyone was still, taking things in. Another one with a thing for black men, Carrow thought. 'Morning all.'

The two girls at the table looked at each other. 'Told you,' one said to the other. 'Told you she'd got someone back. I heard them.'

The boy rose from his seat pushing his cereal bowl across the table. 'Mom!' he wailed. 'You said. You promised you weren't going to be a slag no more.'

'Shurrup, Marley. This man's a friend from work.' She looked over to Carrow. 'Do one for a minute, will you?' As she moved across to her son, Carrow noticed the television screen. The Mendy. A police car outside Walton Tower. 'That's where I live,' he told them. 'On the Mendy. What's happened?'

'They found a baby. Dead,' one of girls said. 'Dumped in a bin. It's been on twice already.'

'Mom you said—'

'Okay, Marley.' Sadie tried to take the boy in her arms but

he squirmed away from her. 'Carra, give us a few minutes, will you? I'll bring you a drink up. My friend's taking them to school for me. They'll be gone in ten minutes.'

'I'm not going to school,' Marley yelled, jumping away from his mother. He grabbed his cereal bowl from the table and flung it towards Carrow in the doorway.

'Marley!'

What we are most concerned about is the mother. She is probably in need –

'He's going to be a right little bastard now, Mom.'

'Shurrit you.'

'Leave him alone, Chloe. Marley—' Sadie crouched down to her son. 'Look at me.'

Carrow turned and went back upstairs.

The water wasn't hot enough. What he needed now was it steaming hot. So hot it burnt. He wanted to wash everything away and he could only do that if the water was so hot it hurt. Instead he just soaped and soaped, kicking the sudsy liquid towards the drain.

A terrible feeling had overtaken him. Dirtiness. Disappointment. He was sliding into a situation he wouldn't be able to get out of. All this craziness over Ruthie Slayte and now he was here shagging some kids' mother. Two voices in his head.

One saying: Why are you getting so stressed up, mate? It's okay. You're a young bloke on the make. That's what you are, that's what you do. An opportunity comes along and you take it. Like all blokes do.

But there was the other voice: is this who you really want to be?

He couldn't see his old mate Jack Stevens ending up in this situation.

It was a good night, he told himself. She was happy. You were happy. Nobody got hurt.

There was a shadow behind the shower curtain, and the girl from last night was back. 'Brought you a drink.' She put a mug of coffee in the washbasin. Turned to Carrow. 'I'd planned for us to do that together. I was looking forward to soaping you down. The kids will be gone in a few minutes. I'll get you something to eat, then I'll just have to see if I can get you dirty again.' She let the curtain drop.

The gym makes everything better. Carrow set ten kilometres as his target and programmed it into the running machine. Kill or cure. He hit Start at 13k: a steady pace. Finley Quaye was playing. For five minutes Carrow held the rhythm of the run. It wasn't hard. Finley played his part, warbling away nicely over his reggae rhythms, a place for Carrow to latch on to. It's always the mind with exercise. You've got to find a place to park the mind. Finley was doing the trick. Those old mellow notes. He would stay with those, then at five kilometres up the speed to 16k – just for two kilometres, then he'd come down a bit. And it was good. Going fast. Going. His body working: all of it, racing, pumping away. A fierce synchronicity. Straining away on the machine. Sweat draining everything out of him. Every unclean thing. His breathing. His heartbeat. That's all there was now. He couldn't hear Finley any more. It was just the sound of himself. Heart. Blood. Lungs. Feet slapping into the rubber track of the treadmill. But then the thoughts arrived. Signing up with Crawford and what that would mean. Ruthie Slayte. He tried to stop thinking – just run, run. Three little kids round a breakfast table. A baby dumped in dustbins on the Mendy because some poor kid couldn't cope. The place had been full of coppers when he had gone back to Toga's for his kit. And more TV vans than there had been in Essex Street last night. Eight kilometres. Perhaps he should let Jack know about Crawford. That his mob was definitely not in on it. Then they could concentrate on the Chinese. Last night he was only able to give a statement about his job at the club. Like all the others. Then just a quick hello with Jack – we must meet up stuff. There hadn't been the opportunity to say anything else. Could he be sure Crawford wasn't involved? He'd give Jack a ring, see if – but the pain was too much. His chest was blinding him. His teeth hurt. His *teeth* hurt. All of them. Every one. He took the deepest pull of air, another gasp, but no, he couldn't. His fist banged down to reduce his speed. 16, 15 flashed past. Stay at 14. Try 14. But his fist didn't move. 13, 12. He pulled it away. You can't go lower than 12. Just for a minute. No. No lower than 12. There was air in his lungs. Eight point eight kilometres. Not much more to go. He took the incline down to 3. He'd stay at 12 until the ten, and then see if he could blast out a further kilometre. Finley was back. So for now. Just listen to Finley.

Weren't you looking the other way when they took the kid?
    Crawford's words from last night were back in Carrow's head. He had fallen asleep after the gym and dreamed of Magnus. A dream he had had many times before.
    But the general impression – over here anyway – was that you were on the payroll somewhere.
    It was where the Dutch police had started from of course. Hours and hours of questioning. Techniques he knew. Sympathetic. Comforting. Then hostile. Downright aggressive. Direct accusations that he was involved.

He knew what they were doing and he knew that they had to do it. He was clean: he had nothing to do with the kidnap. But was he guilty in another way?

He had relived every second of the attack, time and again, but couldn't see how he could have done anything more to protect Magnus. He was sure he couldn't have reacted more quickly – they were armed. A little braver then? But that was stupid – he could have done nothing dead.

The thing was, the subject of them being armed had come up in discussion during one of Martin Okker's regular meetings with his security team. Marjie's cousin who had firearms experience from his army days was in favour. Train all the team and apply for a civil licence as armed guards. Carrow had argued against it. It just wasn't necessary; it was over the top. There had never been any threat made against the Okker family and, if they should suddenly find themselves confronted by someone armed, the last thing they needed was to be in the middle of a gunfight. And the police knew all about the discussion. Why had he not wanted the team armed, they asked. So he repeated to them the view he had expressed. And repeated. And repeated.

He knew that the police believed him a long time before he was officially cleared from the investigation. He knew Martin Okker was sincere when he told him he didn't hold him responsible, that he hoped they would remain friends, that he was welcome to pay a visit any time.

Carrow rose from the settee. He needed a shave. He was having a drink with Jack Stevens tonight and didn't want to turn up looking like a criminal. But the thoughts were still with him as he stared at his lathered face in the bathroom mirror, as he dragged the razor across it.

He had never answered Martin Okker's letter. He had

wanted to but hadn't known what to say. He had thought of sending a Christmas card from Jamaica but hadn't. He had watched his mother die in Jamaica and wondered if all the worry of his troubles in Holland had played a part in her poor health. Can disappointment give you cancer?

Back in Birmingham he told himself that *this* was where he belonged. Rub everything out. Start again. But he could not shake the feeling that there was no way left to redeem himself.

40

Carrow hadn't told his dream to anyone before but he told it to Jack Stevens.

'I'm in some bushes, hiding from someone. I never know who. I'm watching boots wading through a marsh. Squelching through. Muddy water. Reeds. I'm just watching. Getting more and more scared. Then I see a hand. Gloved. And I know it's a copper's glove. Then the other hand. The hands start to part the reeds and I know what's coming: there's the kid, curled up in the dirty water. But I only see him for a second. Just get a glimpse. Then it's his mother, Marjie. She's screaming her head off and she's so close to me I can see inside her mouth. Course, that's when I wake up. Sweating. Like I've done a run. That scream. It always wakes me up. Bang awake.'

Carrow lifted his pint and took a gulp. The Country Girl, next to Selly Oak Hospital, wasn't as busy tonight as Carrow remembered it. When he and Jack had shared a flat together they came here a lot. It had always seemed to be packed with nurses just off shift from the hospital. 'No uniforms in for you tonight,' Jack had said, when Carrow arrived earlier.

This had started them off on an hour of reminiscences about working together on the force and sharing a flat together. Jack's career had traced a steadier trajectory than Carrow's.

Inevitably the story of the time Carrow got his squad car nicked on the Mendy came up. 'It still gets told, that story,' Jack told him. 'It's a legend. If you came back on the force, you'd have to change your name. Or as soon as you said it, it'd be, Carra? You're not the bloke got his car nicked?'

Carrow changed the subject. 'So, where are you with the case? The Norway.' Up until now everything had been personal – catching up, remembering old times. Funny stories. Carrow had laughed more than he had in a long time.

'Everything points to a gangland killing.'

'Turf war.'

'In a way. But it may not be quite as straightforward as that. There are two witnesses, daytime colleagues of yours from the club who saw enough of the gunman to be a hundred per cent certain that he was Chinese. We don't think that happened by accident. Nowhere near CCTV and just enough to show ethnicity. Nothing else in their descriptions is particularly helpful.'

'Could be a decoy.'

'Sure. Someone wants us to believe that it's the Dragons who are responsible – they're the only Chinese outfit of any importance operating in the city now. The gunman is yellow so we go after the Dragons. But equally, it may in fact be the Dragons. And rumour has it there was a security team in —' Jack looked at Carrow.

'Yes,' Carrow nodded. 'Mostly at night, but there was usually a bloke around in the day when staff were in.'

'Armed?'

Carrow smiled at his friend. 'Rumour has it.'

'Well rumour has it that the security cleared off half an hour before the gunman arrived. Those we've interviewed say that one minute he was there, then, when the action kicked off, nowhere to be seen.'

'A better offer?'

'The Dragons want the Norway. That's established. Stretton won't play. More than that he fights back. He gets the club tooled up with East Europeans. So, the Dragons can't have the club. But they can have him. And in so doing stop anyone else having it and—'

'Send out a powerful message that if you ever receive an offer from the Dragons, it's best to accept, because they can always top your security budget.'

'Exactly. The old Corleone message.'

The two men said it together: 'I'm gonna make you an offer you can't refuse.'

'And the decoy theory. Who would set that up?' asked Carrow.

'Crawford is the obvious suspect. It's common knowledge that he was interested in the club. Very different dealing with him though. Just as corrupt, but different tricks. He rang Dowd. First thing this morning. Crawford says he's heard Dowd's on the case. That he knows his name will come into the frame because Kingston Trading – that's the name of what he describes as his development company – has shown an interest in *acquiring* the Norway. Then he gives Dowd the usual stuff: all strictly legit business practices, how shocked he is at what has happened, abhors that sort of stuff. Would we like to go over and have a chat with him? – and his legal team, of course – he's happy to grant us access to all records, happy to assist in any way possible.'

'That sounds like Crawford. Eager to see justice is done.'

'And obviously everyone we get to talk to will have a rock solid alibi. As will all the Dragons' men.'

Carrow liked the way this was going. Like the old days, back at the flat when he and Jack would sit at night and chew the fat about cases they were involved in. 'Too early for the forensics to have come through, I suppose?'

Now Jack hesitated. Then, 'It was a very clean job. Two shots. One in each target. Just two shots fired. Both bullets retrieved.'

'Gun at the bottom of a canal by now.'

'A certainty. There's no way the bullets will have come from a gun with form, not if either the Dragons or Crawford's mob are involved. Far too professional.'

Carrow lifted his empty glass, pointed to Jack's, still a quarter full. 'Same again?'

'Go on then. Three. That's quite a lot for me these days.'

'It always was, mate.'

As he waited at the bar Carrow looked back at his friend. Jack was obviously doing well. The immaculate navy blue suit. Quality white shirt. Silk tie. Maroon. Carrow watched him take his phone from his jacket pocket to check his messages. He hadn't seen Jack since he got the Holland job, but he was enjoying tonight. It was like the old times, talking through a case with him. Except now they were working on different sides of the line. While Jack was climbing the ladder Carrow had fallen off. And he wasn't sure how he was going to pick himself up again.

Listen boss – his words to Crawford last night. Didn't they mean he had made his choice? That's what Crawford had thought.

There was a young woman waiting behind Carrow at the bar. He let her go first. Not out of chivalry, or any attempt to impress – no, he wanted a moment. A moment to consider how far he should go with Jack. Should he come clean? Tell him about his dealings with Crawford? All the bits and pieces he knew about Stretton, the Bulgarians. Could he come up from the murky waters he had been swimming in, take a gulp of clean air and clear out all the filth?

Jack had almost finished his pint of lager while Carrow's glass was still full. Carrow had talked, Jack had listened.

'So you see the position I've got myself into. On the verge of joining the mob. Or as close as it gets.'

'So is this why we're here, me and you? What was it you said in your text? Let's catch up. We've left it too long. Old mates. We should get together again.'

'You sound pissed with me.'

'I think I probably am. Yes. All this stuff about the Norway, not that any of it is confidential – it's all out there for the press. Was that collecting stuff for Crawford, for the boss?'

This was Jack at work. The tone. The way he was sitting now. This was interview room stuff.

'Do you think I would have gone into all those details if it was? This *is* about being mates. I'm telling you where I am. As a mate. Trying to make sense of it for myself.'

'Well it doesn't make much sense to me. It doesn't sound like you're in a good place, Carra. Think about what you are doing. You become part of Crawford's outfit and where does that take you? You know the story, mate.'

It was good for Carrow to hear that word *mate* tucked in there; a touch of reassurance.

'Okay,' Jack continued. 'There's the money. Some good times, no doubt. A buzz. Plenty of women if you're around the clubs. But not many come out with a pension plan. A few years down the line you end up doing a long stretch, or like Stretton with a bullet in your brain, or just a sad old has-been hanging around the gangs doing the jobs no one else wants.' There was a stridency to Jack's tone now that didn't seem too far away from anger. 'I suppose it's possible that you might end up in Jamaica running legit businesses for Crawford but – No, even as I say that, I can't believe it. It doesn't work like that with those blokes. They made their choice about which side of the line they're on a long time ago, and they stay there. You join him and that's where you'll be.'

He paused as if waiting for Carrow to argue with him, deny what he said. 'You had the makings of a good copper. You were decent, probably still are. You put the business of the nicked patrol car behind you. It's more a funny story now than anything. You did good work after that. You left for another job, one a lot of people envied. It turned into a tragedy. But you came out of that clean. I reckon you could come back if you wanted. Dowd would put a word in, so would I.

'Look Carra, you know this already, but I'll say it anyway. The other side of the line is attractive. Good fun, easy money. But in the end it's always about corruption, hurting people, taking things away from people. And being the sort of person who can do that.'

He stopped abruptly. Took a breath. Lifted his glass. Finished his lager. 'I've got to get back. I want to see the *Ten O'Clock News*. Dowd did a piece to camera. It might not make the national, but it'll be a definite for the *Midlands News*.'

Carrow finished as much of his pint as he wanted and pushed the glass away. 'It's been good tonight, Jack. The things you've said—'

'Why don't you come back? Watch it with me.'

'The old flat?'

'Much the same, cleaner and tidier though than when you were there. There may even be a couple of lagers in the fridge.'

'They're probably mine.'

'Could well be.'

They went back together. It made the national bulletin but only as a small item. The angle was simple – local police investigating a double shooting in Birmingham's clubland. The interview with Dowd wasn't used. A glimpse of the staff waiting outside Pinks the previous evening, but Carrow couldn't spot himself. Then there was footage taken this morning: Jack and Dowd in Essex Street, some of Mrs Stretton and her daughters laying flowers on the steps of the Norway.

'Dowd wants her to do a press conference,' Jack said, 'but she's not up for it. He says he'll give it a couple of days to see how things go, then try her again if necessary.'

The local Midlands news that followed led with the story and used the interview with Dowd. 'The brutal shooting of Keith Stretton and Trudy Loop in their place of work is a truly terrible act,' he started. 'Cold. Calculated. Shocking in the extreme. It strikes at the heart of our community.'

'He didn't waste any time,' Jack continued. 'Every PR directive that comes in now states: *stress community; refer to community values.*'

'I want to assure the people of Birmingham, however, that West Midlands Police are pursuing our investigation of this brutal crime with all the urgency, vigour and professionalism that they have come to expect from us.'

'Nice one, Sean. They'll like that upstairs.'

The interviewer asked about the possibility of links with organised crime in the city. As Dowd explained that organised crime was a problem in all big cities, Birmingham no exception, and that all possibilities were being investigated, the screen was filled with a close-up of the blue lamp above the Norway Room before the camera pulled back to show the whole of Essex Street. As the reporter explained that Mr Stretton had left a wife and two daughters, the screen showed them outside the club, placing their flowers on the steps. The shot went into close-up and Carrow knew immediately that he recognised Mrs Stretton from somewhere, grey hair pulled back, into a bun, he was sure he knew that face, had seen her before. A second later he got it – the coat.

41

It was nearly one o'clock when Carrow drove out of the Mendy, three hours since his last drink. He might still be over the limit. But he had to drive. A cab was no good for this.

He cut through Selly Oak. His finger caught the wiper rod and he jumped as the wipers sprang into action. There was a police car outside the hospital. Carrow held his breath as he drove past.

Across the Bristol Road into Harborne and then into Bearwood's dark and silent streets. He was surprised to see a light on in Ruthie's flat. He had expected it to be dark, her in bed now, if she was there at all.

There were half a dozen flats in the old house. Ruthie's was number three, on the first floor. He pressed the buzzer. Held it. He had imagined he would have to ring several times to rouse her from sleep. But the intercom came to life immediately. 'Yes? Who is it?'

And with that the situation seemed completely absurd. He was acting on a hunch – at one in the morning. Pretending to be a copper again. DI Carrow.

'It's Carra,' he said.

'Carra? From the Norway Room?'

'There's only one.'

'Well, he can fuck off.'

'Ruthie! Ruthie?' But she was gone. He back-stepped to see her window. The curtains didn't move. Just panels of yellow light. This was the moment to go. Jack should be doing this, not him. He could call him in the morning – tell him what he knew. But he rang again. Nothing. And again, holding the button for longer this time.

'I told you to go away.'

'You didn't put it quite like that. Ruthie, I want to talk to you.'

'Tough. I don't want to talk to you.'

'Ruthie. You are in a lot of trouble, and I want to help you.'

'I'm not in any trouble.'

'Oh yes you are. You and lover boy Kieran Walsh. And your new best mate Mrs Stretton. All three of you will be up on a double murder charge before morning. If you don't talk to me, squad cars will be here in minutes. I might be able to help you.'

The moment of truth. If he had got it all wrong, she would tell him to fuck off again, tell him she was getting on to the police herself. But she said none of those things. She said nothing. Until, as he heard the buzz of the lock releasing, 'Come up.'

She was wearing an ivory-coloured robe. Her hair was up. A comb plugged into it. Wisps fell loose on to her face. And all he wanted to do was take her in his arms. And the clever girl knew. She knew and there were tears in her eyes.

In the short time it had taken him to mount the stairs she had prepared a strategy.

'You've really scared me Carra. What's all this about?'

'Where's Kieran?'

'Not here. I don't know.'

Carrow wished he could develop a strategy as quickly. 'You don't mind if I do?' And he sat down on the sofa.

She sat beside him. 'So are you going to tell me why you are here? Seriously. Or is this all part of some kinky fantasy to get me into bed. Are you going to put me in handcuffs?'

'I'm not a copper.'

'Old habits die hard.' She held up her wrists and giggled.

So this was her plan. And it meant he had got it right. About Mrs Stretton. The fur coat. Kieran Walsh. If he wasn't right, she wouldn't be resorting to tricks like this. He pushed the wrists gently away. Resisting made things easier. 'Kieran's involved in the shooting of my boss at the Norway.'

'What? Has he been murdered?'

And now it was easy. For the performance had turned to ham. Ruthie could do sex, seduction, but not much else. Certainly not innocent surprise.

'Him, and his PA. Both shot through the head.' There was an attempt at a reaction, shock, horror, but it was still ham. 'Kieran didn't do it himself, of course; he got some Chinese to do the dirty work. A mate. A partner. Or just a hire. But nicely throwing the scent towards the Dragons.'

'The Dragons?'

'You know who they are, Ruthie. And the sooner you level with me the better.' She edged away from him on the sofa.

'I don't. I don't know what you're talking about.' She was crying. 'Even if Kieran is involved in something, it's got nothing to do with me. I'm not even seeing him any more.'

'Ruthie. The game's up. You helped him. Made the link with Mrs Stretton. I saw you with her. Going into the Gables. I've seen you with her and Kieran. Together. I saw her again tonight. On the news. Wearing that expensive fur coat of hers. Mink, would it be?'

Now the acting stopped. She was listening to him.

'Kieran is setting up on his own in opposition to Crawford, isn't he? And his first move is the Norway Room. Linton and the Dobermans are involved, financial investment I guess – and you're the link, Ruthie. The Miss Fix It.'

'I don't know what you're talking about, Carra. Honestly I don't.'

'Stretton won't sell the Norway Room. But his wife will – if she gets the chance. And she'll get that if she becomes his widow. If his fancy piece goes with him so much the better. Kieran gets rid of them, and in exchange she sells to him at a reduced rate.

'He's not daft is he, your mate Kieran? Whatever Mrs Stretton thinks she is going to get for the Norway, she's involved and so will have to sell at his price. And with that Kieran has set up on his own. Your old pals the Dobermans have been trying to get a foothold in the club scene here for a while now I believe, and so I guess you've been able to arrange a little financial investment for Kieran from them; a little bit of funding to help the boy get going.

'You've been a busy girl, haven't you, Ruthie? Crawford, me, the Bulgarians – you negotiated their withdrawal from Stretton's job, I saw you talking to one of them in the club that night you disappeared without saying goodbye – which sounds a bit like accessory to murder to me. And you a member of the caring professions. And you were looking after Kieran and the Dobermans of which your boyfriend, Howie, if I recall correctly, is a long-time member. He'll be out soon and your pay-off should set you and Howie up nicely. Mind if I smoke?'

'I'll have one with you.'

When the cigarettes were lit Ruthie was ready to play her hand. 'If any of this was right? Any of this guesswork?

Because that's all it is, Carra, as you said yourself, guesswork. Hunches. There is no hard evidence for any of it. But, if any of it *was* right – you said you had come to help me. How could you do that?'

This was it. The tipping point they called it. Carrow recalled interview rooms. Hours of denial. Then the tipping point. The recognition they were sussed – the case would stand up. The moment someone says, *Let's switch the tape off for a moment shall we? Take a break*. The time for negotiation.

'I know the men on the case, Ruthie. You turn witness and I'm sure they'll be able to help you out.'

'Are you? How sure?'

'Look Ruthie. It's done. I know. They know. It's just a matter of proving it. Easier if you testify. Mrs Stretton will get cold feet and break down, especially if they give her the chance to ditch the blame. Which they will. And it'll be too late to save yourself then. What the police want are the blokes who did it. Kieran and his Chinese friend. They get them, the case is cleared. That's all they care about.'

She turned and brought her legs up, not as he momentarily thought might be the case, to knee him in the crotch, but merely to close up. Get closer. A feeling of intimacy. She was at it again.

'Look. There is no way I'm going to implicate Linton, the Dobermans. And I don't want to bring Mrs Stretton into it. Her mother's a resident at the Gables, a lovely old lady, that's how I got to know her.'

'And Kieran Walsh. His mom in there too? Is that how you got involved with him?

'Kieran's fancied me for a long time. I went out with his boss, Crawford, a few times. He had a bit of a thing for me. Especially when he knew about Howie, the Dobermans. He collects information like clubs. Like women. He wanted me to find out everything they were up to. He didn't like me leaving him. He's not used to that. Almost stalked me for a time. Sending messages. Phoning. And for Kieran I was a bit of a trophy. He'd got what his boss hadn't.'

'Ruthie. Oh Ruthie.'

'Look Carra, if I told your friends, and then told the jury,' she added with a coy smile, 'just this, and no more, that I had a fling with Kieran, and that through him I knew that he planned to see Stretton off? Except that I never imagined he would *really* do it, or I would have gone to the police. All talk, I thought. I was devastated when I heard about the murders. I can give them info on his partner. Feiyang's his name. He runs a takeaway on the Mendy, the Bamboo Garden. I'll say I had heard them talk of getting in before anyone else and leave it at that. I won't bring up the Dobermans, Crawford, or those other people – what did you say they were called?'

Carrow ignored her question. He was thinking about the guilty people who would go free. Including Ruthie.

'Very good,' he said eventually. 'I think Inspector Dowd might be happy with that. Yes, I think everyone will be very happy with that.'

'Except Kieran. And Feiyang.'

'Well, you can't please everybody. Shall I give my friends a call?'

ASHLEY

42

Ashley was sitting on the bathroom floor. Kieran stood over him, listening.

'I was scared shitless, Kieran. I had no phone, no money. Nothing. I knew I was in trouble. Big trouble. With you and Crawford. What was I supposed to do? I didn't stand a chance against those Paki kids. There were too many of them.'

The Chinese bloke, Feiyang, had Geezbo in the corridor. Geezbo had walked straight through the door into them. There had been nothing Ashley could do to warn him. Now Ashley could hear Feiyang on the phone, talking Chinese.

The right side of Ashley's face was numb where Kieran had belted him. He dabbed at it to assess the swelling. He had been expecting his eye to close up, his sight to become restricted and watery. He hated that, but so far it hadn't happened. Perhaps he'd get away with it.

'So this gaff's Linton's is it?'

'The Dobermans'.'

'He is the Dobermans. And your retarded mate looks after it for them?'

'He's not retarded.'

'He will be when I've finished with him. Tonight's the first time you've been here?'

'Yeah. I'd got nowhere else to go, had I?'

'And what have you heard from next door?'

'Nothing. I told you.'

'Stay there,' Kieran barked.

'I've got no fucking choice have I?'

Ashley was beginning to think things might be all right. Okay, Kieran had belted him a bit. A kick or two. But he had to expect that – in the circumstances. He hadn't really beaten him up. Or worse. They'd both got guns, Kieran and Feiyang. If they were going to take him out they would have done it straight away. Wouldn't they?

Ashley could hear Geezbo yelling. He was getting a beating now. When the door opened again, Feiyang pushed him into the bathroom with Ashley. There was blood on his face. He sat beside Ashley panting. Ashley waited. Geezbo was taking deep breaths. Then he was up on his knees over the toilet bowl throwing up.

Kieran pushed his head round the door. 'D'you think we should tie them up?' he called to Feiyang.

'There's no point. We can't go anywhere. I've got nowhere to go anyway. You've got guns.'

'And we'd have one more if you weren't such a spastic pratt. Wait here quietly.'

Geezbo rose from the toilet. Pulled the back of his hand across his mouth. 'Man, dem goin' be big trouble when Linton learns 'bout dis. Big trouble, man. For evey body.' Ashley liked the way Geezbo spoke. His attitude. He wasn't giving in. Didn't seem scared.

'Don't you worry about Linton, nutterboy. Linton's in with

us. So there'll be no problems – so long as you two behave. Now sit down, and stay here.'

He pulled the door as far as the wires.

Ashley was reassured again. He knew Kieran. That tone. He'd given them a bit of a belting; that was as bad as it was going to get, he was sure of it. Geezbo bent over the bath and rinsed his mouth out then crouched down beside Ashley.

'Push over. Make room.'

'There ain't no room.' The two boys were crammed together beside the bath.

'They got t'Chinaman's wife. In next door. Like a hostage man. That's why they're 'ere. They both 'oldin', man. So they must be 'oldin nex' door too innit. I 'ere im threatin' on de phone. We comin' in. Stansta reason tey holdin' next door or tey jus' go in an blow 'em away.'

Ashley tried to rub his knee that had started to throb. A little blood was oozing from Geezbo's nose. 'Your nose is bleeding.'

Geezbo reached into the pocket of his jacket for a hand-kerchief. 'Not enough room to blow my nose,' he complained.

Voices were raised in the corridor. A yell. A cry. Shocking. Like an animal's howl. It brought both boys to their feet. Geezbo pulled back the door and they edged into the hall.

The curtain was drawn back and in the open doorway stood another Chinese man, older than Kieran and Feiyang, bald, not tall but powerfully built, suited. He wasn't from the Bamboo Garden, Ashley was sure of it. He looked calm despite Kieran's and Feiyang's guns. Kieran held Feiyang around the chest, restraining him, trying to stop him from taking aim. Feiyang struggled to break free, his gun waving about. But the man in the suit never moved. He just watched Feiyang's gun as it swerved and waved. Kieran squeezed Feiyang's chest, shook him. 'Drop it.' Kieran's gun caught

Feiyang's ear. Feiyang held on to his own gun. Ashley held his breath, and saw again for a moment that same gun – he knew it was – resting against Benjy Graham's lips.

The man in the suit remained cool.

'Drop it. Drop the fucking thing,' Kieran bawled. Right into Feiyang's ear. The gun fell from Feiyang's grasp. To the floor. But the bald man didn't go for it as Ashley expected. He's not scared at all, Ashley thought. Supercool. Kieran nudged the gun away with his foot.

'Now calm down a bit,' Kieran told Feiyang. Like a whisper. Tight in his ear. 'Okay? Just keep calm.' Feiyang's head dropped, defeated.

'It is the way.' The man in the suit was talking to Kieran. 'The Dragons' Way. He knows this better than you do. Honour. Revenge. What did you expect? You kill the people we are doing business with. What did you expect? The girl is gone now. It is over.'

'Siyu!' Feiyang's head flew up. Kieran held him as he attempted another lurch at the bald man, who didn't flinch.

'It had to be, Feiyang. You know our history. The Emperor Bang. It is only because we are family that I leave you standing.' He made to leave. Then turned back to Kieran. 'It is not necessary for you to do anything. We will clear everything up. It will be as if nothing happened. No one was ever there. We will talk again – you and I. Another day. Now take him away.'

The man pulled the door behind him as he left. 'Take deep breaths,' Kieran told Feiyang. 'Don't go crazy.'

Feiyang's chest continued to heave. But he was no longer trying to break free of Kieran. In fact it seemed now as if he was leaning against him. 'They killed her.'

'Try to stay calm. There'll be time later. We have to think this out. Okay? Carefully. The whole situation.' He relaxed his hold a little, testing. 'Okay?' Feiyang nodded. Kieran let go. Feiyang did nothing. Kieran spotted the two boys peering from the doorway. 'Get back in there.' He pulled the blackout curtain across and as he did so Geezbo dived. Kieran turned at the sound. But he turned from the shoulder. Geezbo was at his feet. Going for Feiyang's gun. Ashley saw Feiyang move to grab Geezbo. He saw Kieran look from Geezbo to Feiyang. Kieran was looking at him when the gun went off and Feiyang fell to the ground. Geezbo yelled. Kieran raised his gun. But not quick enough. Geezbo fired.

'Between the eyes,' he screamed with glee, 'between the fuckin' eyes.'

He rose and moved backwards towards Ashley. Panting. And sweating. Ashley could see Geezbo's face was wringing wet. He touched his own. Damp, but not wet like Geezbo's. The two boys stood together in the cramped hallway. The buzz of the electrical wiring behind them as loud as gathering flies. They stared down at the two dead men before them.

'Yus uncle ova, man.'

'Let's get out of here,' Ashley said.

'Come on.' But the dead men were blocking the way. Kieran's head had fallen on to Feiyang's foot and so was raised as if he were lifting it to look around, as if to say, *What the fuck was that? What happened?*

'They're in the way.'

'Jus' step ova dem, man. Tey not gonna do nuttin.'

Neither boy moved, but the curtain behind Feiyang did. A quick whisk and the Chinese bloke was back, gun in his hand. Geezbo still held Feiyang's gun, and though he raised it slightly, it was only for a second, instinctive. He was offering no resistance.

*

Ashley thought he was going to be shot, and he cried even as he did as he was told. Shot in the shower, so that the water drains away the blood. He'd seen that in films. It was probably quite common. Geezbo followed instructions too and removed his shorts. 'You gonna execute uz, man?' His attitude, if not defiant, at least appeared unconcerned.

'Just take your clothes off.'

Ashley supposed this was bravery Geezbo was displaying. There had been an urge in Ashley to beg the Chinese not to hurt him. To explain to them that it was Geezbo, not him, who had done the shooting. And he was surprised that he was able to overcome this urge, although he knew that if he were taken into a room without Geezbo he would probably lose his courage.

There were just the two Chinese men with them now in this flat next door to the Dobermans' cannabis farm. One was the bald man who had been arguing with Kieran and Feiyang, the other a younger man, also smartly suited.

'I knows you,' Geezbo told the bald man. 'I seed you before. Comin' and goin'.' Ashley thought this was probably an unwise thing to say. It could make things worse for them.

When they had been brought into the flat there had been a lot of talking in Chinese. Several other men had arrived. All Chinese. There was a lot of activity at the window. Men looking out. Checking what was happening below. Instructions, it seemed, being given over the phone. The bald man waving to someone. Geezbo asked if they were going to be thrown. 'Are we for the drop?' he had said. No one had responded.

'Put your clothes in here,' the younger man said. He held a bin liner. 'We're going to burn everything.'

Once showered they were taken to a bedroom. 'Now, sit on there.' The bald man nodded to a blue futon. The younger added, 'Keep quiet and you will be all right.'

There was always someone in the room with them. But no one paid them too much attention. Eventually they were given a blanket each, some bottles of pop.

When the men lit cigarettes they gave one to each boy. This gave Ashley confidence. If they were going to kill them they would have done it by now. Wouldn't they? Course they would.

Then they were questioned. By the older man. The other standing beside him. Like coppers in a way. Except coppers won't let you smoke when you're underage. They asked about the cannabis flat next door, who ran it, and Geezbo answered truthfully as far as Ashley could tell. It was obvious they knew all about the Dobermans. When the man asked if they knew the Englishman, Ashley said he did. A friend of his dad's. Who worked for Crawford. Then he explained that in fact he wasn't really English but Irish, having come over here as a child.

They called another man to watch over the boys and left. Others came and went from the room. Sometimes their guard changed. If they tried to speak to each other they were told to shut up. Eventually Geezbo fell asleep and then Ashley too, but fitfully and for a shorter time.

The next morning they were given some sandwiches. All Day Breakfast with a Twix bar and a can of Coke each. Later they were given cheeseburgers and another Twix.

Then with dusk came the fear again for Ashley. How long were they going to be kept here? The longer they were kept the worse it was likely to be. That's what they say, isn't it? The fear went when someone arrived with a bin bag of clothes. T-shirts, jeans and trainers. The trainers were good ones. They wouldn't be doing this if they were going to kill them. Geezbo complained when he was given jeans. 'I pride in my appearance, man. I wear shorts. Always. Not this stuff. Nor there ain't no 'oodies 'ere either. I always wears 'oodies.'

The shaven-headed man told him he would be thrown out of the window if he didn't put the clothes on. Geezbo put them on. For the first time in what seemed like forever Ashley found himself laughing – at the new Geezbo, in his jeans and T-shirt. Both too small for him.

'You dead when this is ova man,' Geezbo told him.

The fear returned when they started to take things out of the flat. The blue futon, pictures off the wall. Even a Buddha. They were put in separate rooms. But not for long. The younger man came for Ashley and took him to the main room where Geezbo was sitting on the floor. It was empty now but smelt of joss sticks. The window closed. 'Sit down.' There was nothing in the room to sit on so he sat on the floor beside Geezbo.

The bald man came in. Both men crouched before them. Ashley noticed the black fabric of the bald man's trousers stretch across his broad thighs. Geezbo would probably look a bit like him when he was older.

'You must listen very carefully. You have seen and done many things boys of your age should not see or do. You have stumbled into the world of men before your time, and tried to act like us. Some boys play stupid games on the railway. It is thrilling – but many get killed. Some are lucky. The train whisks by and they survive – by a hair's breadth as the English say. You are like those lucky boys. The train raced past and you have survived.

'Everything has been taken care of. It is our way. The Chinese way. One day you may wish to study our culture. It can only benefit you. But for now, listen carefully. All is over. It is as if it never happened. We will take you back now to this house you live in. Then – you clean your minds. Forget. Not the luckiest amongst us escapes the train twice. Live your lives. Better than before if you can. But if you want to keep them – forget everything. Do you understand?'

Ashley was shocked at the words he heard from Geezbo before he could say a thing.

'Yes, sir.'

43

What had he dreamed about? He must have dreamed about something; you have to, don't you? Ashley lifted his arm and looked at his watch. It was eight o'clock. There was sunshine outside his bedroom window at Cecil Road. He could see blue sky. It was weird. He had slept right through. Last night he didn't think he would sleep – probably never again, but he had and now he didn't know what he had dreamed about.

Downstairs Geezbo was still asleep on the settee. Curled up. His hands sandwiched between his knees. His shoulder rising and falling. Not snoring, but the sound of his breathing audible.

Ashley went through the kitchen to the bathroom and took a piss. Then he made a cup of tea. He buttered two Weetabix and piled jam on top. He would have liked a proper breakfast, a café fry-up, big and greasy with lots of tea, but this would do for now.

He sat on the upright chair beside the table to eat his Weetabix and drink his tea. He looked around. He had sat on this chair doing this lots of times. A thousand times. What happens now? he thought. Everything looked the same, but everything was different.

He wished Geezbo would wake up. But he didn't know what they would say to each other when he did, so he left him – just watched him sleeping. Last night when they got back he had been full of shit, as high as a kite. Talking all the time. About his nan's prophecy, about his relative who was hanged, about evil, about destiny. Then he'd left Ashley on his own while he went for some clothes. He wouldn't say where. Ashley thought he wouldn't come back. But he did. 'Weez in dis togetha, man. Destiny's made uz like bruvvas, innit. Destiny funny ting, man. Me an a puny white kid.'

Ashley knew he should try and get away from Geezbo – leave now before he woke. Fuck knows what was going to happen otherwise. This was the time to head for London. For Manchester. Anywhere. There were Weetabix crumbs in his lap. He brushed them away, remembering how St George used to pounce on any crumbs or bits of food he dropped. He remembered his dad. Sitting on this chair playing with the dog, rubbing her head. Telling him stories when he was little about dogs and pigeons, about winning races. St George was never even entered for a race although that was once the plan. His dad was all talk, that was the problem. That's probably why his mom went. But he wished he were here. Perhaps he would go and visit him soon. But without Kieran he didn't know. It would have been easier with him. And now he was filled with sadness. He liked Kieran. He was sorry he was gone. He *was* like an uncle – in a way.

Geezbo started to shake. His legs at first. His legs mainly. But then the rest of him. Shaking like mad. Ashley watched. Then Geezbo's head fell back, his mouth opened. It started as a yawn, but turned into a noise, like a cry. He opened his eyes. Looked around. The shaking stopped. He scratched his belly, then squirmed to a sitting position. 'Wha' you munchin' on?'

'Weetabix.'

Geezbo rose and made his way to the bathroom. Ashley heard him piss, then heard him washing, for ages.

'Why there no 'ot water, man?'

'You have to use the immersion.'

'I adta take a shower wiv cold water.'

'We had a shower yesterday.'

'I 'ave to wash away everythin', man. Cold water probably good for that. Little pain. Good ting.'

Geezbo insisted he was going back to the sixteenth floor of Nimrod House. 'Need to see if any damage done to the plants – 'fore I face Linton.' He had already told Ashley that he knew now more than ever that he wanted to be with the Dobermans – properly, a full member. He would have liked to be a Dragon. He knew that for certain when the Chinaman talked to them – 'He cool, man. Wise.

'But your race is your race, your colour your colour.' The Dobermans were his place in the world. And now he had experience. 'Tha' worf a truckload a shit man, that iz.'

'He told you he put everything back the way it was.'

'I needs to see. There waz a lota blood – bot' ya uncle an de utta guy. Dem Chinese boyz professionals, man. But I needs to see if dey left anytin', miss anytin'. Incriminatin', innit. I need to know Linton don't know I waz involved. If they clear away like they say, it puts me in the clear. An I wan' to see where it 'appen. One more time. Where I did the deed. Understand? It not been on the news nor nuttin. Like I neva did nuttin, man.'

'That's good.'

'Good and bad, man. Good and bad, innit.'

*

276

Ashley and Geezbo made their way down the Tallis Road to cut across the grass bank to Nimrod House.

'Now yus uncle gone, you can stay where you iz,' said Geezbo. 'And I can use it as one of my bases now weed linked.'

'We're not linked.'

'Oh yes an we are. We stick togevva, ord we swing togevva.'

They stopped. 'Shit! They've set us up.' On Nimrod car park there were three police cars, a television crew. 'Quick. Come on, Geez.'

''Old on, man. We don't know whaz goin' on.'

'We do. We've been set up. They never did what they said they would.'

'Stay cool, man. Look. Don't look like no scene of crime to me. Nuttin taped off. Jus a few cars. Probably jus' a bust. Come on, man. Stay cool.'

Ashley followed Geezbo, who had started to saunter in the exaggerated way he sometimes had. Ashley expected they would circle the cars, give them a wide berth, but Geezbo led him right through them. 'Ooze you bustin' today? Not my friends on the fourth floor izit? They ain't done nuttin'. I was widdem all de time. I tell de jury so innit.'

This made the police officer laugh. 'We're not busting anybody today. Unless maybe you if you get too cheeky. We're here for the soldier's funeral.'

Ashley waited outside in the corridor, smoking and drawing in the dirt on the window. He started his name and rubbed it out. Did a couple of question marks and rubbed them out. Then tried to form a question mark with the smoke he exhaled from his cigarette. But he still couldn't do it. He thought about how cool it would be if he could do writing. The word Sophie slowly taking form from the smoke he exhaled.

Geezbo was taking his time. Ashley couldn't go into the flat with him. He never wanted to go in there again. He didn't think he'd ever be able to smoke weed again. The smell would make him want to puke, just like the other night. He considered how calm Geezbo was, had been since the shooting. Even more confident than before. Ashley wondered if you could become addicted to killing. If it was like crack. Once you tried it you were hooked for life, that's what they say.

Geezbo came out of the flat and joined Ashley at the window. 'Deys did a good job, man. Respect. Big respect. I seed a few tings. Touches ony a expert eye would see, man. But can't see no blood. All de wiring still workin. No trays of dead plants. Evertin in order. We in de clear man. Big respect to em.'

He went to the door of the Chinese flat. Put his ear to it. Knocked, and the door swung open. Ashley followed Geezbo in. The flat was empty. The boys wandered round each empty room. 'Mus' be an old Chinese trick. Makin evertin disappear. Chinese magic.'

Mel looked smart in a black suit. 'I'm glad you've turned up love. Soph's not feeling so good. I'm not letting her go. She's pulling a face. But I've definitely said no. She'll be all right now she's got you to stay with her.' She led Ashley through to the lounge. 'Soph, your friend's here.'

'Where you been? Haven't seen you for ages.' Sophie was in her pyjamas, lying on the settee, a blanket covering her feet.

'A few days. Nowhere really. Are you all right?'

'She's just a bit off colour, love. I wouldn't leave her otherwise. But if I don't go to this funeral she will.'

'You only want to go because Gareth's on duty. You didn't even know Wesley.'

Ashley sat down on the floor beside Sophie. 'What you watching?'

'*Trisha*. Why aren't you going?'

'Forgot it was today.'

'You could still go.'

'No. I'll stay here with you.'

'You can watch it from the window. Both of you. It's coming right past.'

When Sharon arrived she was also dressed in black. There was a black band on her head from which three wands bearing small black butterflies waved. She bundled across the room to kiss Sophie on the top of her head. 'How's my princess? A little bit poorly woorly is we?' The butterflies wobbled above Sophie's face. 'I won't get too close. Just in case. Do you think you've got a cold?'

'I don't think so.' Mel answered for her. ' Just one of those days you get.'

'What do you think of my fascinator?' She shook her head and the butterflies went mad.

'A bit over the top,' Mel said. 'But nice.'

'Over the top!' She took her hand to her chest in mock shock. 'Moi?'

'Makes you look like Miss Piggy,' Sophie said.

'I keep forgetting I'm on the Mendy. Wouldn't recognise class up here if it crawled into your underpants.'

'We don't wear 'em up here, love.' Mel took her bag from the chair.

Ashley loved listening to this. He wished he could live here with Sophie and Mel. It would be magic to be able to stay here.

'Talking of crawling into one's underpants, has one heard from our young police officer recently?'

'She had a text half an hour ago,' Sophie answered for her mother.

'Are they supposed to do that on duty? Personal texts.'

'He's going to be at the crem. They think there's going to be some anti-war demonstrators. So there'll be a few of them there, just in case.'

'Anti-war demonstrators. How disgusting. At the poor boy's funeral. They won't need the cops if I see them. Come on. I want a fag before we go. But I'll have it outside. I don't want to encourage her.'

Sophie made him some dinner. Ashley said he would do it but she said she was fine. Spaghetti hoops on toast. The funeral was due to go past at half two, and while Sophie rested on the settee Ashley stood at the window watching. There were small groups of people, half a dozen or so, at various points along the road. A few more on Tallis Corner.

'Here it comes,' he told Sophie when he saw the undertaker turn into Walton Road, hat and cane held aloft, the hearse slowly following. Sophie joined Ashley at the window.

'Why does that bloke walk in front?' Sophie asked.

'It's what they do.'

As the first limousine appeared Ashley wondered if Karl's mom had stopped cursing the war. He tried to imagine Wesley, flat and stiff inside his coffin, in his uniform. And in that instant he saw Kieran again. Not dead like he'd last seen him, his broken head propped against Feiyang's boot, but Kieran sitting on the settee in Cecil Road texting, Kieran carrying a bin bag containing school uniform, listening to Green Day in the car, the Kieran who had said to him quietly: *Yeah. It's a gun, Ash*.

The people on the corner started to applaud as the hearse drew level with them. Two people stretched a union flag between them. Ashley tried to imagine Karl and his mom in the black limousine passing below, but he saw instead his dad in a prison cell, tried to stop a picture of his mom forming in his mind.

'You're crying, you mong.' Sophie was taking the piss. But not in a bad way, not mean. 'I knew you were soft.'

'I was thinking about my mom,' he said.

'Oh sorry.'

And what he wanted to do now was take Sophie's hand and tell her everything. *My mom's not properly dead. She left us, years ago. Never seen her since. So she might just as well be. Easier to think of it that way. But now. I thought I might try to find her. What do you reckon? Will you help me. After the baby.* But even thinking it was pointless.

'Is it all right if I have a fag? Or shall I go outside?'

'You've got to give me one.'

'You sure?'

'I haven't had one today.'

There was a long trail of private cars following the funeral cars. 'The crem's going to be packed,' Ashley told her. 'They won't all get in.'

He lit Sophie's cigarette, then his own. Through the cigarette smoke he watched the procession moving away. There were tears in his eyes again, but Sophie hadn't seen them.